HEIRS

Cassandra Pierce

EROTIC ROMANCE

Siren Publishing, Inc.
www.SirenPublishing.com

A SIREN PUBLISHING BOOK
IMPRINT: Erotic Romance

HEIRS TO DARKISLE
Copyright © 2010 by Cassandra Pierce

ISBN-10: 1-60601-690-3
ISBN-13: 978-1-60601-690-9

First Printing: May 2010

Cover design by Jinger Heaston
All cover art and logo copyright © 2010 by Siren Publishing, Inc.

ALL RIGHTS RESERVED: This literary work may not be reproduced or transmitted in any form or by any means, including electronic or photographic reproduction, in whole or in part, without express written permission.

All characters and events in this book are fictitious. Any resemblance to actual persons living or dead is strictly coincidental.

Printed in the U.S.A.

PUBLISHER
Siren Publishing, Inc.
www.SirenPublishing.com

HEIRS TO DARKISLE

CASSANDRA PIERCE
Copyright © 2010

Chapter 1

A century had passed since Sebastian had fled Darkisle, but Morgan House itself had hardly changed. Musty blood-red carpets still lined its gloomy halls, while solid Victorian-era doors still opened into airless, over decorated rooms. A month earlier, Edgar had died at the unlamentable age of one hundred eight. Now the house, with all its sundry ghosts and legacies, belonged to Sebastian. Again.

He found his former dressing room transformed into a storage area, with a heap of moss-green vinyl furniture jumbled up in one corner and a broken box of outdated clothing in another. To his relief, the room's best feature remained intact: a small terrace that jutted out from the house's worn façade to yield an unobstructed view of the sea. Gingerly he stepped out, cautious of cracks or loose brick, and leaned on the worn stone railing.

The punishing waves had done their best to grind away the rock-strewn shoreline, but he could still distinguish the line of jagged rocks that formed a delightful network of caves and fissures whenever the tide went out. He was thinking back to his frequent boyhood climbing expeditions when Ruby charged into the room.

Her thickly penciled eyebrows slanted upward in surprise. With her spiky dark hair rumpled from travel and the buckles of her leather jacket swinging at her sides, she looked like any ordinary college student who'd just arrived home on break. Only in this case, her absence had lasted almost sixty years.

"Sebastian, you won't believe this! My room is exactly the way I left it!"

He nodded sadly. "Edgar always hoped you'd return."

"And now I have."

She darted out, no doubt off to raze all traces of her human existence from her old quarters. Sebastian returned his attention to the sea, and a twinge of weakness rippled through his limbs. Odd: the injection should have held him for the night. Possibly the stress of travel had worn him down. He no longer had the stamina of those who took their nourishment from more traditional sources.

He was about to close his eyes, will his metabolism to a near-complete standstill, and draw fresh strength from the crisp night air when a movement on the beach below caught his attention.

Only senses sharpened to and by the darkness, like his, could have detected the two shadowed figures clambering along the jagged rocks. A small boat bobbed on the slippery froth nearby.

"What happened?" Ruby emerged from her room, an antique tennis racquet in one hand and a pair of saddle shoes in the other, as Sebastian stormed past her open door. "Where are you going?"

"Stay here," he commanded. "We have our first visitors."

* * * *

The woman leaped from the dinghy the moment it nudged the rocks. The man, knee deep in churning black water, struggled to tie the boat to the concrete plug he'd heaved overboard.

Curses punctuated his efforts. The rope felt slippery in his wet hands, and he could barely see in the darkness. The spots dancing in front of his eyes didn't help, either. The surf bubbled like the foam on the beer he'd drunk too much of yet again.

The woman squirmed out of her red midriff shirt and flung it onto the wet sand as she raced ahead, braless. The shirt caught in his feet and tripped him as he left the boat and scrambled after her. Lurching forward, he grabbed her arms and turned her to kiss him. He moaned as her bare breasts pressed into his chest. Clinging to one another, they staggered toward the rocks.

"This doesn't look safe," she complained as swells of dark water snatched at their ankles.

"Course it is. All the high school kids used to come up here. It was a great place to make out."

He maneuvered them both into one of the cramped spaces tucked between the boulders. Sheltered by the overhanging rock, the upper portion looked flat and dry enough for several adults to stretch out comfortably.

"A perfect little hideaway," he said, sweeping his hand out in a grand but clumsy gesture.

"I see what you mean." The woman started to giggle. "I'll bet you snuck up here all the time."

"Nah. I wasn't like that back then."

"And now?"

"Now I'm all grown up." He spread his body on top of hers. "And a lot more adventurous."

"I'm counting on it." Giggling again, she raised her thighs and crushed him against her. Her kneading hands worked his t-shirt over his head. As his mouth went to her bare nipples, a particularly rough wave sprayed them with cold salt water.

"Ooh, I'm getting all wet," she squealed.

"I certainly hope so," he rasped as she tossed his shirt aside and reached for the zipper of his jeans.

"That isn't what I meant." She paused to slap his half-bared rear end. His mouth dug at her hardening nipples while his hands pushed at her leather microskirt.

"Hey," she gasped as he fumbled with the laces. "What'd you say your name was again?"

"Huh?"

"You shouldn't have bought me all those drinks if you expect me to remember every detail."

Funny, he didn't recall her drinking all that much. He'd gone totally overboard, as usual. In more ways than one. "It's Todd."

"Bet you don't know mine, either," she teased.

"'Course I do. It's Ami."

"Very good." She arched her back, raising her taut nipples toward his face. "So give me a reason to remember yours next time."

Unable to undo the laces on the skirt, Todd finally gave up and just rolled the garment up Ami's writhing hips. Their breathing grew ragged as Todd rubbed his sweaty flesh against her in clumsy, desperate movements.

Suddenly, the cavern grew noticeably darker. A silhouette moved toward them.

Todd's head snapped up. "What the—"

"Who the fuck are you?" Ami demanded. She sat up, totally unconcerned about exposing all of her best features to plain view. Todd toppled off her and onto the rocks.

"It is I who should ask you that," the tall man growled. "How did you get up here?"

"Same way everyone else does," Todd retorted. "Same as you, probably. By boat." Briefly his mind flashed on the dinghy they'd borrowed—to use the term in its loosest possible sense—and the way he'd left the rope swishing even more loosely around in the water. Or maybe he had paused to tie it down more securely. He just couldn't remember.

"Leave this area immediately," the stranger ordered. "You are trespassing on private property."

"My naked ass I am!" Todd scrambled onto his hands and knees indignantly. "Old Man Morgan died months ago! This place doesn't belong to anyone now!"

"Let us approach the problem logically, not that I would assume you are in any condition to do so. You are correct that Edgar Morgan departed this sorry world four weeks ago. Therefore, since this is Morgan Point and I am the owner, it follows that I must be a Morgan. My goal is a simple one: to dwell here in peace. Therefore I am advising you to collect your things—and your, ah, companion—and leave at once. Swim if you have to."

"Kiss my ass!" Todd lunged to his feet, fists clenched, and felt his left foot skid on a wet lump of sea grass. When he tried to catch his balance, he instead felt himself pitch forward. Interpreting the movement as an assault, the new arrival met him straight on.

His actions brief and decisive, the stranger tilted his upper body to one side, avoiding Todd's flailing arms, and easily captured his left wrist. A single forceful twist flung Todd to his knees. Before he even had time to shriek in pain, the stranger began dragging him out of the cave. His long strides forced Todd to skitter and crawl after him in a crouched position. Pain ripped through his legs, feet, and his floundering right hand as unforgiving stone and debris lacerated his skin.

Back on the beach, the man dumped him onto the hard, wet sand. To his dismay, Todd spotted the dinghy, untied, moving slowly out to sea. He really would have to swim for it if he had any hope of retrieving it now.

"I'm gonna call the cops," Ami announced, struggling to wrap herself in her wet clothes. Todd didn't have the heart—or, at that moment, the capacity—to explain that her cell phone was most likely drifting away in the dinghy with her purse.

"Please do," said the stranger. He withdrew a cell phone of his own from the pocket of his tailored pants, handed the device over, and stepped back to wait. Ami indignantly stabbed at the numbers.

"Hi, 911? We're out at Morgan Point," she shouted at the dispatcher, "and some maniac is beating up my boyfriend, Tom. Get someone out here to taser this creep!"

"It's Todd," Todd moaned, wondering if the guy had dislocated his shoulder. He supposed he ought to put some clothes on before the cops arrived, like Ami had, but every movement filled him with pure agony. Besides, he needed to throw up. He shouldn't have drunk so much at The Chum Bucket. How many times had he told himself the same thing? The end result was always disaster. He didn't even want to imagine what Briana would say this time.

Frustrated rage boiled up in him. He couldn't stand up, so Todd braced his hands in the sand and kicked wildly out at the man who still towered over him.

A booted foot stomped down hard on his ankle.

"Try that again." The man's voice rumbled through Todd's spinning head. "A single step can break your leg in several places."

Todd slumped back into the sand. What a lunatic! Best to let the cops deal with him. As the victim of a calculated assault, Todd knew he'd get the last laugh on both this maniac and his overbearing sister, Briana.

Moments later, rough hands hauled him to his feet. Cold steel touched his wrists as a pair of cuffs clicked around them.

"Come on, Todd." He recognized the soothing voice as belonging to Deputy Joel Tanner, a guy he'd known since high school. "You've been down this road before. Come sleep it off and we'll figure out the rest later."

"Hey, wait just a damn minute! That guy attacked us!" Ami shrieked. Todd saw the cops hauling her toward the police car, too. "I want him arrested!"

"Man's got a right to protect his own property," the older cop said. Todd knew him, too. Sheriff Garvey had busted him for DUI and taken away his license, and for all intents and purposes, his freedom, over a year ago.

"Don't worry," Garvey said. "I'll call your sister for you and let her know what's happened. You probably won't have to spend the night in the tank."

"Assuming you didn't already piss her off this week," Joel added. The two of them laughed.

His cheeks—both exposed sets of them—burned with shame as they shoved him into the back of the police car. Jail would be a cakewalk compared to what his sister would do to him when she heard the particulars of this little episode.

* * * *

Briana took the call at the front desk of The Dunes Motel. She'd actually meant to head home hours ago, since no one had checked in or out of the motel all day. She didn't expect anyone to show up now, either.

Maybe things would pick up in a month or two, when the tourist season started, but she held little hope of turning a profit then, either. Darkisle just wasn't a very popular destination—and it wasn't even an island strictly speaking, just a little crooked finger of land wedged between far more desirable spots like Bar Harbor and New Brunswick. With its inhospitably rocky coast and the fishy smell that lingered in the air, their ramshackle town wasn't the stuff vacations were made of. Most of the locals—at least those who didn't own tourist-centered businesses—preferred it that way.

The ringing phone stirred a pang of excitement in her. Maybe an old friend would invite her somewhere, or a year-round resident had sent an unexpected visitor over to rent a room.

Her hopeful mood soured as Will Garvey gave her the rundown on her brother's latest escapades. Morgan Point...new owner...trespassing...possible assault charges....

She slammed down the phone, steaming mad. Not forty-eight hours ago, after she'd confiscated a six-pack and made him pour it into the kitchen sink, Todd had promised once again to stop this nonsense. Losing his contracting business two years earlier hadn't stopped him nor had surrendering his driver's license for driving drunk. Now he'd not only taken a head-first tumble off the wagon of sobriety, but he'd landed back in jail and needed her help. Would he never learn?

She locked up the motel, the only thing her father had left her aside from a last request for her to look after Todd, climbed into her Land Rover, and drove the few blocks to Darkisle's tiny police station.

Sheriff Will Garvey himself manned the front desk, while Joel sat in the corner, typing on an old computer. Updating her brother's arrest record, no doubt.

At the far end of the room, a woman with wild red hair and wet clothing that left little to the imagination sat cuffed to the ring in the center of a long wooden bench. She smirked as Briana approached the counter.

"You got here fast," Will observed.

"Slow night at The Dunes," Briana explained. "Believe me, I considered leaving him here to think about his behavior for a few hours. I might have if I thought it would do any good."

Nodding, the sheriff reached for a ring of keys stashed in a pigeonhole near his coffee cup. "I'm sorry about what happened, Bri. We didn't have a choice."

"I know. I don't blame you."

Will seemed to understand that Briana was in no mood for a lecture. He led her toward the steel door that separated the lobby from the two holding cells in the back.

He hesitated before pushing it open. "When you see him, Briana…uh, just so you know, we did what we could. I don't want you to think we take pleasure in embarrassing anyone."

"I know that, Will," she replied, puzzled. She couldn't imagine why he looked so grim until he waved her back to the same cell she'd confronted Todd in a year ago, after his drunk driving arrest.

Her brother lay facedown on the cell's narrow, sheetless cot. His back and legs sported a maze of scratches and ugly red welts. He wore nothing but a pair of denim cut-offs several sizes too big for him. When he saw Briana, he sat up too quickly and had to secure the pants with one hand.

"You must hate me," Todd began as soon as the sheriff had left them alone.

Briana clenched her fists at her sides. She couldn't decide whether she should tear her own hair out or reach through the bars to grab his. "Hate isn't even the word I'm thinking of right now. Homicide might be closer to the mark."

"I'm sorry, Bri. I just…I don't know what came over me. I only went down to play pool, I swear. There was this girl, Ami…."

"The charming specimen chained to the wall out front, I presume." Briana's eyes narrowed. "And I suppose she's the inspiration for this new look of yours?"

Todd's blush crept all the way down to his chest. "We went swimming."

"I assume a strong current carried away your bathing suit." She pointed to the shorts he desperately hitched up with one hand.

"Hey, that wasn't my fault. The guy took my clothes—with my wallet in my pants."

"Who?"

"Some asshole who says he's one of the Morgans. Struts around like he owns the Atlantic Ocean."

"Todd, you know Edgar was the last of the Morgans, and I doubt he came back as a ghost to patrol the shoreline. Either this person pulled your leg or you imagined the whole thing. I wouldn't put that past you, considering the state you were probably in."

Her brother's eyes grew moist. "I didn't mean to drink anything, I swear. But she invited me to sit down with her and I...you know, I had to buy her a round. It was the gentlemanly thing to do." Alcohol-tinged tears trickled down his face. "We've got to get my stuff back, Bri! I had almost thirty dollars left! And I lost my favorite jeans, too."

"Your wallet? Your jeans? How many times are we going to go through this, Todd? One day I won't be taking a call to pick you up from the jail. One day it'll be the hospital—or the morgue."

Chastised, Todd gazed at the floor. Eventually she caved, just like she always did.

"All right. Much as I think you deserve to stay here tonight, or even longer, I don't want to have to come back tomorrow. Let me talk to Will and see what we can do."

Back in the lobby, she motioned Will to the far end of the front desk so Joel and the woman in handcuffs couldn't hear them.

"Okay, Sheriff. What's the fine this time?"

Will scowled. "It's a little worse than usual. We might have a stolen boat to deal with, though we haven't recovered that yet. For now there's the matter of yet another public intox, trespassing, and worst of all, attempted assault."

Briana tilted her head toward the red-haired woman. "On her?"

"No. On the owner of Morgan Point."

"That's impossible. Edgar Morgan died. He's been the only owner since my grandfather was a kid. He had no heirs. Surely the place is going to some kind of public trust or something."

"Nope. His grandson, Sebastian Morgan, just moved in today, and he's pretty keen on keeping rubberneckers off his property. You might want to do your part to spread the word. I don't want to run up there again anytime soon. Place gives me the creeps."

"So what exactly are you planning to do with my brother?"

"Well, it's up to the man he attacked to press charges. So far, he hasn't. As long as Todd promises not to skip town, I'll release him into your custody for tonight and hold off on anything more serious."

He tossed the keys to Joel, who got up and disappeared behind the steel door.

"I'll talk to Mr. Morgan," Briana said. "I'll just have to convince him to drop the whole issue." She noticed the red-haired woman leaning forward in an attempt to hear them. "What's with her? Is she being charged?"

Will shook his head. "She was pretty animated when she got here. Just giving her a chance to settle down. I couldn't put them in the cell together."

Joel returned with Todd while Briana signed the paperwork. Todd still struggled to hold up his baggy shorts.

"Hey," Ami piped up from across the room. "Tom told me you guys own a motel. I've been living in my car since my old man threw me out. I need a place to stay. Got any rooms available?"

Todd perked up and nearly let his pants fall. "Please, Bri?"

"I'll be a model guest," Ami promised.

Briana rolled her eyes. Todd wasn't about to give up though.

"I guess you could stay at the house," he reflected. "We've been using the third bedroom for storage, but there's always the couch. Or I could clean out my room."

Shocked, Briana held up one hand. "We have plenty of space at the motel. The rooms are twenty-five a night, off-season rates. First sign of trouble, you're out."

Ami's smirk returned. "No problem. I never look for trouble."

She waited by the desk while the sheriff brought out another release form, and Joel walked over to uncuff Ami from the bench. The moment Ami got up, free, Todd rushed over and swept her into his arms. The two of them clung to each other as if they'd been separated for years instead of minutes.

Mystified, Briana shook her head. Despite his utter lack of maturity, ambition, and self-control, Todd always managed to find an endless stream of friends and lovers. He didn't attract the sort of people she would choose for herself of course.

Still, she couldn't help but imagine how nice it would be to have someone look at her with the kind of reckless, smitten passion Ami and Todd exchanged as she marched the prisoners out to her car.

Chapter 2

Briana swung by The Dunes on her way home with Todd to check Ami in. Her demands for up-front payment went unheeded, since Ami's purse, wallet, cell phone, and other sundries remained in the dinghy they'd lost, drifting on the open sea toward Canada.

She groaned aloud when Todd confessed where they had gotten the dinghy in the first place, giving her one more fence she didn't look forward to mending. Todd understood the situation, yet he had put her in this awkward position anyway. Why did she put up with him?

Once they'd tucked Ami safely away for the night, Briana drove up to their house and helped Todd into his room. Briefly she considered locking him in—the motel lay only a few hundred yards away—but decided that in his present condition, he wasn't much of a flight risk. He couldn't even stand long enough for her to turn down his blankets, so she let him collapse on top of the covers. Thankfully, the oversized shorts remained more or less in place.

"My wallet…" he moaned into his pillow as he drifted off to oblivion, "…in my jeans. Want them. Gotta get'm back, Bri. Help me."

Briana pulled Todd's door shut behind her and grimaced. A half-empty wallet and a grungy pair of jeans should be the last things on Todd's mind. He should be more worried about whether or not he would be charged with assault and battery. Unfortunately, his fate rested with the new owner of Morgan House…a man her brother had insulted and attacked.

Was there any point in trying to talk him out of pursuing the matter? If they ended up in court, Todd's previous arrests for alcohol-related infractions would doom him. Maybe he wasn't much help around the house or the motel, but she didn't want to see him carted off to a year in the county lockup. Besides, she'd be the one footing the lawyer's bills and any fines imposed.

Well, what the hell. She had nothing to lose by talking to the guy. Sometimes the simplest apology did wonders. Could he be worse than a disgruntled customer at The Dunes?

Heading back into the kitchen, she grabbed her keys off the counter and walked outside. With old man Morgan dead, the new owner probably planned to fix the place up and sell it at a huge profit. His gripe no doubt involved property damage more than personal affront. She just hoped he didn't demand a significant wad of cash to forget the whole thing. The DUI episode had already sucked up half her bank account.

Ten minutes past midnight, she stood on the crumbling front steps of Morgan House, a place she'd never seen up close despite living out her entire twenty-eight years in Darkisle. While she waited, she studied the pitiable state of the three-story house. The stone façade loomed grimy and cracked, with several windows boarded up from inside. Greasy black residue covered the front door and smudged her knuckles when she knocked. Disgusted, she wiped the back of her hand on her jeans. If the newcomer wanted to put the place on the market, he'd definitely be swimming upstream without flippers. Edgar Morgan, eccentric and reclusive, had let the once-grand estate home erode into a heap of dirty bricks and fractured glass.

Several minutes passed before the door cracked open to reveal a young woman's pale face. The wife or daughter of the man Todd had confronted, perhaps?

"Yes?" Huge dark eyes, made to look even bigger by a generous application of inky eyeliner, studied her. Then again, Briana thought, maybe she was the kind of guest one hired for a single evening.

"I'm Briana Dempsey. I came to talk about the…ah…incident that took place here earlier tonight."

"Are you a cop? Or a reporter? Because we're not interested in making a statement."

"Neither. You had my brother arrested. I wanted to talk to you about what happened."

The woman smirked. "I don't think there's much to say. The police took the man away. He became violent."

"But he isn't—that's what I want to discuss. Please, I only want a moment of your time."

"Ruby!" A male voice barked the name, and Briana heard staccato footsteps on bare floor. "What are you doing? Close the door."

"Someone's here," Ruby protested. The door banged shut, and Briana heard the two confer in hushed tones. Stung by such rudeness, she raised her fist to start pounding again, dirt or no dirt, when it suddenly heaved all the way open.

Briana found herself looking up at a tall man who had planted himself in the middle of the oversized doorway, his arms spread so that he resembled an oversized painting about to leap out of the frame. Instinct prodded her to take a step back, but she held her ground. "Come in," he said. She did.

Once inside, she studied him in greater detail. In the light, his resemblance to an inanimate work of art faded, mostly because Briana couldn't imagine a portrait that could secure her attention so completely. His face, had it been painted, could only be captured by a skilled combination of bold, yet sensitive brushstrokes. Any artist would relish the stark planes of his narrow cheeks and his high, aristocratic forehead, streaked with a few tendrils of dark hair. And only an expertly blended palette could reproduce the color of his eyes: icy green, as murky and foreboding as a winter sea. His silk shirt matched their color perfectly. Briana also decided that the two people standing in front of her were not man and wife. They looked too much alike not to be related, but too close in age to be father and daughter.

Ruby seemed to be in her early twenties, and the man in his mid-to-late thirties.

"Ruby," the man said, "this unfortunate event did not involve you directly. I will therefore speak with our visitor alone."

Ruby's full lips parted as if she were about to argue with him. Then, abruptly, she vanished, gliding from the room so fast that Briana's senses didn't quite register the movement. She seemed to evaporate into the house's veil of dusty air.

Briana shook her head, disoriented. The stress was making her hallucinate now. Todd would pay for this.

"I…ah…I'm sorry for showing up unannounced like this, and so late, but considering the situation, I thought it best to act right away. You're Mr. Morgan, I understand?"

He nodded. "Sebastian Morgan."

"Are you Edgar Morgan's nephew, or something?"

"Ruby and I are his grandchildren. Did you know him?"

"I knew of him, of course. Everyone did. He was sort of a—" hastily, she caught herself from making a serious faux pas— "a legend around town. Very reclusive."

"Yes. He preferred his own company to that of other people. I tend to share those sentiments."

"I guess we all do now and then." He didn't respond to her attempt at lightness, so she pushed on. "I know he'd been married a few times. I never heard about any children though."

"Six times, to be exact. Only his first marriage produced any offspring," Sebastian said. "Unfortunately, the family became estranged long before your birth."

"Oh. Well, I was sorry to hear that he had passed away. My condolences."

"Edgar Morgan lived far longer than most mortals have any right to expect. After a certain point, death becomes a natural, even desirable, culmination. No doubt many greet it with relief."

Briana supposed he had a point, given Edgar's advanced age and apparent senility, but Sebastian's nonchalant attitude sent a spidery chill through her.

"I'm sure you've already guessed what I came here to say. Of course I want to apologize for my brother's behavior. There's no excuse for what he did, but please realize that he isn't a bad person. Life's been a little...well, a little difficult for him lately. He just lost control of the situation."

"We all have our sad stories. I grow tired of people who refuse to behave in a civilized fashion and then use their hardships as excuses."

"I'm offering a reason, not an excuse." Briana felt her cheeks redden as she struggled to keep her anger in check. What did this man, with his obvious wealth and social standing, know about hardship, emotional or financial? About having only one other person to depend on, to feel close to? "He's far from perfect, but he's my younger brother, and it's my duty to look out for him."

"If I may say so, your willingness to do so is probably the direct cause of his lack of control, as you put it."

"It most certainly is not," she shot back. "You know nothing about either one of us."

"Your brother is hardly unique. He indulges his baser nature at the expense of others. Because he feels entitled to his pleasures and is assured of your protection, he sees no reason to moderate his behavior." He flashed a smile she found infuriating. "Your expression suggests that you agree."

"My expression should tell you that I am offended by your presumptions. Todd posed no threat to you or your new home. You didn't have to call the cops on him!"

"As it happens, the young lady with him dialed law enforcement. I simply provided my cell phone—as any gentleman would have."

Briana opened her mouth to say more—along with a few things she fully expected to regret later—but this revelation stopped her in mid-sentence. "Ami called them?" she asked, mortified. "I—I hadn't realized that."

"I'm sorry she and your brother were not more forthcoming. Perhaps their memories are to blame. Admittedly, the scene became a bit chaotic."

"I heard."

"Miss Dempsey, you may believe that Todd was in no position to harm me, but had he and his companion injured themselves, or even drowned, on my property, you would no doubt be here demanding to know why I did not intervene when I had the chance."

She fidgeted uneasily. Todd could easily have capsized the stolen boat, passed out in the surf, or struck his head on the rocks. And who knew what kind of story Ami would spread around town once she sobered up? Todd might have found himself facing a very different charge. Much as she hated to admit it, in this case Sebastian Morgan had done a better job safeguarding Todd than she had.

"All right. So I didn't consider all the angles. Please, Mr. Morgan. I'm asking you not to press charges against my brother. It would be terribly embarrassing for him—for both of us. And to be blunt, I just don't have the resources right now to bail him out of trouble again."

He folded his arms over his broad chest and studied her. "I have no desire to inflict any unnecessary hardship on you. However old-fashioned this might seem, I cannot respect a man who hides behind his sister's skirts." His lip curled upward as he glanced at her legs with obvious appreciation. "Or dungarees, in this case."

Before she formulated an answer, he crossed the foyer, retrieved an object from atop a chair, and handed it to her. "Speaking of which, I suspect these items belong to your brother."

Briana looked down at the jeans, faded t-shirt, and a single red high-top sneaker rolled together in a soggy bundle. Black strands of seaweed and a gritty coat of sand covered everything. Her fingers brushed over a lump in one of the jeans pockets: Todd's wallet, safe after all.

"My apologies for the loss of one shoe. I scoured the beach for some time, but its mate failed to appear."

"Don't worry. I needed an excuse to throw this one out. Thank you for saving what you did," she said. "You'd have been within your rights to let the stuff wash out to sea."

"I told you: we all have an obligation to be civilized. I have lived by that maxim for a long time."

She took a chance. "Does that mean you won't file a complaint against Todd?"

To her surprise, a genuine smile lifted his face. "I must consider my decision. Bring your brother tomorrow evening, and I will discuss the matter with him personally."

"We'll be here," she promised.

Moments later, she picked her way back down the worn stone staircase, one hand ready to grasp the moss-covered railing should the structure give way under her. The whole way, she carried Sebastian Morgan's gaze like an open palm resting on her shoulders. At one point, she felt compelled to glance back, convinced that he had followed her. But she saw only his lean silhouette, shutting the heavy door as he retreated inside.

* * * *

In the morning, she drove into town for breakfast. Even after a surprisingly peaceful sleep, she didn't trust herself not to pulverize her brother the moment he staggered into the kitchen demanding strong coffee. Forcing him to brew his own, given his probable condition this morning, seemed a fitting first step in his punishment. She'd figure out the rest later.

Before she got out of her car at the restaurant, she pulled her cell phone from her purse and dialed a number she knew by heart. Though she had hoped to get voicemail, the familiar voice came on the line after the second ring.

"I'm at the diner. Meet me in ten minutes. I need to talk to you."

"Okay. I'll be right over."

She shoved the phone back into her purse with a sigh. The public wharf hosted plenty of dinghies Todd could have untied, but only one whose owner wouldn't notice right away, and wouldn't make too much of a fuss when he did. Even with three sheets to the wind, Todd had realized as much. Maybe Sebastian Morgan had a point about the whole enabling thing.

At the diner, she took a seat at the counter and toyed with the pink and blue packets of sugar substitute, arranging them in colorful patterns while she waited for her food—and her guest—to arrive.

When someone slid onto the stool next to her, she didn't have to look up to recognize Graham Smith. "Hey, Bri."

She forced herself to pivot around to face him. "How are you, Graham?"

"Holding my own."

She watched him while he gestured for the waitress to bring his usual fare. Briana remembered it: a toasted blueberry muffin and strong black coffee she smelled across the counter. She used to brew it thick for him in the mornings and then add more water to the pot for herself. They'd enjoy it together while his boat rocked under her feet and the brisk wind whipped her shoulder-length hair against his face.

"You must have been out in the bay," she said. "I haven't seen you around."

"Had to bring the boat in for some work. Want to be ready when the tourists come back. They don't like the smell of a real fishing boat. Or a real fisherman for that matter."

Briana smiled. He always smelled good to her. Salty, manly, like a tide pool warmed by the sun. She reminisced about rubbing her soft jaw against his stubbly cheek, and to feel his work-roughened hand on her thigh. Now that same calloused hand propped up that same half-shaved cheek as he watched her watching him. Maybe he was revisiting some of those memories, too.

"Todd behaving himself?" he asked between bites of buttery, skillet-browned muffin.

"Not really. Graham...I'll get right to the point. Todd stole your dinghy from the pier last night. He took it up to Morgan Point and let it float away. I'm sorry."

Graham put down his muffin. "Son of a...are you kidding me?"

"I'm sure he planned to get it back to you safely. He didn't act alone, so for all I know it wasn't even his idea. Don't be too hard on him."

"That little piss-ant needs the wind knocked out of him. Might scare him into acting like a man."

"Don't start, please. I've been through this already once."

"Okay, sorry," he grumbled. "I know it's none of my business anymore."

"No, it isn't," she agreed.

"Still, I don't see why you don't just throw his sorry ass out on the street. Let him fend for himself a while."

"You know I have no authority to get him out of the house. My dad left it to both of us, fifty-fifty. Todd has just as much right to throw me out. Same goes for the motel."

"Yeah, that damn motel. He should at least help you fix that dump up so you can sell it."

"Who says I want to sell it?" They ate in silence for a while. She watched Graham's jaw muscles pulse, as if he were chewing nails. "Listen, Graham. I'm worn out making excuses for Todd, so I'm not even going to try any more. I'll pay you back for the dinghy as soon as I can."

He finished his coffee and set the ceramic mug down with a thump. "No need. Some guys found it floating in the bay this morning. ID'ed the tag and called me. I'm going out to get it this afternoon."

Briana stared at him in disbelief. "Jeez, Graham! You could have told me the truth at the beginning! Here I've been beating myself up all morning."

"Well, then—I'd say mission accomplished." He lifted his coffee to his lips, hiding a laugh. For a moment, Briana allowed herself to look past the problems of the previous night and let the tension melt from her body. She picked up her own mug and did the same.

They put down their cups in unison. Their smiles faded slowly.

"Come down to the docks and see the boat," Graham said. "I want your opinion if it's ready for tourists. You know them better than anyone, working at the motel."

"Since when did you value my opinion so much?" His wounded look made her regret her words. She always spoke to him too sharply. "All right," she relented. "Just for a minute."

He paid for both of their meals—by way of apologizing for the trick he'd played on her, she supposed—and they walked the short distance to the wharf without talking. Morning fog swathed the entire village in a silvery cloud. Briana almost didn't see his fishing boat until he touched her hand and pointed. *The Reelentless*, named for a playful pun she'd come up with in happier days, nodded beside the pier, cottony orbs of mist rolling across the deck. Graham hopped in first and then reached back to grasp both her hands and guide her aboard.

Despite the limited visibility, the boat did look better than last time she'd visited. He'd applied a coat of wax and straightened up the tackle, which he tended to scatter around the deck. Each seat and bench featured a fresh new canvas cushion.

"It looks terrific, Graham. You'll do a lot of business this summer."

"There's more. Come on, check out the cabin."

His innocuous tone disarmed her, so she followed him down the narrow steps that led below deck. Here she found new paint on the walls and a new full-sized bed in the corner. Feather pillows and a blue Shaker-style quilt made the area look like a cozy loft instead of a cramped berth on a twenty-year-old fishing boat. "This is nice. I'm impressed, Graham."

"I wanted to make it more homey. I got spoiled spending the winter in your motel. Of course, it's a little lonelier here."

She ignored the latter half of his remark. "Makes sense."

"If you get tired of running that fleabag, I could always use a first mate." His hand drifted to her hair. His fingertips traced the contour of her ear.

"You know that isn't a good idea, Graham. One of us would end up tossing the other overboard, and I hate to swim."

His hand tensed against her cheek and slid down to cup her chin. In the split second before his lips met hers, she considered pulling away and starting that same old care-about-each-other-but-just-can't-make-it-work routine, letting him down in a kind and responsible way. But already her body started responding to his touch, her pulse quickening in a way her mind continued to warn her against. Raw physical need raged through her, not just trampling logic but leaving it smashed, broken, and scattered across the deck in tiny, shimmering pieces.

Their kiss felt rough, hurried, hungry. Graham unbuttoned her shirt as they fell together onto the bed. His coarse fingers kneaded her breasts, traced the outlines of her nipples, and then pinched and rolled them more aggressively. Briana moaned when she felt the urgent bulge in his pants push against her left thigh. Her palm moved to cover and knead his desire.

"It's been so long," he groaned. "Too long."

In no time, she lay shirtless and braless and her pants were open down to the last notch on the zipper. His lips now roved over her body, the light growth of whiskers on his chin scratching her flesh in a way that aroused her to the very edge of tolerance.

Then the pants came off, bunched around her boots, and his tongue took her to places she'd thought she'd been exiled from forever. Almost before she was ready, the sheer force of his ravenous need flung her over the precipice into sweet, hot oblivion.

Afterward, Graham rested his head on her middle. Briana stroked his hair while delicious aftershocks ripped through her. She continued shuddering when he slipped something from the nightstand drawer, fumbled with the wrapper for a moment and then crawled back up and fitted himself against her. Her legs curled around his waist and pulled him closer. The scruffy hair dusting his abs scraped the soft flesh of her stomach as the treacherous current of sheer desire swept them out to open waters.

All too soon, they ran aground in the shallows again, flung flailing on the pebbly shore and gasping for breath. They lay twined together on the bed, her bare legs tangled in his and the plaid quilt twisted around them both.

How easily she could fall back into this pattern—spending the morning on *The Reelentless,* slipping into one of the motel rooms to wait for him after her shift at the front desk. If only she could forget the quarreling, the insecurity, and the control issues that burned alongside his sexual passion.

Graham's fingers traced circular patterns over her bare breasts and down her pale midriff. "Your skin would darken up if you spent some time on the boat."

"You want me to go topless in front of the tourists?"

"Absolutely. Business would boom." They laughed. "Seriously. Come out with me this summer. We'd make a good team."

Briana's amusement trailed off in a sigh. "We tried that, Graham. We weren't any kind of team at all. You might need—or want—a first mate. The problem is, I'm not looking for a captain."

"A ship needs a chain of command."

"That's why I choose to stay on land. I'm sorry, Graham." She kissed his shoulder and got up. "This was wonderful. You were wonderful. No one can make my body do the things you can. But I think I need to go now."

He lay silent while she dressed and headed topsides.

"I hope you change your mind," he called after her.

"I know. I'll see you around town, Graham."

"No doubt about it."

She trudged back to the diner where she'd left her car. Graham Smith proved a pleasant diversion, as always, but she had to get back to reality. First and foremost, she had to set her brother on the right track and, hopefully, keep him there.

* * * *

"No effing way!"

Not to her surprise, Todd detested the idea of returning to Morgan Point in the evening. Rumpled, bleary-eyed, dressed in a pair of plaid boxers instead of the shorts from the police station, he stood beside the open refrigerator and raged at her. "I'm not groveling to that stuck-up jerk, no matter how deep his pockets are, or how much of this godforsaken dump of a town his ancestors owned!"

"I went to bat for you and this is how you thank me? Look, I'm going up to the motel for a few hours. I don't care what you do in the meantime, but if you want to stay out of jail, you'd better be shaved and dressed and in my car right after supper. And I'm telling you, this is the last free ride you'll ever get from me. It's time you learned." She addressed both of them as she left the kitchen.

Chapter 3

"Dragging your feet isn't going to get you out of this." Briana stood on the top step, arms folded, and stared down at her dawdling brother. "Stop prolonging the inevitable."

She'd experienced such relief when she returned from the motel that afternoon and found Todd dressed to impress in a white button-down shirt and a pair of black jeans he'd ironed himself. Sadly, his cooperative attitude had faded by the mile as they drove out to Morgan Point. Now, literally only a few steps away from resolving the whole matter, he'd turned petulant and obstinate.

Todd kicked at a loose paving stone, and Briana held her breath in fear that the entire structure would slide down in a small avalanche. "If the Morgans are so rich, how come they don't have a gardener?"

Briana rolled her eyes. "Just be glad they don't have an armed security guard. Besides, they moved in yesterday. You can't expect miracles."

"I think I'd rather do the jail time than hang around here."

"Fine. Go back and tell Will. You'll have to walk though, because I'm done helping you make an idiot of yourself."

Grumbling, Todd hooked his thumbs in his empty belt loops and followed.

Before Briana had even knocked, Ruby appeared at the front door. Tonight she wore eyeliner the color and texture of pitch, bright silver lipstick, and earrings shaped like tiny daggers. A skin-tight black tube dress, featuring the shortest hem Briana had ever seen outside of a risqué magazine, and chunky police-style boots completed the effect.

"My brother is expecting you. Come in." Her frank gaze swept Todd's body as they stepped inside the foyer. "So you're the man Sebastian sent to jail. Wish I'd gone to the beach with him. Things might have turned out different."

For the first time that evening, Todd's mouth tilted in a grin. "Then that makes two of us."

"My brother is waiting for you in the study. I'll take you to him." Ruby glanced at Briana with far less interest. "You can wait here. I'll come back and keep you company in a moment."

"Can't wait," Briana said under her breath.

Left alone, she studied her surroundings. Sebastian and Ruby had straightened things up since her earlier visit, but in truth, she didn't notice much improvement. A creepy gargoyle-footed table sat beside a dusty overstuffed divan, while a four-foot marble statue of some half-naked Roman goddess stretched eerily elongated fingers toward her. She half-expected Edgar Allen Poe to stroll in with a raven perched on his shoulder.

Maybe Todd had a point about preferring jail.

Ruby soon returned. "We'll leave those two to work out their differences. Men are such egotistical creatures."

"They have their quirks," Briana agreed.

"Base appetites rule them." Ruby flashed two rows of spellbinding white teeth. "We should pity them, I suppose, but I admit I despise them for their weak natures."

"Including your brother?"

"At times. Sebastian is unique. He works hard to control his urges. You know, if the ancient matriarchies had survived, the world would be a different place. The tragedy is that the same qualities that enlightened our primeval mothers guaranteed their destruction. They valued cooperation over competition, peace over bloodshed. Brute force trumps intellectual achievement every time."

"I...uh...guess that's one interpretation."

"Don't get me wrong. I would love to watch Sebastian and Todd fight it out. It's good for men to fight. They're a bit like animals in that regard—physical danger toughens them, sharpens their instincts. Have you ever seen a man battle for his life? It's exhilarating."

"I'm afraid I wouldn't find that entertaining." Was Ruby trying to shock her? "I'll have to take your word for it."

Ruby poked the goddess statue's nose. "I wish she could come to life and speak. Bet she'd spin us some juicy tales from the Coliseum." She laughed irreverently. "So tell me about your brother. Why does he get into so much trouble?"

"Mostly because he doesn't listen to me."

"I can sense that just from looking at him. Willful and self-destructive. Quite a deadly combination."

"Tell me about it." Genuine interest flickered in the young woman's expression, so Briana seized the opportunity to further her cause. "He wasn't always like that, you know."

"What changed him?"

"Well, for starters, our father died two years ago. Things got a little…unstable. We have a motel to run—"

"A motel? Oh, how depressing. All those ridiculous people with their petty ways and idiotic demands. I can see how that might drive someone to drink."

"You have experience in the field?"

"I've never stayed in one, if that's what you mean. And I never want to."

Briana wasn't sure whether to take offense or agree.

Luckily, Ruby hadn't expected an answer. "We'll have to put our heads together and figure out a way to rehabilitate Todd."

"Not pressing charges might be a good start."

"Oh, Sebastian would never do that. He doesn't want that kind of publicity. I'm sure you know that small towns like this thrive on gossip. Most Americans don't understand the difference between a desire for privacy and rudeness. It's different in Europe."

"You spent time in Europe?"

Just then, Todd returned to the foyer and jerked a thumb over his shoulder. "Your turn, Bri. He wants to talk to you now."

"Me? Why?" When Briana hesitated, Ruby slid behind her as if to prevent her from bolting.

"First door on your left." Her cool whisper glided over Briana's ear, making her shudder. She moved quickly, glad to get away from the strange young woman and her intrusive manner.

The room she entered, some kind of library or office, was also in a transitional state. Sebastian Morgan sat at a heavy antique desk, surrounded by old-fashioned, leather-bound books. Tonight he wore a black silk shirt with a banded collar, left open to expose a simple gold chain that glittered between a few dark chest hairs.

Sebastian himself looked ruddier and more cheerful than he had last night. She wondered if he noticed a similar change in her, though he would never have guessed the reason. Or would he? The intense way he stared at her suggested that he could read all her thoughts in an instant. Just to be on the safe side, she temporarily banished all memories of how she and Graham had spent the morning.

"Will you sit down?" Sebastian waved at an ornately carved wooden chair.

"No thank you. I'll stand. I can't stay long."

He didn't insist. "Your brother offered me a very pretty apology. But sincere? I wonder."

Briana felt herself becoming annoyed. If Ruby had told the truth, Sebastian had never planned to press charges on Todd in the first place. This entire visit was just an exercise in manipulation.

"Accept it or don't." Her anger flared. "We promised to show up here, and we did. We'll deal with the consequences of whatever you decide to do, but we won't grovel."

He steepled his long fingers under his chin. "Todd tells me he once worked as a handyman of sorts. Was he a good one?"

"Yes, he was. And is."

"I'm pleased to hear it." Sebastian lifted his gaze to the frayed black and maroon wallpaper surrounding them. "As you can see, Morgan House is sorely in need of some first aid."

It took a moment for her to catch on. "Are you offering to hire my brother?"

"I have a few tasks we can use as a sort of trial run. If he performs well, more may follow. I must insist on a few conditions: no drinking on the premises. He must be punctual and obedient. Also, the hours will be unconventional: dusk to midnight, when I am at my leisure and can supervise his progress."

Secretly, Briana felt overjoyed, but she saw no advantage in seeming too eager. "The terms are sort of unusual, but I guess it's up to Todd."

"Not entirely. He informs me that due to certain…excesses in his past, he is no longer allowed the use of a motor vehicle. Therefore, you will be responsible for delivering him to and from the job site."

She pretended to think it over.

"I'd be willing to drive him, as long as it doesn't interfere with my work at the motel. I usually lock the office up right around dusk, so it should be all right unless we get a sudden influx of tourists."

"You have a great deal of family loyalty. I admire that."

"Yesterday you said I let him take advantage of me."

His lips curled in genuine empathy. "I took issue with your methods. I don't fault your motives."

Unexpectedly, Briana felt herself warming to him. "Thank you for saying that."

"No doubt some would criticize the actions I have taken to protect Ruby. When our loved ones are involved, though, what choice do we have?"

"That's pretty much the way I see it. On the other hand, I've been thinking about what you said. Maybe I do baby Todd too much. That hasn't helped him in the long run. From now on, it's going to be nothing but tough love."

He stood as she left the room. Briana found the gentlemanly gesture quaint but endearing. Back in the foyer, Todd and Ruby chatted about the relative merits of the party scene in Europe and Darkisle. For once, Briana was glad they lived in a town with only one bar and one motel.

Todd followed her out to the car with a spring in his step and a grin on his face.

"So what do you think?" he chirped as he buckled himself in. "A real job and everything! This could be a new start for us, Bri."

"I guess it could be...if you don't screw up."

"I won't. Promise."

His voice held so much hope that she decided to give him the benefit of the doubt...until the route home led them past The Chum Bucket and his face lit up like the tacky neon sign over its doors. Briana's hands tensed on the wheel.

"Please, Bri? It's Diablo Hot Wing night. I'm starving." She flashed him a look so lethal that he raised both palms in surrender. "You can guard me the whole time. I won't drink anything but soda, I swear."

Sighing, she swung the car into The Chum Bucket's unpaved lot. If she refused, Todd would probably just sneak out later. And the Diablo wings tasted pretty good, considering the bar provided them free. "Okay. Chicken wings and soda I'll allow. You got that? Soda."

"Yeah, I got it. Trust me, I'll even go Diet if it'll make you feel better."

"Well, no need to go overboard."

He began scanning the crowd the moment they walked in. Sure enough, Ami already stood at the bar, signaling to him.

"A setup. I knew it!" Briana could have kicked herself for being so gullible.

Todd donned an expression of utter innocence. "I swear I didn't realize she'd be here!"

"You know, Todd, I wish you'd stop swearing. I don't want to be standing next to you when lightning shoots down and fries your lying butt. Go ahead—talk to her for a few minutes, then tell her we're leaving. And I'd better not see a glass bottle in your hand at any point."

"Looks like you've managed to stay out of trouble since we last met," Ami said as she approached him.

"Maybe I just haven't been caught." Todd laughed nervously.

"Give him time. It hasn't even been twenty-four hours yet." Briana rolled her eyes. Abruptly, she focused on a different problem. Graham stood by the jukebox, staring right at her. He tipped his beer bottle to them—to her—in a mock toast.

"Let's get a table." Ami took Todd's hand and pulled him towards the wooden booths lining the wall. "You can come, too, Bri," she added without much enthusiasm.

"Gee, thanks, Ami. Todd, remember. Soda."

"I sw—I mean, I promise," he said, and then shuffled off after Ami.

Graham wasted no time sidling up next to Briana. His stern gaze followed Todd across the room. "Is he okay?"

"Yes. For now."

"I don't suppose you want to dance?" he asked. Briana glanced at a few people gyrating beside the jukebox as it blasted oldies. Nothing on earth would inspire her to embarrass herself so thoroughly, but she also felt no desire to be close to Graham again. Somehow this morning's escapade had provided unexpected but welcome closure.

"I'm sorry, Graham. That wouldn't be a good idea. I've had a long day."

"You're telling me. I can't get this morning out of my head." His hand crept up her arm. She gently moved away from him. "But it looks like you have."

"Look, Graham, you know I care about you. We're just too different to be anything more than friends. As for the rest—well, it wouldn't be right to pretend we can have something when we both know it's impossible."

His eyes dropped to the half-empty bottle he still held. "Guess I have to accept that, for now at least."

"Come on," she said, "let's sit down and have some wings. As good friends."

They joined Ami and Todd at a corner booth. A paper plate of wings already sat in the middle of the table, oozing pungent red Tabasco sauce. Ami nursed a pale pink drink with a green paper umbrella sticking out of it, but Briana felt relieved to see a cola in front of Todd.

"Hey, man, I'm really sorry about your boat." Todd darted a sheepish look at Graham. "I got into a little trouble last night. Did some stupid shit."

"You'll have more than a little trouble if you pull a stunt like that again." Graham crossed his arms over his chest and leaned back against the vinyl-covered seat. "Not just for what you did to me, but to your sister."

Todd nodded in obvious misery. "I can't do anything to change what happened, but I'm not going to make the same mistake again. I promise you, and Bri, that much."

Ami twirled her paper umbrella between her fingers. "Well, you got your boat back in one piece, and I got my purse. What more do you want?"

Briana could see Graham getting hotter than the sauce on the chicken wings, and she didn't want a replay of the brawl on the beach, with Graham taking Sebastian's role in the fracas. "All right, why don't we let the whole subject drop, once and for all? The boat survived, both wallets showed up, and Todd's making amends to everyone involved. For now, I'm content to leave it at that, and I hope the rest of you are, too."

Ami dropped the umbrella back into her glass and raised it. "No need to put that one to a vote. Onward and upward, I always say." It didn't take her long to reduce the pink concoction to a glob of crushed ice. She banged the glass back down with a flourish. "Come on, Todd, let's cut a rug. The tension around here is driving me crazy."

The two of them crossed the room and took their places among the other couples on the tiny parquet dance floor.

While Briana sat silently beside Graham Smith and waited for Todd and Ami to return, The Chum Bucket's front door opened several times to admit new patrons. Most of them were regulars, though a few seemed to be natives of other towns, presumably even duller than this one. Suddenly, to Briana's amazement, Ruby and Sebastian Morgan walked in.

They still wore the same clothes they'd had on back at the house. Ruby's provocative attire instantly attracted plenty of male attention, but just as many women turned to look at Sebastian. He'd donned a knee-length leather jacket over his black shirt and jeans, and the hem of the coat swung around his long legs as he strolled through the crowd. Briana felt as though a magnet forcefully drew her eyes toward him.

Soon she began sweating again.

The pull between them seemed to work both ways. He spotted her immediately and headed straight for their booth. Ruby followed him.

"Please join us," Briana said, motioning to the seats Todd and Ami had vacated. Graham's steely expression never changed while she introduced them. "I have to admit, this is the last place I expected to see you."

"It was my idea," Ruby announced as she slid into the booth. Sebastian sat down next to her. "Your brother told me about a bar in town called The Chum Bucket. I insisted that Sebastian take me. I wanted to see if it really attracts bloodthirsty predators."

"I'm sure plenty of them are here already. You can't always tell right away," Briana said.

"Agreed," said Sebastian. Neither he nor Ruby so much as glanced at the wings in the middle of the table, even when Briana offered them some. She assumed they found messy American finger food distasteful. They didn't want to drink, either, since they made no effort to walk to the bar or flag down any of the servers who periodically swept by.

"So how do you like Morgan House?" Graham asked. His voice held a touch of suspicion. "You guys took on quite a project there. Not many people would have the patience to clean up the mess that loony old man left behind."

Briana gaped, shocked at his rudeness, but Sebastian remained unfazed.

"Or the money, you mean. To me, Morgan Point is more than just an investment. It is a matter of family pride. My great-grandfather, whose name I carry, built the house. It seemed fitting that I undertake the restoration personally."

"This isn't your first trip to Darkisle, then," Graham pressed. "I mean, if you're into your heritage and all."

Sebastian shook his head. "My sister and I lived in Amsterdam for many years. We never found the time to visit before now. Our loss, I'm sure." He spoke to Graham, but focused his attention on Briana. His stare bored into her until she felt the top of her scalp prickle. "Unfortunately, we are still unfamiliar with local customs. I assume the citizens of Darkisle amuse themselves here?"

Briana spoke up before Graham offered another boorish comment. "I'm afraid our entertainment can't compare to what you're used to. Once the tourists come, a few more places open up along the coast. You're probably not too interested in beachside clubs and video arcades, though."

"Personally, no. My sister is the one who gets restless. I need to maintain a store of diversions to keep her occupied."

Graham snickered. "I've heard about the diversions in Amsterdam."

"Debauchery exists in every corner of the world. Perhaps Amsterdam does offer extra temptations, but I am in no position to say. Such pursuits hold no fascination for me."

That train of thought reminded Briana to check what Ami and Todd were up to. Peering over Sebastian's shoulder, she saw that they had abandoned the dance floor and moved to the bar. "Excuse me for a moment," she said, and started to get up.

Ruby held up a hand to stop her. "Please. Let me."

Leaving the table, she breezed through the room and cut across the dance floor. At the bar, she greeted Todd as if Ami weren't present at all, neatly wedging herself between the two. Briana couldn't hear what the three of them said, but Ami's infuriated expression spoke volumes.

"I see your brother and his friend picked up right where they left off," Sebastian observed, arching a brow.

"I suppose." Briana scowled. "I'd be lying if I said I was happy they found each other."

"You never know," Graham put in. "Sometimes the least likely relationships last the longest."

"And sometimes they destroy both people involved," Sebastian said.

"Anyway, I think it's time we got going. Todd and I only came in to sample a few wings. They're very good; I'm sorry you don't like them, Mr. Morgan."

"Please call me Sebastian. 'Mr. Morgan' makes me sound as decrepit as poor loony Edgar."

Briana blushed at the reference to Graham's insult, but Graham only grunted. "I guess I'll see you tomorrow, then," she said quickly.

"I look forward to it. Be there at sunset."

Briana noticed Graham's disapproval and hastened to explain. She hated the way her blush deepened. "Todd is doing some restoration work for them."

"Great." Graham shoved his empty bottle aside and got up. "Time I got moving, too. Nice seeing you, Bri. Take care."

"You, too." She avoided Sebastian's gaze as he followed her to her feet. No doubt he wondered about her relationship with Graham, but she suspected he was too polite ever to ask. She hoped he was perceptive enough to understand that their connection belonged to past history, and she intended to keep it that way.

"Tomorrow, then," she said, and hurried away. She resisted the urge to look back at Sebastian.

She reached the bar just as her brother opened his newly recovered wallet.

"Don't bother. We're leaving," she informed him. "We've both had enough soda for one night."

"Your sister is very kind to look out for you the way she does." Ruby grinned, flaunting those glistening white teeth of hers. She could have been a model for those foul-tasting little plastic strips Briana found totally worthless but kept buying. Apparently they did work on some people.

To her relief, Todd didn't put up a fuss. If anything, he looked grateful for an excuse to extract himself from the uncomfortable social sandwich he'd ended up in the middle of. "Sorry, guess my ride's leaving," he said to both Ami and Ruby. "Maybe we can do this another time."

"No matter. I'll have you all to myself tomorrow evening." Ruby looked directly into Ami's defiant face as she said it. Briana and Todd discreetly slipped outside while the two women glared at each other. "Thanks for not embarrassing me in there," Briana said as they settled back into the car. "Well, except for the dancing."

"I dance better when I'm drunk. Anyway, I'm the one who should say thanks. Who knew I was so irresistible to women?" His eyes gleamed in wonder. "I expected them to start a catfight over me right on top of the bar."

Briana resisted her natural inclination to share in his flippant humor and to go on pretending that none of this was a big deal. "Todd, listen to me. We don't need any more fighting. You don't need to hang around with people like Ami. She'll drag you down. I know the Morgans are weird, but they're trying to help. Just focus on one thing at a time."

"And one woman at a time, you mean? Now you're really going too far."

"I'm not suggesting that you get involved with Ruby, if that's what you think. I mean the work on Morgan House. Give it your best shot. Romance can wait."

"Yeah, I hear you there. I don't need to end up bare-assed in the pokey again anytime soon." Todd dropped his head and raked his hands through his hair. "I know you're right. I'm sorry. I'm going to do better."

"I want this to be a new start for you, Todd. Maybe for both of us."

Without warning, her mind flashed back on the way Sebastian Morgan's intense stare had zeroed in on her at the bar. Once he sat down at the table, Graham Smith had totally ceased to exist. . Even now, the armpits of her shirt felt damp. No man ever had that strong an effect on her before.

"A new start." Todd's good humor quickly returned. "Let's not drink to that."

Chapter 4

Sebastian waited until Todd and Briana left The Chum Bucket and then approached the bar and drew Ruby aside. Ami continued to glare at them as they moved to a private niche beside the jukebox.

"Time to go," Sebastian growled in her ear.

Ruby's eyes remained fixed on the dance floor, where a tipsy man ground his hips and sang along with the music. "Not now. I'm having fun. Besides…you know what I need."

"We've been through this. You can't feed here. Don't ask."

She glanced at him long enough to scowl. "You might consider it noble to starve yourself, but I want, and like, to feed. I don't intend to wait much longer. I get crabby when I'm hungry."

"I don't object to you enjoying your existence, and your appetite, within reason. However, I draw the line at compromising our safety."

"You know, that's the trouble with guys from your century. So freaking paternalistic."

Sebastian raised a brow. "I believe I've adapted to the twenty-first century quite well."

"Well, I'm glad you think so."

"Actually, I'm prepared to prove it to you. It just so happens that I have a solution to your dilemma. Note that I said you couldn't feed here…not that you couldn't feed at all. Come on. Let's drive."

"Awesome." She flashed her pointed teeth at him, so quickly that no one else could have registered the movement. "You're the best."

"Now will you take back what you said about my being old-fashioned?"

"I'll defer judgment until dawn. Now let's go. I've been cooped up in this dive long enough."

He couldn't blame her too much for being young and famished. Fifty-nine years was not so long by their standards. No doubt many more decades would have to pass before his attempts at guidance sunk in.

Minutes later they were roaring up the coast in Sebastian's dark green Maserati, following the curve of the sea. Salty night air blasted their faces through the open windows. Ruby was deep in thought as she watched the scenery flash by: long lines of dingy vacation cabins, boarded-up tourist attractions, and rows of fishing boats bobbing in the darkened bay. After a while, she turned to him.

"I've been meaning to ask you. Why are you letting those humans move in on us?"

He feigned confusion. "What humans?"

"Please. That woman, and her brother."

"Ah, the Dempseys. Simple. We need the work done. Edgar left the house in a shameful state. It's likely to crumble around our heads if we don't do something."

Her amusement faded to incredulity. "Now you've really lost your mind. You preach and carry on about discretion and safety, and you invite humans to poke through our house—to hang around us all evening? It's just a matter of time before they see or hear too much!"

"I intend to stay and supervise them. You're free to go out."

"Supervise, huh?" She made the word sound dirty. "You want to feed on her, don't you?"

"Of course not." His hands tightened on the steering wheel. The Maserati already traveled at breakneck speed, but he edged it up another notch. The road seemed to consume his attention.

"You say that now. In time, you'll admit the truth. You hunger as much as I do. Probably more. How long have you gone without real blood? A couple of years?"

Sebastian sighed. "Two years, six months, four days...and seven hours," he confessed miserably.

"That's insane." Ruby opened her mouth wide and licked the sharp points of her teeth as if to taunt him. "Don't think I'm upset to see you come to your senses. Quite the opposite. The man looks delicious to me, too. B negative, I'd guess. Not my favorite, but he'll do."

"Ruby! How often must I remind you to be cautious? This is our home now. We must do our best to fit in. We don't want a repeat of Amsterdam."

"Oh, who cares?" Ruby squirmed. "I wanted to leave anyway. All those nasty canals and stupid bicycles everywhere. You got bored, too. Don't bother to lie."

Sebastian let the matter drop. He wasn't ready to ask himself how close Ruby had come to the truth. He had no intention of debating his emotional or nutritional needs with her.

"Where is this place, anyway?" she griped.

"I suggest you pace yourself. One day, your impatience will get you into trouble."

"So what else is new?"

At the very end of the beach the hushed darkness gave way to the hazy glow of tiki torches and the callous beat of industrial dance music. The club itself came into view as they crested the hill. Jutting halfway over the cliffs, its open deck functioned as a dance floor, strung with festive party lights and vibrant with activity.

Ruby's enthusiasm increased by the minute. "Now we're talking!" she chirped as Sebastian pulled into the gravel parking lot.

"We've driven almost a hundred miles," he said. "No one here will recognize us. We must also be sure they don't remember us. Therefore, I ask you to comport yourself with discretion."

"You can trust me."

Sebastian laughed to himself as Ruby bounded past him, pushed through the double glass doors, and charged into the club. As he followed her inside, he saw several pairs of male eyes turn to her with interest. She would enjoy herself here.

The space, so modern and loud like everything these days, dazzled him. Neon-blue strobe lighting flashed across a crowded, circular bar, while a wall-sized video screen blazed a kaleidoscope of random images. The music blared loud and fast, and the patrons were on the move, dancing or slipping from one shadowy part of the room to the next. Some huddled in pairs or groups. Some partied alone.

A young blond man in a midriff shirt and white jeans paused to tilt his head at Ruby, exposing his slender neck. His skin glowed purple in the artificial light. She stared back at him with obvious lust.

Sebastian caught up to her and leaned over to whisper in her ear. "Go," he told her. He didn't have to repeat himself. She plunged into the crowd without so much as a backward glance.. He took a seat at a small table near the bar.

Sebastian had to admire her style. Back when he still hunted, it often took him the better part of an evening to interest a mark—unless he offered cash, a ploy he used only if desperation gnawed at his empty stomach. Tonight he intended simply to observe.

"Care for something?"

A young woman had stopped at his side, holding a tray of colorful drinks toward him. She was scantily attired, even by twenty-first century standards, with shoulder-length dark hair that reminded him of Briana Dempsey. His senses twitched as her enchanting scent reached his nose.

"No thank you."

Smiling, she bent close to him. Her almost-bare breasts hovered inches from his face. "Are you sure? I can mix something special for you. Just ask."

Sebastian struggled against the emotion that squeezed his throat and the raw physical need that swelled his dried-out veins. Most of all, he fought back the image that blossomed in his mind at the sight of those soft, upturned lips as they spoke to him. His own lips could capture them so easily and then drift lower, toward the throbbing vein that creased her milky throat. He could see it, trembling just beneath the surface.

Averting his face from her, he shook his head sadly. "I think not."

"Okay, then. Suit yourself."

His entire body slumped in relief when she shrugged and finally walked away. The smell of her hormone-laden blood thankfully faded, along with the pounding in his lifeless guts.

But an image of Briana remained.

Ruby, as usual, had guessed the truth before he did. Years ago he not only would have wanted to feed on her, he probably would have done so by now.

But times had changed. He had changed. Coming to places like this reminded him how much.

Soon he spotted another woman eyeing him, this time from across the bar. Long ago, she would have seemed a desirable prospect: brunette, late twenties, wearing a sleeveless dress that revealed an intricate tribal tattoo slithering up her right bicep. Her florid complexion suggested a sugary flavor and a strong constitution. He'd always preferred donors who could handle a more aggressive session. Somehow it lessened the guilt he felt even when the woman participated willingly. This one obviously would.

She rolled the edge of her highball glass over her coy smile.

Sebastian stood, trembling, and ventured farther into the club to find Ruby. He saw no sign of her, nor the man in the white jeans, but several women turned to look at him as he passed. He recognized their interest as an overture to much more.

He continued his search outside the club. A few people milled about, some of them carrying drinks. One couple leaned against the side of the building. The woman's hand was boldly roving over the front of the man's pants. The sight startled him, and he looked up and away. The sky had begun to change: dawn would come in a few hours. He and Ruby would be home by then, safely ensconced in their sunless bedrooms and safe from their compulsions for another few hours.

Eventually, he found Ruby beside a tree at the far end of the parking lot. She sat cross-legged, her spiky hair mussed, her mouth swollen and wet. The young man from the club lay crumpled in the dirt. His head was propped on a root that protruded from the ground like a monstrous limb. His discarded midriff shirt lay beside him, the collar dark with spatter.

"Is he all right?" Sebastian stood over the man, relieved to see the narrow ribcage rising and falling under the pale skin. Except for the stained shirt, he might have been sleeping off a long night of partying.

Ruby shrugged. "Yeah, but he'll be out for a while. He had so much beer in him that I'm a little tipsy myself." She extended her hand. Sebastian helped her up.

"Time to go." He led her back to the car. Sated and happy, she didn't protest.

"So, did you enjoy yourself?" Ruby asked as they flew back down the same winding roads they'd traveled earlier, moving even faster this time. Her speech sounded a bit slurred, the result of her partner's high blood-alcohol content.

"I'm not sure I'd go that far."

"You're hopeless."

"Perhaps." Luckily, she didn't ask him if he'd fed. Sebastian didn't want to consider how close he'd come. And he didn't want to think or talk about Briana again.

Finally, they crossed the long, narrow bridge that separated Darkisle from the more accessible villages along the coast. Despite the late hour, a few hazy lights still sprinkled the landscape.

"You know…." Ruby licked her lips. "I keep thinking about those humans you invited over. I know I wasn't too enthusiastic before. But I've changed my mind. Now I think it might be nice to have them around. Convenient. Safe."

He didn't answer.

On their way to Morgan Point, they passed The Dunes Motel and then the Dempsey's small Cape Cod-style house. The night air had grown cool and still. Sebastian tilted his head and listened for Briana's heartbeat as they drove by. Soon enough he picked up the muffled throb, mixing with the distant whisper of the sea.

Chapter 5

Briana felt relieved to see Ami's car parked outside The Dunes the next morning. That meant she hadn't skipped out on her bill, or at least not yet. Briana just hoped her guest hadn't driven here drunk from The Chum Bucket. The awkward angle at which she'd parked didn't look promising, but the sides of the motel appeared intact and no other cars sat in the lot. Paying for new siding or being sued for vehicle damage was the last thing The Dunes needed at this delicate fiscal moment.

Fortunately, business began to pick up that very morning. Around noon four college boys pulled in on their way back from a spring break excursion to parts unknown. Privately, she wondered if they had been thrown out of their previous digs.—Why else would they show up at Darkisle? Still, as long as they paid the bill, she wouldn't pry.

Sandy, the older woman who came in once a week to do the housekeeping, expressed less enthusiasm about their new crop of clients.

"Young people like that are always trouble," she declared as she entered the office with a load of linens for the laundry room in back. "You can be sure they'll leave me a mess to clean up when they finally check out. And they're already blasting that awful music."

"Ah, give them a chance," protested her teenaged grandson, Reggie. "They're just having fun."

"Their kind of fun we don't need around here. I suggest you keep your eyes on that laundry basket and steer clear of Briana's guests."

Reggie sighed and took the laundry from her. Along with Sandy, he'd become a mainstay at The Dunes, taking shifts behind the front desk when Briana was otherwise occupied, or helping his grandmother wash, fold, and redistribute towels and sheets to all the rooms, rented out or not. In some ways she felt sorry for him. Young people in Darkisle tended either to flee, cutting all ties, or hang around forever, generally nothing in between. As she watched Reggie meekly carry the basket off to the washer, Briana predicted he would fall into the latter category as she had.

Sandy stumped back out to continue her rounds. She returned within moments, looking even more annoyed.

"That woman wants to talk to you," she told Briana. "Some problem with the room. No doubt she caused it herself."

Briana could guess as to whom *"that woman"* referred. Assuring Sandy she would take care of the crisis, she walked down to Ami's door and knocked. Sandy followed, uninvited.

Ami emerged in a pink bathrobe, a towel wrapped around her head.

"Something's wrong with my shower," she complained. "I tried to turn up the hot water and look what happened." She held out her hand to display the chrome knob, broken clean off the wall. "How about sending Tom over to fix it? Isn't he some kind of plumber?"

"No, *Todd* isn't." Briana emphasized his name. "He works with wood, paint, and things like that."

"Well, he told me he's going to rebuild that old haunted house on the cliff from top to bottom. I'm sure he can fix a shower."

"I'd say he exaggerated a little. All right, though, I'll send him over...provided you put some clothes on."

Ami batted her false eyelashes. Somehow, she'd had time to apply those, along with plenty of other makeup, but no chance to get dressed in the wake of the great shower catastrophe. "Of course I will. What kind of a girl do you think I am?"

"We need to collect the towels," Sandy said, stepping forward as if prepared to forcibly wrench the one from Ami's head.

"I'll drop it outside when I'm ready."

She closed the door on them. Briana and Sandy walked back to the office. "Wouldn't kill these people to make our lives easier once in a while," Sandy grumbled.

"Her hair was dry," Briana said. "If she took off the towel, we would have known."

Naturally, Todd agreed to come right down and assess the problem. Sandy pretended to sort through the clean linens Reggie had brought out to them while she listened to every word.

"Is he really going to fix up Morgan House?" she asked.

"Yes. Why?"

"It's just strange, considering Edgar kept it locked up for so long. I'm sure the place is filthy and probably full of dry rot and termites."

"Well, the new owners seem to be surviving all right. Maybe it's not so bad. In the old days, they built houses to last."

Sandy frowned. "I wonder about those people, too. What have you heard?"

"Not much. I've only seen them in town once." Briana thought it best not to mention where. "They're Edgar's grandchildren."

"Or so they claim."

"Why do you say that?"

"Only because I can't imagine how Edgar Morgan could have any grandchildren. When I was little, my mother worked part-time in the kitchen up there. Before the old man went crazy, they used to have guests and parties and things like that."

"Really? I had no idea."

Sandy nodded. "Edgar had only one daughter I knew of, and she was a few years older than me."

Briana ran a quick calculation in her head. Sandy was almost 70 years old, making Edgar's mystery daughter a bit old to have had children the age of Sebastian and Ruby. Unconventional, but not impossible.

"Well, she probably married at a late age. Look how long Edgar lived, and how many wives he had."

"I doubt she had any children. She disappeared, you see. Right after her first year of college."

"Disappeared?"

"Ayuh. High and mighty little thing, she was. Spoiled rotten, though I blame Edgar and his wife for that more than I blame her."

"You knew her personally?"

"Heavens, no. A servant's girl didn't travel in her circle. She didn't go to the village school either. Edgar sent her to some fancy girl's academy in Boston, and then she went off to college. In the summer, she'd go off to Europe and shop. One day she left with some of her friends and didn't come back. Edgar never saw or heard from her again. Losing her almost killed him. My mother said he was never right after that."

Briana gaped. "Her friends didn't know what happened to her?"

"So they said. Not everyone believed them."

"But no one found proof she died either. Could there have been a man? Someone she knew her father wouldn't approve of?"

"I suppose. She always was a wild thing. Or so people said anyway."

Briana digested this information as she helped Sandy fold the linens. "People covered things up in those days—like an illegitimate baby. Maybe that's the story behind this current generation. They might not even know the truth themselves."

"Might be. Then again, Edgar was married so many times that he might have had a son and just never mentioned him. These two carry the Morgan name after all."

"I guess that would explain a lot."

Todd showed up a few minutes later, strolling down the path that connected their house to The Dunes. He carried his big metal toolbox, which Briana hadn't seen in a while. "Just on my way to take a look at Ami's shower," he said, stepping into the office.

"Make sure that's all you look at," Briana reminded him. Sandy's expression broadcast her disapproval, though she said nothing. They went on folding in silence.

A few minutes later, Todd returned. "Ami's going to drive me up to the hardware place for some new fixtures. We'll be back soon."

"Todd—"

"Fixtures, Bri. Fixtures. I may as well grab a few things for Morgan House, too." His cheeks reddened a bit. "I...uh...I'm going to need some cash."

Briana sighed. "I figured as much." Taking a key ring off its hook on the wall, she went into the office and unlocked the bottom desk drawer. She extracted three rumpled twenty-dollar bills from the petty cash tin.

As she carried the cash back to the lobby, one of the college boys wandered in.

"We wondered if you had some ice," he said.

"Go back out, take a left. Machine's right outside the laundry room."

"Thanks." The young man ducked out again.

"I can imagine what the ice is for," Sandy grumbled. "I don't want to see the condition of that room when they get finished."

Briana handed the money to Todd.

"Get a few packs of light bulbs, too, would you? Never too soon to start fixing the place up. The tourists will be here before you know it."

Through the glass door, Briana spotted Ami, fully dressed for travel, coming up the walkway. She didn't come into the office but waited outside for Todd. He stuffed the money in his jeans and hurried out to her, grinning.

Briana saw nothing more of Ami, her brother, or the college students for the rest of the afternoon.

* * * *

Sebastian spent his first waking moments out in the salt-laden night air standing motionless behind the eroded railing with his head tilted back, eyes half-closed, and arms stretched out at his sides. He had wasted no time in claiming the room with the small stone terrace as his own. Now that he had chased away the trespassers and replaced the tawdry furnishings he could finally enjoy his private sanctuary.

Slowly, the strong rays of the moon penetrated his cold flesh and invigorated his muscles. The caress of the night air moved over him with the nurturing grace of soft fingertips. His body opened to the shadowed world around him like a night-blooming flower.

He supposed the closest thing to this tranquil ritual was what humans called sunbathing—something unknown during his own mortal days. Sometimes he regretted that, especially when he viewed photographs of nearly—or fully!—naked women stretched out on bone-white sand or floating carelessly in water, their flesh sparkling under a brilliant sun. Still, the night held sensual pleasures aplenty and all without the pain of burns or the chafing of sweat.

He shifted comfortably as blue light spilled over his bare chest, warming the ridges and hollows. How strange to be back in this house, back on this familiar slab of weather-beaten stone. Amused, Sebastian envisioned his parents' horrified reaction if they saw him now, their treasured heir, his modesty preserved by nothing but a bed sheet around his waist.

Not that they could imagine such a spectacle: both had now been dead for well over a hundred years, and to them the concept of a vampire, if they had ever heard the term at all, belonged to the world of their servants' lurid dime novels.

Sebastian's intimate knowledge of the moon's positions told him when to quit. Now came the part of the evening ritual he hated. Gliding back into the room, he dropped the sheet, retrieved his dressing gown from a peg by the door, and pulled it on while he padded downstairs. As he'd expected, Ruby waited for him at the dining room table. His syringe rested on a folded linen napkin, which in turn lay on an ornately engraved silver tray that had once been his mother's. How disconcerting to see all these familiar objects again, but in so different a context.

"Ugh." Ruby wrinkled her nose as Sebastian settled himself into a chair, picked up the needle, and fitted the point to the tender flesh inside his wrist. "As many times as I've watched you do that, I can't get used to it. How can you stand putting that sludge into yourself?"

Sebastian pushed the plunger, filling his dry veins with the special nutrients that would relieve him of the need for blood for another night. The pain snaking through his body was temporary; he'd learned not to wince. Ruby averted her gaze.

"When you reach my age, you'll realize that small discomforts are worth the greater conveniences."

"I don't consider my hunger an inconvenience. I find it exciting. It motivates me."

"It will become an inconvenience if you don't learn to be discreet." He put the empty syringe aside and pressed the bloodless hole on his wrist with his thumb, forcing the chemicals into his body. "Anyway, I never said the drug took the hunger away."

Ruby clicked her tongue in disgust. She continued to pace. "I hoped that was why you invited them. A feast for both of us."

"Ruby!" Sebastian brought his open palm down on the table in sudden anger. "I will not repeat myself. You must learn to conduct yourself in a way that does not expose either of us, or the humans around us, to danger. Please arrange to be elsewhere when Todd and Briana arrive if you don't believe you can do this."

She smiled, baring her sharp teeth in precisely the way he had always warned her not to. "Are you kidding? I wouldn't miss their visit for the world. By the way, do you plan to put regular clothes on, or do you want to be ready for action the moment Miss Briana walks in?"

Jaw clenched, Sebastian rose from the table. The formula had not quite dissipated into his body, causing a slight rush of dizziness. He braced himself with both hands so Ruby couldn't tell.

His tone of voice left no room for disagreement. "Stand by the door in the event they arrive before I return. If that is the case, you will be polite and demure."

"Assuming they show up at all. Maybe you're the one who needs to slow your roll, Sebastian. Everyone in that sleazy bar saw you hit on her."

She seemed determined to annoy him this evening. Sebastian resolved not to give her the satisfaction of losing his temper with her. It only made her push harder.

Instead of answering, he turned and headed back upstairs. Ruby was right: it would be a bit awkward for Briana to come upon him in a state of undress.

The thoughts that flowed all too naturally from that mental image proved even more awkward.

* * * *

Briana left Reggie in charge of the desk and headed back into the office after she and Sandy had refitted all the motel rooms with fresh sheets and clean towels.. She spent the afternoon cleaning out the desk and sorting the mail. To her relief, she found no overdue bills.

She got home just before sundown, expecting to find Todd there, getting ready to call on the Morgans. She didn't. Figuring he'd return at any moment, she killed some time by going through her closet, finding an outfit suitable for her visit to Morgan House that evening. Not that she wanted to impress anyone but she could hardly wear the jeans and t-shirt she'd worn to clean the motel.

Suppertime came and went with no sign of Todd. She forced herself not to worry as she microwaved some frozen pizza slices and watched the sky grow darker. Surely Todd would be home soon.

He wasn't.

Not sure whether to be angry or frightened for Todd's safety, Briana headed back to the motel, driving this time in case he was there and ready to head directly up to Morgan Point.

She had barely pulled out of the driveway and started down the road when she spotted Todd ambling along the dirt shoulder, carrying his toolbox.

She pulled up alongside him. "Where have you been?" She realized she didn't need to ask as soon as he'd opened his mouth. His breath reeked of cheap beer.

"Those guys from the motel," he stammered. "They invited Ami and me to come out with them for a while. They offered to buy us a round. I didn't want to be rude."

"You never got to the hardware store, did you?"

Todd hung his head in shame. Briana wanted to reach through the window and strangle him.

"I can't take you to Morgan House like this!"

"I'll be okay. Just need some coffee. I didn't have much, Bri, I swear! Only one. Two at the most!"

"Get in."

She drove along the waterfront, stopped at a take-out sandwich shop near the pier, and bought two extra-large cups of coffee. She handed one to Todd.

"Start drinking," she told him.

He finished both on the way up the cliff.

Sebastian Morgan himself opened the door. "I expected you twenty minutes ago, Mr. Dempsey," he said coldly.

Todd spread his hands in a clumsy gesture of surrender. "I'm all yours. Show me what to do."

"Very well. My plan is to renovate this house one room at a time. We shall start with the rooms we use most. The foyer is the first thing guests see when they enter. As you know, first impressions are hard to revise."

Briana surveyed the foyer along with Todd. Though a hint remained of its former grandeur, the space was now a sorry jumble of peeling, outdated wallpaper, warped walls, and scuffed wood flooring.

"Make a list of what you require in terms of materials, and I will have it delivered tomorrow. At that point you may begin work. If I am satisfied with your skills, we will arrange further tasks."

"Okay, I got it covered." Kneeling, Todd opened his workbox and removed a flat pencil and a small spiral-bound pad of lined paper. His hands shook slightly when he held the objects up. "See? I came late, but prepared."

"Then by all means begin. I shall return to consult with you after I walk your sister to her car."

"Go for it, man."

A stony-faced Sebastian accompanied Briana back outside. She appreciated the darkness, so that Sebastian couldn't see her utter embarrassment at Todd's behavior.

"I'm sorry we arrived late," she said as they walked toward her car. "I let him run an errand for the motel, and it took longer than expected."

"You needn't fabricate excuses for him. Your brother must take responsibility for his actions. He and I have an agreement, and I expect him to fulfill it."

"He will. At least, I'll try to make sure he will." Briana fought to contain the emotions bubbling up inside her. She saw no point in denying it any longer. Her brother was desperately, dangerously ill. Covering up for him would never work.

Worst of all, she'd been looking forward all day to seeing Sebastian again. Now Todd had ruined that for her, too.

To her horror, she burst into sobs.

"It isn't your fault." Sebastian touched her hand. Slowly, his fingers curled around hers. His skin chilled her, but Briana found that refreshing compared to the grief boiling inside her. "I warned you before not to claim his failures as your own. That is a sure path to madness."

Appalled at her own loss of control, Briana was nevertheless unable to stop herself. She rested her face against Sebastian's firm chest and cried into his black silk shirt.

"I'm sorry," she said, lifting her head and wiping her eyes. "I'm not usually this foolish."

"You care about your brother's future. Your reaction makes sense."

"It's not just the beer. I'm also sorry he's insulting you. You tried to give him a chance. He isn't the least bit grateful for that. But I want you to know that I am."

Sebastian paused. He seemed genuinely caught off guard and moved by her concern for him.

In a way, that made things worse. Revealing too much of herself usually got her into trouble. Something told her this time wasn't going to be any different.

* * * *

Todd felt relieved when Sebastian left him alone, especially since his new boss had probably seized the opportunity to flirt with his sister. Maybe if Briana finally got some, she'd lay off his and Ami's case.

For a few minutes, he occupied himself by measuring corners, testing wood for rot, sketching out floor plans, and taking notes. While he worked, he could wrestle away the demon that nagged at him. Eventually, though, that familiar aching thirst swelled his tongue.

Todd set down his measuring tape, removed the top tray of his toolbox, and took out the bottle he'd concealed there. He used a small claw hammer to pop the top. Then he knelt in a corner with his back to the door and a few props arranged beside him. Anyone coming in would assume he'd bent down to record some measurements.

After a furtive glance around he lifted the beer to his lips. He was about to take a sip when someone seized his wrist and jerked it back so roughly that a jagged pain shot up his arm. Todd hit the floor, his shoulder colliding with the discarded hammer. He somehow managed to hang onto his beer.

"We can cancel this arrangement if it's going to be too difficult for you," Sebastian growled down at him. "Of course, we will still have the matter of a trespassing and assault charge to settle."

Todd moaned as Sebastian's fingers tightened. "Come on, man! I'm entitled to a little break!"

"You're entitled to what I allow you, and nothing more. If you fail to respect my home, the consequences will be unpleasant." As he spoke, he began to squeeze Todd's arm—hard. The bottle fell, cracked against the side of the toolbox, and rolled across the floor in pieces. A circle of foam spread around Todd's prone form. "Am I speaking in a language you can understand?"

"Y-yes," Todd whispered. The skin on his wrist had already turned fish-white, while the rest of his arm quickly went numb in Sebastian's unbelievably powerful grip. *The guy must do martial arts or something,* Todd thought. For a minute it seemed like he might just wring Todd's hand right off the joint.

"You may not realize I am watching you, but I have ways of knowing what you are doing–always. Never attempt to humiliate me again."

Finally, he let go and stepped away. Todd's eyes filled with tears as he rubbed the circulation back into his stiff fingers.

Sebastian stared down at the puddle of spilled beer. "Now clean up this disaster. My floor is in dreadful condition already. No need to make things worse."

Todd stayed on the floor, whimpering, while Sebastian turned and clomped upstairs. A few moments later, someone else entered the room. Todd froze, prepared to be brutalized again.

He breathed a sigh of relief to see Ruby. "Was my brother hard on you?" she asked innocently.

"No more than I deserved, I guess." Todd struggled to his feet. He'd cut himself on the bottle, though he hadn't noticed it before. Now that his veins were plumping up again, a trickle of blood began to course down his forearm. Ruby stared at the flow, mesmerized.

"Don't worry," Todd said. He covered the wound with his hand. "I'm all right."

Ruby's eyes flicked to the beer bottle. "Why do you crave alcohol?"

"I don't know. I guess because it tastes good. It makes me feel relaxed."

She tilted her head with curiosity. "Does it? How interesting."

"You mean you've never tried beer?"

"No…not exactly."

He finally succeeded in stanching the trickle of blood down his arm. "Well, don't. It's not worth the trouble. Stick to herbal tea."

"Your love for this substance has cost you a lot, I guess."

"Oh, yeah. Big time. Sometimes I think I need someone to control every minute of my life. Then I'd get into a lot less trouble."

"But when your sister tries to do so, you become resentful."

"Yeah. I get into this rebellion thing. Makes no sense, I know."

Ruby's lips curled in a tight smile. "You know, that actually does make sense to me. Perhaps I can help you."

She moved closer and ran her fingers along his injured arm. Her thumb stroked the shallow cut from the bottle. Todd felt the pain ebb. His eyes drooped as a wave of exhaustion washed through his body.

Laughing, Ruby took her hand away and licked at her thumb. Then she winked at him and walked back out of the foyer.

This chick is too much, Todd thought. He realized that, in spite of everything that had gone wrong, he felt peaceful enough to smile.

Maybe this gig would work out after all.

Chapter 6

The next week ranked among the least stressful, or even the most pleasant, of Briana's life. The motel took in some decent business as a group of mature bird-watchers descended on Darkisle in search of a rare gull, Todd no longer complained about working nights at Morgan House, and both Graham and Ami apparently found other people to pester.

Only one problem remained. She had to find a way to get Sebastian Morgan into her bed.

Or herself into his. She didn't care which. She'd fallen in lust.

She couldn't pinpoint the exact moment when her longing for Sebastian had ignited. Maybe the first time she saw him swaggering around in his knee-length leather coat, or maybe when his fingers first gently curled around hers, or even when she had rested her tear-washed cheek against his shirt. Ultimately, though, what did that matter? She only knew that she had to feel him against her. She wanted to slide her hands through that thick dark hair, which she imagined would dust his entire body, and arch herself into those muscular arms while his strong thighs gripped hers.

More than once during the days that followed, she found herself flashing back to the visit she'd paid Sebastian in his study at Morgan House. The visions grew more detailed each time she mentally replayed them. Before long, lusty phantasms haunted her almost constantly.

In real life, the two of them had conversed with decorous formality and restraint. In her fantasy, though, Sebastian didn't simply peer up at her from behind his stately desk. Instead, he pulled himself up to his full, impressive height, reached across with both hands, and pulled her onto its polished surface.

Moments later—her subconscious skipped over the awkward details—they were naked, twined together, their bodies slick with sweat. The image was so vivid that she could feel his fingers skimming her moistening crevice and then sliding inside to stroke her pulsing inner walls. His thumb rolled against her swelling pleasure pearl, strumming her nerve endings raw, urging her to the very peak of desire.

Desperate to join their flesh more completely, she reached between them to close her hand around his surging shaft. The rigid column of flesh filled her palm, the needy pulse within quickening until it matched her own heartbeat.

His cockhead bulged with need, replacing his groping hand at the apex of her spread thighs. Gasping, Briana guided the plump organ toward the flames that raged between her legs.

He rocked his hips and speared her quickly, mercilessly, filling her with a single, needy thrust. He plunged so deeply inside her that the coarse fringe surrounding his cock tangled with the softer nest that cushioned her pulsating feminine notch. Her quivering inner folds closed over his flesh and drew him inside with such force that the breath rushed from her lungs and her body slid halfway across the desk.

Pleasure more intense than any sensation she'd ever experienced blasted through her in a searing explosion. An instant later, she and Sebastian dissolved together in a shimmer of liquid fire.

Though her logical mind never quite forgot that she was merely daydreaming, her body's responses burned painfully real. Imagining the silky brush of his skin against hers sent waves of tangible bliss rushing through her, sometimes with enough force to leave her hot, wet, and shuddering. After two such experiences, she made sure she was in private before allowing her thoughts to wander down that particular twisted path. Then her own fingers took the place of

Sebastian's lips, hands, or cock and acted out the scene all over again. Such interludes provided some relief but made her burn that much more for the real thing

Whether Sebastian sensed the electricity between them, too, she couldn't be sure. Yet he'd gone out of his way to maintain their connection when he could easily have dismissed Todd from his service forever. The compassion he'd shown her that night at his house went beyond gentlemanly protocol. At least, she hoped so.

Maybe she needed to give things a little push. The first step involved Todd and his work at the house.

For a few nights after her humiliating crying jag, Briana had kept her distance, dutifully leaving Todd on the front steps and waiting until he disappeared inside. At midnight, usually after checking on the motel, she would return to find him by the mailbox, dirty and exhausted, but on the whole in an upbeat mood. It proved simple enough to ask for a glimpse at his progress. Most likely contact with Sebastian Morgan would follow. She tried to think up witty conversation openers as she accompanied Todd up the stone steps, now cleaned and swept free of loose pebbles.

To her surprise, Todd pushed the door open and walked right through without so much as knocking. "Ruby leaves it unlocked for me," he explained. "She checks on me later. Come on in."

Briana was impressed to find the entire foyer transformed. The wooden floor had been re-laid, sanded, and polished. Todd had scraped away the old musty wallpaper and replaced it with rich hardwood panels. A few cans of paint stood pyramid-style against the wall.

Briana picked up one of the unopened containers. The label showed a deep-sea green, the shade of the kelp strands that sometimes drifted ashore.

The shade reminded her of Sebastian's eyes.

"I like it," she said.

Todd grinned. "Picked it out myself. Sebastian wanted something subtle but dramatic," he said proudly. "Ruby says I have an eye for color."

"It's true," Ruby herself declared. As in the past, she had appeared virtually out of nowhere. She strode toward Todd and leaned a little closer to him than etiquette permitted, but he didn't seem to mind. "Todd is the most skilled worker my brother and I have ever employed. And to think he does everything on his own."

"I prefer to work alone," Todd said. "It might take a little longer, but I know it's done the way I want."

His voice sounded strong, confident. Briana could hardly believe it. "Thank you for giving him the chance," she said to Ruby.

"And thank you for driving him here every night." Ruby flashed her perfect white teeth. "I don't know what we'd do without him."

"Speaking of your brother, where is he?" Briana attempted to sound casual.

"He should be down momentarily. I'm sure he'll be thrilled to find you here. Come and sit with me while Todd gets busy."

Briana hesitated. The thought of being trapped in a small room with Ruby for an unspecified period made her uneasy. She always felt as though the girl were laughing at some private joke with Briana as the punch line. "Oh, no, I don't want to be a nuisance. I shouldn't even have invited myself in."

"Nonsense. The Morgans might be antisocial by some people's standards, but we don't object to the occasional guest. Sebastian won't mind at all. Follow me."

The two women walked into a room that might have been a sort of parlor in a more formal era.

"Pretty soon I'm going to get this place fitted out right," Ruby announced. "Big screen TV, wall speakers, real furniture." She indicated a set of overstuffed Victorian chairs with obvious disdain. Briana wasn't sure whether Ruby expected her to sit in one or take part in deriding them. "As soon as Todd finishes the foyer, he's going to get started in here."

"I think you are mistaken," Sebastian's voice interrupted. "His next task is to refurbish my study."

"If you expect ladies to visit you here, you have to give them somewhere to sit and be comfortable," Ruby shot back. "Besides, at the rate Todd is going, it won't even take him a week. He can rearrange your boring old books after that."

"My books are already arranged to maximum efficiency. I was thinking instead of the ceiling plaster. If it comes loose and rains down on us, we will spend months cleaning up the debris. Besides, I need the office to conduct estate business. Electronic entertainment must take second place to practical requirements."

"I see this room with a chandelier," Ruby went on, ignoring him. "Something contemporary, of course, though I'm sure my brother will argue about that, too. He's determined to turn this place into some kind of museum. The past is gone, I say—let it stay that way."

"Ruby considers candles and fireplaces hopelessly moribund," Sebastian said. "I, on the other hand, believe such things lend character to a home."

"Never mind—she's going to agree with you," Ruby sniffed.

"Personally, I've always wished my house had a fireplace," Briana said. "I never thought of asking Todd to build one until now."

"When it gets cold, perhaps you could come over and enjoy ours." Ruby glanced at Sebastian. "Once everything is finished here, we'll have five operational ones."

"That's very kind of you." Briana felt a touch of embarrassment that Ruby saw through her so clearly, but she should have realized that women picked up on things men didn't. Time to change the subject. "I want to thank both of you for your kindness. Todd seems to have found a purpose in life again. That's something I couldn't give him on my own."

"I would call the arrangement mutually beneficial," Sebastian assured her as Ruby stifled a giggle. "You don't need to thank us."

Ruby seemed in no hurry to leave them alone, so Briana scanned the room in search of fresh fodder for discussion. A framed nineteenth century print of the house caught her eye. She walked over and pretended to study it. "You know, back in school, the kids used to say that Morgan House was haunted. Every year around Halloween, some of the boys would dare each other to knock on the door and ask Edgar Morgan for candy. They always came running back down the hill as fast as they could."

"And are you frightened now?" Ruby asked pointedly.

"Of course not," Briana said. "I never believed in such nonsense."

Sebastian gave his sister a chastising look. "Perhaps you'd like to see the rest of the house," he said to Briana. "I'd be happy to show it to you."

"I have to admit that I am a bit curious."

Ruby's expression made it clear she had become bored with the entire conversation. "Why don't I go and check on Todd?"

Sebastian motioned for Briana to precede him into the hall. "I believe we've seen enough of this room. Time for the tour to move forward."

For the next few minutes, Briana accompanied him through several ground-floor dining, smoking, and sitting areas. In the era when the house was built, Sebastian explained, families liked to have a separate space for each activity, not to mention for each gender. After dinner, he told her, the gentleman would retreat to discuss politics and economics, while the women would gather to share more genteel pursuits. Nannies and servants would usher away any disruptive children. Briana rather liked the sound of that.

A pair of French doors opened onto a small patio overlooking the rock-strewn beach. Noticing her interest, Sebastian pushed them open and motioned her outside. Briana headed straight for the sand. He caught up to her as she made her way toward the water.

Finally, things were falling into place tonight. They were alone. The Morgans' private beach was quiet and romantic. Even the weather was cooperating. The moon was glowing a vibrant amber, and the wind was blowing off the ocean, strong but pleasant.

Sebastian tilted his face and let the salty gusts tousle his hair. "Storm's coming. I can feel it."

Briana nodded. "Well, we get a lot of those in the spring. One of the bird-watchers at the motel told me the winds can get strong enough to blow tropical birds up here. Amazing, isn't it? You might wake up to find a flamingo on your roof."

"Unlikely, though appealing." He smiled, but looked back as if to make sure. "So how do you like Morgan House, with or without rare ornithological specimens?"

"Makes me realize how small my own place is. I'd be embarrassed to show you around the way you just did for me."

"Not at all. I would be delighted to be your guest."

"You know...I feel I should do something for you, considering all you've done for Todd. I'm not much of a cook—my idea of a big meal is a frozen pizza—so I don't quite dare to invite you for dinner."

"A meal would not be necessary. I'd enjoy your company without any food at all."

"That's nice of you to say. Have you met many people since you got here?"

"Your brother and Ami were the first. Aside from you, though, none have been as memorable."

Briana hoped the darkness obscured her hot blush. "This probably isn't the easiest place to start over. Darkisle is one of those towns where everyone knows everyone else, as the old saying goes. If you haven't lived here all your life, it can be tricky to fit in. Boredom is another issue. Fall and winter get pretty dreary, believe me."

"Yet you choose to stay," Sebastian observed.

"Mostly because I don't know any other way of life. My family has lived here for generations, just like yours." She paused as a sudden thought came to her. "I wonder if they knew each other, way back when."

"An intriguing possibility."

"I doubt my great-grandparents traveled in the same circles as yours. Still, it's an amusing thought."

"Quite."

They had strayed close to the waves. The sand here felt wet and hard.

"I'm going to take off my shoes," she said. "The water will destroy them."

Sebastian watched her pull off her boots and socks and toss them as far as she could onto dry land. With a murmur of pleasure, she thrust her bare toes into the sand and burrowed them in deep.

"Do you like the water?" she asked Sebastian.

"I'm afraid not. I prefer to observe from a distance."

"I can deal with boats as long as the waves aren't too rough. But you're right. Looking at it from here is perfectly fine."

He murmured noncommittally and slid his hands into his pockets. Briana casually swung her gaze along the water and ended up staring right at him. There was no question which view pleased her more.

"You probably won't mind spending the winter here. I get the feeling the isolation won't bother you at all."

"Why do you say that?"

"Because you always seem so content, so self-assured. Like now. You look like someone who prefers being alone."

He removed his hands from his pockets and gingerly stepped through the rocks, making his way cautiously toward her. He settled himself beside her, careful not to submerge his feet the way she had. "It may look that way because I am so used to being alone."

"Then I'm wrong?"

"Not entirely. I admit I've spent most of my…existence…on my own. With solitude comes safety. You've probably discovered that for yourself."

Briana nodded. "To some extent."

"I won't deny my interest in self-preservation. At times, it has become an obsession. I have desired it above everything else—money, position, even love. That particular door closed for me long ago. I made a conscious decision never to pry it open."

"Why?"

He turned his face to the night sky, and Briana took the opportunity to study his profile. By now, everything about him had begun to arouse her: the firm, aristocratic planes of his cheekbones, the graceful way he moved, the controlled rhythms of his speech. He was utterly unlike any man she had ever met.

"Over the years, I've come up with a number of reasons. Perhaps I should call them justifications. No doubt some seemed legitimate, at least at the time. Strangely enough, at the moment I can't remember a single one."

"I'm glad to hear that."

Suddenly, he fixed his eyes directly on hers. That she felt herself drawn into those mysterious, dark green depths came as no surprise. What she did find inexplicable was the giddiness that crept over her, the slight blurring of her own vision that accompanied his interest. She felt grateful for the solid rock beneath them.

"Sebastian," she whispered. Her voice grew husky with need.

"Shh."

She fell silent. The longer his gaze held hers, the more lightheaded she became. She didn't move as his right hand came to rest on her shoulder, fingers stroking the side of her neck. The contact only intensified the need that swept through her with the force of a wave swamping the rock they perched on.

Briana sucked in a quivering breath as he toyed with the buttons on her shirt, easing the first few open and then caressing the exposed skin. Despite the breeze, she felt warm sweat pool in the hollow of her throat. Slowly, he undid another button, then another. His hand slid inside the gap, palm cupping her left breast.

The slow, deliberate movements of his flesh against hers drove her mad with need. Sliding her arm around his neck, she arched her back and pulled him to her, the rocks serving as a natural, if coarse, resting place. The coolness of his cheek grazed hers, followed by the quick rasp of razor stubble. His lips dragged along the curve of her jaw. The blunt edge of his upper teeth nudged her earlobe and began a slow sweep downward.

Everything felt exactly as it had in her erotic daydreams, only indescribably more intense. The pressure of his hand on her breast, the measured drag of his thumb over her nipple, the startling cool of his lips on her skin all combined to inspire a sudden, mind-numbing flash of pure need.

Suddenly, his hand dropped from her breast to the waistband of her pants. The tips of his fingers curled over the fabric's edge and then dipped lower, finding the waistband of her panties. She gasped as he defied her expectation and pulled it up instead of down, just enough that the silky panel between her legs caught against the sensitive folds of flesh it covered. Clenching his fist, he ratcheted the fabric higher, prompting a rush of wet heat from her center.

He grumbled against her ear, a sort of half-laugh, half-moan that prompted her to press her body closer to him. Releasing his hold on the panties, he reached lower, pretending to pat them back into place. Next his fingers spread out, still on top of the cloth, poking and prodding with a feather-soft touch designed to arouse. And arousal certainly resulted. Her hips tilted toward his roving hand, her dampening crevice enfolding his splayed fingers through the slick textile barrier.

When she mimicked his seductive gesture and placed her hand in his lap, she found all the evidence she needed that he felt the same. The bulge behind his fly pressed upward against her palm, nuzzling it as if seeking release. Eagerly she stroked the rigid mound, moving toward the tab of his zipper. A lusty rush of breath escaped her lungs as she began to pull it down. Awareness hit her like jolt of electricity when she felt his heavy crown thrust through his open fly, tenting his own undergarments against the crook of her thumb. A few backward strokes and she could free it from its prison of white cotton.

Closing her thumb and forefinger into a half-circle, she pushed back on the briefs, steering the Y-shaped flap toward his straining cockhead. She moved slowly, grating the cloth along the flesh of his shaft, hoping to tantalize him the same way he had done to her.

She couldn't resist glancing down as she unveiled him, just the briefest fraction of an inch at first. She caught a glimpse of the flat, round tip as it poked through the opening at the front of his briefs. Then it seemed to stretch forward, serpent-like, and brush the underside of her wrist.

She gasped again, this time in surprise. The part of him that had touched her didn't feel like lust-warmed skin at all. It felt like a bar of cold, unyielding steel. He noticed her reaction and immediately stopped what he was doing to her— and with her. For a moment they remained motionless, touching each other in ways that suddenly seemed awkward, embarrassing, even intrusive. Then, as quickly as it had ignited, the fever between them melted away. The vertigo that had kept her clinging to him faded abruptly. Sebastian raised his head and drew back his hand. Methodically, he rebuttoned her shirt and refastened his trousers. Her senses returned to normal while the trail of moisture his open mouth had left on her skin rapidly chilled.

That chill…it permeated every inch of him, it seemed. Or had her senses begun to play tricks on her again?

"So we're going to play it safe after all." Though it took every ounce of emotional strength she could muster, Briana kept her voice casual. She didn't want Sebastian to see her disappointment. "I guess you're not ready to break down that door just yet."

He leaned back on the rock, his lips still parted as if either words, or his breath, had deserted him. "We should go in," he said finally.

"I guess so."

He climbed off the rocks first, reaching out to assist her to her feet. His long fingers snapped shut around hers as he drew her up to him. That same thrill snaked its way through her again, leaving every nerve in her body frazzled and raw. Her hands felt numb as she retrieved her boots and pulled them back on. Too distracted to bother with the socks, she shoved them in her coat pocket.

They trudged up the beach side by side, never touching. Briana's emotions roiled like the storm Sebastian had predicted. So much for the grand seduction. Did she disgust him? Maybe where he came from, that kind of forwardness in a woman was an insurmountable faux pas.

Only when they reached the house did a fresh possibility occur to Briana. Maybe it wasn't her forwardness he worried about, but someone else's. Someone they had let out of their sights a bit too long for comfort.

"I want to talk to you about something," she ventured as they let themselves back into the study. "Ruby and Todd seem to be getting along very well, don't they?"

"It would appear so."

"Well…what do you think about that? I mean, my brother's made mistakes…."

"And Ruby has, too. I see no point in denying that."

"So do you have a problem with them—I don't know how to put this, exactly—seeing each other?"

His jaw tightened. "I do have a few concerns. But not for the reasons you might think."

Despite the vow she'd made to herself to be more realistic and less protective when it came to Todd, Briana felt herself slide into that old and ugly defensive mode. "I hope it's not because you consider Todd nothing more than hired help," she said. "Because that would explain a lot."

His expression stiffened. "I assume you are referring to what just happened between us."

"You bet I am." Somewhere in the back of her mind, she knew she wasn't just shielding Todd. "I assume that if Todd isn't good enough for your sister, then I'm probably not good enough for you either. I was only half-kidding when I made that remark about my great-grandparents not traveling in your circles. No, I've never lived in a huge house on the ocean or traveled overseas. In fact, I've never been farther than the other side of the bay. Don't tell me you never thought about that, because I know you have."

"You are misinterpreting the situation."

"Am I? I took a real chance this evening. I put my emotions right out there for you to see, Sebastian. I offered you—" She caught herself and took a calming breath. No need to completely humiliate herself. She began again, in a much steadier voice. "I offered you my trust. That doesn't come easily to me. But now I see that you really aren't interested in anything I have to give you."

"Briana, please. This isn't about social standing, I promise you."

"Then maybe I don't interest you. I'm not sure if that's less insulting or not."

He reached for her, grasped her shoulders. She fought the physical sensation that pulsed through her the instant he made contact. The man was cold as a fish and conceited as a king. How could she still want him so desperately?

"Believe me when I say that you are not comprehending the real situation," he insisted. "There are factors here you cannot possibly understand."

"Then explain them to me. Tell me why you rejected me just now."

His hands slid away. He averted his eyes. "I cannot."

"I thought as much."

She stormed ahead of him, barging out of the study, and striding purposefully toward the foyer. If Todd wouldn't leave with her, she would go home on her own. She wasn't about to spend another minute in Sebastian Morgan's presence.

Her confident steps slowed as she approached her brother's workspace. The faint moaning and rustling sounds mortified her. Todd was at it again. Couldn't that man learn to keep his pants zipped? His total lack of discretion had gotten them—her—into this mess in the first place.

Ignoring Sebastian's admonition to wait, she pushed ahead into the foyer. Briana had no doubt what she would see when she turned the corner.

She couldn't have been more wrong.

Todd lay stretched out on the floor, his t-shirt balled up beside him. Ruby rested on top of him, her clothes rumpled but mercifully still on her body. There the resemblance to any normal human coupling ended. Ruby's mouth was fastened on Todd's throat like an attacking animal's. Fresh red blood bubbled up around her lips. She drank, lapped, and sucked with overt delight. Todd murmured in pleasure, while Ruby did the same.

"Briana!" Sebastian's urgent whisper came from directly behind her. Ruby heard him, and looked up from her sanguineous feast.

In a full-blown panic now, Briana spun and crashed directly into Sebastian's chest. The collision startled her. She screamed.

Then Sebastian's powerful hand slammed down over her mouth.

Chapter 7

Briana woke up late the next morning with the immediate sense that something was off. She lay in her own bed, slightly sweaty, wearing panties and the shirt she'd had on the day before. Oddly enough, she still wore her bra. Why would she forget to take it off? She must have been exhausted. She couldn't remember going to bed or much of anything else from the evening before. She'd driven Todd to Morgan House so he could start his work...she'd exchanged a few words with Ruby...and after that, her mind went blank.

Puzzled, she changed into her bathrobe and set off to take a shower. On her way past Todd's room, she felt a sudden urge to check on him.

Fortunately, she found him peacefully asleep in his bed. Quickly she shut his door and leaned against it. She must have had some weird dream, she decided, one that had melted into her subconscious and influenced her waking behaviors. What had it been about? She closed her eyes and tried to remember even a single detail. All that came to her was the impression of candlelight, crisp ocean air...and Sebastian close, so very close to her.

After her shower, she put the robe back on and made a pot of extra-strong coffee. While she waited for it to brew, she leaned against the sink and stared out the window. The sky swelled with steely grey clouds that held the promise of torrential rain. Vaguely she recalled someone warning her about a storm in the works.

Jumbled images clawed at her mind. They came in no particular order and made no sense at all. One of them featured Sebastian, who seemed to be carrying her through her house and up the stairs to her own bedroom. It wasn't a romantic interlude though. He placed her on top of the bed, pulled off her shoes and jeans, and then stepped back and looked down at her. She had the sense of her panties left askew. Sebastian started to touch them, but he caught himself and abruptly pushed her legs underneath the covers. His tense expression seemed more alarming than alluring. Somehow he looked...hungry.

Of course, that had been a dream. Hadn't it? No way had she gotten drunk enough to invite Sebastian Morgan into her bedroom and then forget it. Unless she'd been in some kind of car wreck and suffered a head injury? She rushed to a mirror, relieved to find no sign of bruising or laceration.

The whole thing was beyond weird.

Eventually, Todd walked into the kitchen, freshly showered as well. He'd changed into jeans and a t-shirt, but kept a damp towel draped over his shoulders.

"How are you doing?" Briana asked him as he poured some coffee and sat down at the table. "Feel okay?"

"Sure." He tilted his head at her. "Why?"

"I don't know. It's just that—well, I think I'm coming down with something. My head hurts, and I'm kind of tired."

"Could be. You stayed on the beach for a while last night. Maybe you caught cold."

"The beach? I don't remember that," she confessed. "It must be this headache. Things are kind of fuzzy."

"You'll feel better after you eat," Todd suggested. He slid off his chair and headed back to his room, as if he feared catching something from her. Briana hoped he was right. She'd never felt so disoriented—almost as if this were the dream and reality a hazy phantom.

She heard Todd close his door and put some music on. The muffled thump of the beat started to bring her headache back. She made toast and munched it half-heartedly. Eating seemed to help a little, if only to convince her that she really was awake.

Her relief increased when the phone rang.

Reggie had called from the motel. "My Gran needs to talk to you. Some kind of party in room 16. Place is trashed apparently. She's threatening to quit if someone doesn't help her clean it up."

"All right," Briana said. Her voice still sounded groggy. She finished her coffee, washed out her mug and Todd's, then grabbed a baseball cap and jacket and walked over to The Dunes. The rain on her face revived her a bit more. By the time she reached the office she felt fairly coherent again.

Reggie lounged behind the front desk, reading a magazine he rolled up as soon as Briana entered.

"Where's your grandmother?"

Reggie shrugged. "Making the rounds, I guess. She's pretty ticked off about the mess in the rooms."

"The college students, I assume?"

Reggie stifled a laugh. "Nope. The bird-watchers. Apparently those old fogeys went on quite a bender last night."

"You've got to be kidding me."

"Did you hear about the storm?" Reggie called after her. "Supposed to be a real doozy. Not safe to be on the road once it starts."

She found the older woman pushing her cart down the side of the building, taking care to stay out of the rain, which had picked up considerably. The clouds had swelled darker and thicker, and wet silvery needles slashed at their feet.

"Everything okay?" Briana asked.

"Not on your life," Sandy growled. "Room 16. Hooligans practically tore the paper off the walls. Cigarette burns all over the bed and rug. I get paid to make beds and vacuum, not disinfect cesspools."

Briana sighed. "I'll get the carpet cleaning service out here." Hiring outside assistance would eat into what little profit she'd made that week. "For now, just put the spread in the washer. I'll send Reggie to help you pick up the bottles."

"Wouldn't hurt to be more choosy about who we rent to." Sandy wrinkled her nose.

"We're not really in a position to be choosy right now."

"Hmph." Sandy marched off to retrieve her cleaning cart. Briana returned to the front office and sent Reggie off to Room 16 with a black contractor bag. He looked unhappy about having to abandon his magazine, but perked up when she told him to go ahead and take his grandmother home as soon as they finished.

Briana set the service bell out on the front desk and went into the back office to find the number for the rug cleaners. No sooner had she started rooting through the files than she heard someone ringing it.

Through the open office door, she glimpsed a man waiting at the counter. Her pulse quickened as she hurried out to greet him. Her excitement waned when she saw Graham Smith leaning against the counter, his hair and sweatshirt spattered with rain.

"Oh, it's you, Graham."

"Nice to see you, too. What's going on? You sick?"

Was it that obvious? And here she'd been feeling better. Maybe that assumption, too, resulted from delirium.

"Not really."

"Well, you look like hell. It's the stress of this place. You need more help around her. Where's that skinny kid? And why can't Todd pitch in once in a while?"

"Reggie's cleaning rooms. Todd's busy. Don't worry, I'll be fine. Did you want to rent a room?" In the past, that had been his usual practice in the face of a storm. It had led to many a night she now wanted to forget. Briana decided that if he said yes, she would put him in Room 16. That would keep him busy for a while.

"I just came to check on you."

"I don't need you to check on me, Graham."

"You can say that all you want. You haven't convinced me. Look at yourself!"

He pointed to the round security mirror hanging on the wall by the desk, which allowed her to monitor the counter area while she worked in the back office. Briana glanced up and paused. She did look wan, almost malnourished. She'd be lucky to escape the flu or pneumonia. Why had she gone down on the beach alone?

Only she hadn't.

Sebastian had been there. He'd been walking with her, and she had an equally strong impression that they'd done more than stroll. Briana shivered as she recalled the sensation of his hands on her—drawing her close—his mouth sweeping close to hers, only to turn away at the last moment....

The image dwindled and vanished.

Graham was saying something she'd failed to catch. In fact, she'd forgotten him altogether. His sentence ended with "...because I still care about you."

He didn't seem to realize that her thoughts had drifted miles away. "I care about you, too, Graham. We had a good time together. But some relationships aren't meant to last."

He winced. "I know, friends forever, blah blah blah. Things change. I accept that. But for crying out loud, Briana, get a few hours of sleep. I'm not kidding. You look like something that washed up on the beach."

"Thanks for the compliment."

"You know I didn't mean it that way. Truth is, you're running yourself ragged around this place. You need someone to help you."

"Graham, I have some work to finish up in the back. Be careful out on the water."

"I've slept through a coastal storm before. Nothing to it."

She stayed behind the desk and watched Graham slouch away and head down the street on his way back to the mooring where he kept his boat tied. He disappeared from view within moments, the lowered clouds now almost totally masking the sun. Before long, she also spotted Reggie's car pulling out of the lot with Sandy in the passenger seat. Everything went quiet, except for the occasional whine of the wind and the gargling sound of the rain draining off the roof. The glass door dripped with rain, the walkway out front transformed into a deep, dark puddle. When she double-checked the registration cards Reggie had placed in the metal file box by the register, she found that, except for Ami, all of her guests had now checked out.

It was the perfect time to get some paperwork done. Retreating to the office, she took out the ledger book, a sheaf of bills, and a box of business cards that hopefully contained the current number for the carpet service. One of these days, she vowed, she would get everything on computer and retire her late father's filing method, which relied heavily on manila envelopes and paperclips.

Given the stillness of the air and the stuffiness of the office, Briana wasn't all that surprised when her mind began to wander. Though she no longer felt dizzy she found it difficult to concentrate. She longed to clear a little space on the desk and rest her head on her hands for a bit—or, better still, retreat to the cot in the back of the office and lie down until her senses stopped swimming.

The bed was nothing much, just a lightweight aluminum frame with a flimsy roll-out mattress on top. Right now, though, it looked more appealing than a king-sized feather bed in a five-star hotel. She stretched out and closed her eyes. Just for a moment, she told herself.

When she opened them again, the office had gone dark. The rain drummed even harder on the roof.

Sebastian Morgan stood over her.

"Briana?"

Briana sat up when he reached out and flipped on the lights. The wind had tousled his dark hair, and he had turned the collar of his jacket up against the rain. The leather, like his pale skin, glistened with silvery droplets.

"You didn't lock the door," he said. "That isn't safe."

"It's all right. I only lay down for a few minutes."

"I don't think so. I've been at the counter for almost half an hour, waiting. I finally decided to come back here and check on you."

She glanced at the clock on the desk and was startled to see that, indeed, several hours had passed. She got up and rubbed her hands over her face. "Oh…guess I lost track. This weather makes it easy to sleep. I'm sorry you had to wait."

"That isn't the point. I was concerned."

She smiled weakly. He'd arrived, just as she'd been hoping, and now her common sense had deserted her. Witty and charming would have to wait. Barely coherent would have to do. "Uh…What can I do for you?"

His eyes pinned her in place. "I came to tell you that you need not deliver Todd to my house this evening. The storm will make the road treacherous. Besides, you look unwell."

"No…no, I'm…wonderful." Even to herself, her voice sounded distant and dreamy. But suddenly she knew that she wasn't falling ill and never had been. What she felt was more like the hazy peace that followed an intensely satisfying sexual encounter, similar to the mind-blowing rush after an orgasm. Usually, a sensation like that would end within moments, but this one had lasted for almost twenty-four hours. No wonder she felt worn out.

And something told her Sebastian was responsible.

"You were with me last night," she blurted. "On the beach. Todd tried to convince me I was alone, but we all know that I wasn't. Why did you ask him to lie? And why can't I remember everything? What happened to me out there?"

She remembered Sebastian standing close to her, looking down into her eyes. Her hands rested on his chest. His hands cupped her face. While he started at her, her body seemed to go limp. The image faded but left behind a painful throbbing in her temple. And Ruby—she had to tell Todd something about Ruby. What was it? She didn't know. But she'd certainly known the answer the night before.

She could come up with only one explanation for this disconnected web of sensations. "You hypnotized me."

He flashed a rueful smile. "Most people recover almost immediately with no aftereffects. Your will is a bit stronger than I expected. I should have realized that. It's not exactly something you keep hidden."

"But why? What am I not supposed to remember?"

He stepped closer and slid his hands along her wrists. His fingers tightened as he drew her near. "You can hardly expect me to tell you, knowing how much trouble I went through the first time."

"You think this is some kind of game," she stammered. Already she found herself lost in that dark, penetrating glare again. It really felt like a vicious undertow at the beach. The more she struggled against it, the deeper she felt herself sucked in.

"No! I'm all too aware that it isn't. I'll try to put things right. If I succeed, you'll remember this only as a peculiar dream. You'll forget it completely within a few days. After that, you will be as you were before you met me. But you and I must never again spend time together."

Panic surged through her. She grabbed at his sleeves. "Sebastian, no! That isn't what I want!"

"Believe me, I understand the strength of your urge. I would be lying if I said I didn't share it."

"Tell me, then—tell me what you feel. What I feel. I'm so...confused."

The last part was a lie, and both of them knew it. There could be no question at all about what she felt and what she wanted. Her desire for him almost oozed from her pores.

"What I feel?" His voice dropped to a whisper. "The sensation is like a virus, twisting through my body. It's like a choking thirst. The only way to slake it is to possess you, taste you. And it's driving me mad to know that I cannot."

"That's the way it is for me, too." She pulled herself to him, resting her lips against the corner of his mouth. His lips were swollen but cold to the touch. "Why should we fight it? Come and be with me now. No one will disturb us. The storm is the perfect excuse. We can stay here all night."

As if to underscore her plea, a fresh torrent of rain lashed the glass door until it seemed to bulge and shake in its metal frame. Sebastian's eyes grew bright and glassy, like someone afflicted with fever. His palms snaked up her arms and came to rest on either side of her neck. His fingertips stroked the tender flesh there, gently enough to coax her to tilt her head back. She closed her eyes as his chilly kiss brushed against her burning skin. Far from cooling her, the contact only fanned the fire.

Her own fingers clawed at his hair and shoulders. She began peeling him out of the wet leather coat while he pushed her shirt down and away from her body. She realized that this was exactly where their encounter had stopped at the beach. What they had left unfinished would not be ignored.

"I need you," she murmured, tilting forward again, easing herself into his kiss. Her lips caught his suddenly, and her tongue unfurled into his mouth. She skidded it along the inside plane of his teeth, intent on tasting every morsel of him. Nothing, nothing existed outside of him at that moment. Her own pulse thudding in her ears even blocked out the storm.

He tunneled inside her consciousness as forcefully as his hands roved over her half-bared breasts. She felt the psychic space between them open—only a crack at first, just enough to offer her a glimpse of the desperate need dragging his mind into hers. He hadn't exaggerated: the emotion alone overpowered her. The concurrent physical ache was nothing less than frightening. That ache became part of her, flowering darkly in her innermost core.

Gasping, she pushed one of his hands against the front of her jeans and clamped down with her thighs. The added pressure brought her so close to orgasm that she didn't know if she could wait for him to tear her clothes away. She held back only by reminding herself of the sweet release that surely awaited. Reaching it would take the kind of patience that would be rewarded a thousand times over, if any justice existed at all in the universe.

Then, just like before, a heavy door slammed shut between them just as she readied herself to slip through the gap. Her mind and body alike grabbed for him as he tugged himself away. Both efforts failed miserably.

"I'm sorry, Briana." The words seemed torn from some deep part of him that bled. His pain hit her in waves, though it mercifully faded as he took a few steps back and shrugged back into his coat. "Perhaps I had to see for myself what a terrible idea this was. Forgive my weakness. I will regret my actions for the rest of my impossibly long life."

He turned to go. His face had gown damp. The water must have dripped from his hair onto his cheeks. Already the connection between them began stretching, breaking. Every word he spoke turned to a hollow, tinny echo without meaning or substance. He'd told her she would soon forget. Briana felt her life dwindling along with the memory of what they had almost shared.

"You can't go out in that storm," she called after him in desperation.

"I've been through worse."

"Sebastian!" Shameless tears spurted from her eyes. Her heart seemed to freeze in the middle of her chest.

Pausing only to adjust her disheveled clothes, Briana ran after him as he opened the front door and stepped out into the gloom. When she tried to follow, a solid sheet of wind and rain pushed her back inside. By the time she recovered her balance and charged out again, Sebastian had disappeared.

She scanned the parking lot in desperation. How had he managed to move so fast?

From the shadows, a figure loomed in front of her. He'd changed his mind. She sagged against the doorframe with relief. "Sebastian—" she began, and then stopped.

The man in front of her wasn't Sebastian. Nor was it Graham. This person was much shorter, thinner, with a black hoodie pulled up to his face, presumably to shield him from the rain. He pushed past her into the office, eager to escape the downpour. She could hear him panting as he attempted to shake himself dry.

Nothing about him looked familiar. A tourist who got trapped on the road, she decided, since she'd neither seen nor heard any car pulling up. The soaked and muddied state of his black pants and high-top sneakers suggested he'd trudged quite a distance.

"You must need a room," she guessed. The man nodded. Briana handed him a registration card off the stack by the register. "Just fill one of these out."

He murmured something affirmative.

"Would you like smoking or non-smoking? There are three of each available, so you basically get your pick of the place."

"I don't care," the guest stammered. His obvious nervousness made her look up. The hood, still pulled over his face, obscured everything but his nose and chin. His skin showed no hint of razor stubble, confirming his young age—probably no more than a teenager.

"Do you mind showing me some ID? We can't rent to anyone under eighteen without a parent or guardian present. I'll need a credit card, too."

"ID? Yeah…sure." He stooped a bit as he reached into his pocket. Too late, Briana realized her mistake. When he straightened up again, he wasn't holding a wallet, a license, or currency in any form. Instead, he'd pulled out a switchblade.

"Give me all the money you have," he barked. "Now! Do it now!"

"I-I don't keep any cash out here. It's in the office." Instinctively, she began backing away, though she recognized the poor strategy.

After all, where could she go? The only exit lay in front of her. The assailant, and his weapon, —blocked her path.

"Then get it!" He came around the counter, waving the blade in her face, forcing her a few more steps backward. If he trapped her in the back room, she'd have no way out. Her hesitation made him angrier. "Hurry up!" he shouted.

"I-I'll need the key to the strongbox. It's here somewhere." Wildly she cast her eyes over the counter and the shelves underneath, as if looking for something. "I'm telling you, though, there isn't much money. We're off season. Business isn't exactly booming."

"Just do what I say! I know how to use this, you know!" He waved the knife again, in a way that suggested the opposite.

"Okay, okay. Give me a minute." She backed away, pretending to search for the key.

Unleashing a volley of curses, he grabbed her wrist and slashed the blade back and forth in the air, no more than an inch or two from her face. Terrified, she went to the counter and retrieved the tiny key taped underneath. "Better," he said. "Now get me the money and hurry up!"

Briana realized it would be unwise to turn her back on him even for a moment. Given his edgy state, he might go off and do something crazy. "The box is in the bottom drawer of the desk. I'll have to go into the office to get it."

"Then do it!"

Taking slow, deliberate steps, Briana entered the office. Never taking her eyes from the knife, she crouched in front of the drawer in question.

"I'm telling you right now, we don't have much money. Thirty-five dollars at the most."

"Shut the fuck up and just get it for me! I'm sick of hearing you talk!"

"Okay, okay! Hang on. I'm getting the box out now."

Still moving in slow motion, Briana slid open the drawer and removed the nondescript tin box. As she did, her mind flashed on the last time she'd taken it out: the afternoon she'd handed Todd money for his trip to the hardware store. How many people had watched her? Had one of them tipped off a friend?

Balancing the box on her lap, she inserted the tiny key and pretended to fumble with it. From the corner of her eye, she could see the kid getting antsy. He glanced over his shoulder. She hoped an accomplice wasn't waiting for him outside.

"Hurry up!" he repeated. His gaze flicked backward yet again. Briana saw her chance.

She jumped up from her crouch like a runner exploding from the starting line. She slammed into him with her whole body, sending the knife flying, and sprinted for the door. Swearing, he grabbed the weapon off the floor and darted after her.

She reached the door and yanked it open. A blast of icy water gushed inside, slicking the floor. Her feet slipped as she hurled herself outside. The knife flashed as the kid launched himself after her.

Just before the blade sank into her flesh, Sebastian stepped out of the downpour and seized her attacker's wrist.

Chapter 8

"Drop the weapon," Sebastian growled, "and I may spare your life."

Briana watched his fingers tighten and winced at the creak and pop of bones being crushed. The knife hit the floor with a clink.

With his free hand, Sebastian tore the hood from his face. Briana didn't recognize the bewildered teenager, but she recognized the ashen look of pain so extreme it robbed him of his voice.

"Now I know who you are," Sebastian said in a slow, quiet tone that made her tremble. "If you do this again, anywhere, to anyone, I will hunt you down and destroy you. Do you understand?"

The kid nodded, tears spurting from his anguished eyes, and clutched his arm to his chest the moment Sebastian let go. His fingers sagged like the tentacles on a beached jellyfish. The intruder loped out into the rain, the wet door banging shut behind him. Sebastian made no effort to follow.

Briana reached for the desk phone. "I'll call the police."

"To what end?" Sebastian moved it out of her reach. "He took nothing from you. I promise he will be unable to bother you, or anyone else, again."

She considered his argument. The hold-up attempt had been pathetic, at best, and perpetrated by someone who looked too young to be prosecuted. The pain in his hand would give him plenty to think about the next time he wanted to scoop some easy cash. Besides, if the cops did respond, hours might pass before she and Sebastian found themselves alone again. And given today's mixed-up legal system, Sebastian might well find himself the one facing assault charges.

"Why did you come back?" she asked, still trying to make sense of everything. Half a lifetime's worth of excitement seemed to have passed in a matter of minutes.

"I saw him sneak in as soon as I left. He'd been pressed up against the wall, waiting for me to go. No normal customer would do so."

"Well, I'm glad you did. Believe it or not, we've never been held up before. We have almost no crime in Darkisle, aside from occasional petty vandalism—and my brother's exploits, of course." She met Sebastian's gaze boldly. "Was crime prevention your only reason? Or did you have something else to say to me?"

"I'm not sure anything else needs to be said. You should be safe now." His expression sagged as he turned away for the second time that evening. "Goodbye, Briana."

"You're not even going to take me home? I mistook you for a gentleman."

The accusation stung. His back stiffened. "I recommend you wait a bit. The elements are somewhat in turmoil. When the weather permits safe passage, I suggest you contact your brother."

While she struggled to come up with an adequate response, he stepped outside. Briana watched him through the water-streaked glass. Oddly, he wasn't moving forward. He simply stood in the rain, getting soaked to the skin, as if he couldn't quite bring himself either to go on or come back inside.

She pulled open the door and strode into the night after him. Five steps onto the walkway left her drenched. The rain fell so hard that each droplet seemed to bruise her skin.

"Take care, Sebastian. I'll miss you. But as you said yourself, I'll recover."

She saw his shoulders move as if he were nodding, or possibly shivering in the rain. Slowly, he raised his head and turned to look at her. His skin looked bluish in the storm-filtered light.

"This thing between us…" She paused to swallow. She refused to let her voice, and her resolve, trail off. "I mean, it's distracting, even painful. Ignoring one another doesn't seem to help. Wouldn't we be better off if we confronted our curiosity? Worked through it?"

He spoke through gritted teeth. "Giving in once might lead to a desire for further experimentation."

"Would that be so bad?"

"Possibly. There are things you need to know, Briana. About me."

Her mind flashed back to the image of Sebastian's powerful fingers casually demolishing those of her attacker. The expression on his face seemed almost exultant as the violence surged within him. Her own horrified fascination puzzled her even more. "I-I realize that," she stammered.

"No—you have no idea. Even to imagine the situation would force you to question everything you know…even your own sanity."

"I've always considered sanity overrated. Besides, maybe I'm stronger than you give me credit for."

His hands curled into fists at his sides.

"I know you're strong, Briana. I know you are more than capable of protecting yourself…under ordinary circumstances. We are not dealing with ordinary circumstances in this case."

"I don't see what you're getting at."

"Does that frighten you? Do I?"

He loomed over her now. The cold cutting into her body was not only the result of the rain. It seemed to radiate from him. The more Briana tried not to shudder, the more intense the shaking in her arms and legs became. She drew herself up tight in an attempt to control the tremors.

"Of course not." She wasn't exactly fibbing. What she felt toward him wasn't fear in the usual sense. He unnerved her and awed her, but when he was this close to her, getting away from him was the furthest thought from her mind. How could that be fear? "I know you wouldn't hurt me. You just saved my life."

"For tonight. Tomorrow could be different. You have no way of knowing. That is my point."

"I know enough not to trust the future. But what if I said I trusted you? Even if I don't quite understand why?"

Briana gasped when he wrapped his hands around hers and brought them up to his chest. His fingers were icicles. She clutched at them, trying to give him her warmth. Her efforts produced little, if any, effect.

"Then I would tell you that trusting me might be the most foolish, even the most dangerous thing you will ever do. How can I ask that of you?"

"Maybe you should stop trying to figure that out and just try."

Careful not to break her grip on his hands, Briana drew him back inside the motel, standing in the doorway, dripping wet, while the storm threatened to wash away everything outside. At that moment, with her body pressed against his and his attention focused on her, she didn't even care.

His jaw tightened; he fought the words. Briana tilted her head so her lips would brush his when she spoke. "Ask me," she whispered.

"Briana." Her name came out in a ragged groan. He tugged one of his hands free and let it slide along the curve of her back. His fingers prodded the juncture of her drenched jeans and shirt. Flesh met flesh as he skimmed the waistband and slipped his palm inside. "I cannot deny that you affect me in a way few women ever have."

Briana used her own freed hand to part the front of his shirt and stroke his chest. "You heard me. I want you to ask."

"Very well. Briana...Will you have me?"

It wasn't the question she had expected. Graham had never spoken to her with such deference. Hearing him express his desire that way, with such quaint old-world innocence, melted her from the inside out.

Her laugh emerged tremulous, husky. "Not in those clothes. They're wet."

"There is an obvious remedy for that."

"I know." She unbuttoned his shirt eagerly. He didn't resist. Not until she had reached the last button and reached up to push it back from his shoulders did she realize that they still stood in front of the door. Only the spatters of rain on the glass and the grey fog rolling outside concealed them from the street. "Um...we should probably take this to a more private setting."

"I agree."

"It just so happens I know the perfect motel." Briana gestured toward the rack of keys on the back wall. "We can have any room we want, and for a great price."

With a slight shake of his head, Sebastian turned and locked the door, flipping over the *Closed* sign. He moved toward her, peeling away his shirt and leather jacket in a single motion. Then he slid one arm around her waist and crushed her flat against his bare chest. His other hand went to her face, where he caressed her cheek with an air of wonder.

"I have yearned for you since the moment we met," he murmured. "I struggle every night with a need so intense I can hardly comprehend it."

"I want you, too, Sebastian. More than I've ever wanted any man on this earth."

"You may come to regret that," he murmured into her hair.

"Maybe. Let's worry later."

With his body still wrapped around hers, Sebastian guided her into the back office, where the intruder had terrorized her just minutes ago, and kicked the connecting door shut. He didn't take her to the cot in the corner, as she expected. Instead, he hoisted her onto the desk, knocking aside the ledgers and paperwork she'd collected, and positioned himself between her legs.

Her boots came off at the same instant, one in each of his hands. Next he went straight for the button of her jeans. He swept them, along with her panties, away with brusque efficiency. Wearing only her shirt, she reached forward and grasped his belt buckle, fumbling with the clasp while her naked legs locked around his waist. Sebastian stopped caressing her long enough to push her hands aside and finish undressing himself. She watched him kick his damp trousers and shoes into the corner of the office. Then she settled back on the desk and allowed him to strip her flannel shirt and tee away. Moments later those rain-soaked garments joined the others on the floor.

For a long, maddening moment, they stood in motionless silence, savoring each other's nakedness. The paleness of Sebastian's body struck Briana first. Underneath his almost translucent skin, and the dusting of dark hair that extended from his chest to his groin, his muscles twisted firm and finely sculpted. Casting her gaze lower, she found his masculine contours equally solid—and his plump cock rose between them visibly, robustly aroused.

A sudden thought struck her. "Do we need...you know...protection? There's a first aid kit in the drawer, and I always keep a few condoms on hand. You never know what guests might ask for."

"As far as contraception is concerned, there is no need. I am sterile. As for the other...modern anxieties, I am without a doubt the safest partner you will ever have."

Coming from anyone else, that would have sounded like a sleazy line. Sebastian, though, was not like anyone else. Briana didn't just want—or need—to believe the things he said. Her faith in him drove her like a compulsion. When he spoke, the words seemed to flood her mind as well as her ears.

"Then take me, Sebastian." She hardly needed to say it. Both of them knew she already belonged to him.

She wasn't sure if he nodded or if they agreed so completely that she imagined the gesture. Either way, the time for banter and flirtation had ended.

Extending his fingers, Sebastian ran his hands over the length of her, like an artist smoothing his sculpture or a dreamer testing the reality of his vision. Overcome with the urge to devour him whole, she tilted her head to lick at his nipples.

Her tongue bathed the hard, blunt tip and nipped at the dark hairs curling around it. The rain had chilled him to the bone. His skin remained cool and tight against her lips. The sensation struck her as startling but pleasant, like a splash of cologne after a hot shower.

"Wait," he commanded. His hands circled her shoulders, encircled her arms, and slid to her wrists. Suddenly he pushed forward and pressed her flat on the desk. The movement brought her knees higher around his waist. Briana gasped when she felt his swollen erection touch the tender spot between her legs. Sebastian leaned over her, flattening his body against hers, pinning her beneath his weight. Being completely at his mercy felt delicious. "Stay still," he rumbled from deep in his chest. The tremors massaged her bare breasts. "Let me please you."

"Yes." Briana closed her eyes and luxuriated in the unfamiliar concept of someone taking care of her for a change. She knew she wouldn't be disappointed. "Yes, I will."

Sebastian's palms cupped her hips and pulled her forward. Her legs opened wider as she balanced herself on the edge of the desk, her thighs bracketing his as he moved closer to her circle of warmth. She'd never felt more exposed. Or more safe.

She found his skin's continued frostiness a little strange, considering how long they'd been inside and the fact that she herself teetered on the brink of bursting into flames.

"You're so cold," she whispered.

"Then warm me," he pleaded.

Briana examined his face with new interest: his lips swollen and parted, his eyes wild. What secret did she need to know about him? The answer seemed so close, as though it should be obvious to her in this most intimate situation. Yet for some reason her mind couldn't wrap itself around the truth long enough to make sense of his constant allusions to the threat their attraction posed.

She sucked in a breath as his cool, rigid shaft nudged the shallow folds of her hot center. He made no move to enter her, though. Instead, he let the underside of his cock skate over her supple crease, the chubby crown tilted up and away from the part of her that craved it most. As badly as she wanted to buck her hips up and force him inside, she remembered that, for the moment, this was his show to manage. She wasn't at all surprised to find that he was more than capable of managing both it and her.

He rocked lightly against her, wedging his hips between her thighs. His raw shaft, thick and textured with vein and muscle, swept the length of her crease, and then slowly dragged away again, leaving her gaping and wet with need. Ignoring her desperation, he pushed forward once more in the same calculated manner, pulling back just as deliberately. Soon her free-flowing nectar coated the circumference of his organ. With each pass of his hips he painted her with her own slickness. Slowly, she became his work of art, opening herself to him by degrees, both physically and emotionally.

Sebastian continued this languid sawing motion for a few minutes until she could barely control the tremors raking her body. Her midriff had turned into one heavy ache. Briana's legs squeezed his in lusty convulsions, trying to force him inside. At one point, she heard him hiss, perhaps with the strain of holding himself back while her need grew even more obvious. Finally, his muscles seemed to tense and then loosen in a sort of surrender. He relaxed his balance and let her draw him into position. His stiff tip stroked her open, as if parting a flower's delicate petals. His self-control amazed her, though hers had slipped almost into oblivion. He was resting fully against her now, no more than a tiny shove away from full immersion in her roiling center. Her most intimate muscles constricted, trying again to pull him in closer and deeper. Still he held himself in position, tormenting her. The pressure of her ankles around his waist didn't hurry him at all.

"Come inside," she begged. "I can't hold out much longer."

In response, a flicker of amusement passed over his face. He'd been testing her, she knew, trying to find out which of them would surrender first to the raging need that bound them together. Normally, Briana hated to let anyone get the best of her, but this was a contest she wouldn't mind losing.

At last, his stony determination to tease her to the point of anguish seemed to weaken. Her heels dug into his thighs and aided in his forward motion as, at long last, he gave in and thrust himself deeply into her. More than ready by then, she took him all without the slightest hint of pain or resistance. A moan burst from her throat— guttural, primal.

At last, when he was fully immersed in her swollen depths, some of her heat seemed to seep into him. The change came over him immediately and perceptibly: a blush rose in his cheeks and chest, and his muscles grew supple and more responsive. Even the color of his eyes seemed to melt into a warmer shade of greenish-blue.

The rush of heat energized him, drove him. His member curved upward, stretching out to thread its way through her moistened tunnel. Yielding to the welcome invasion, her ripe folds expanded, parted, and closed up again, flesh enfolding flesh in the most intimate of embraces.

He imbedded himself with a single lunge, stretching her to bursting on every side, filling every corner of her womb all at once. She cried out with pleasure as their hips began to move in tandem, his powerful thrusts lifting the lower half of her frame into the air and then banging her rear end back down on the desk. The thud of her bare skin against its surface marked the rhythm of their coupling.

For one wonderful moment, she lost consciousness of everything but the explosion of pleasure far inside her own body. Her desire peaked, crested, and sent her plummeting into the incomparable delight of pure oblivion.

At the exact point of climax, she did something she had never done before, had never even fantasized about doing. Briana lifted her mouth to the sinewy ridge that joined his neck to his shoulder and bit him. Hard. She heard a slight tearing sound as her teeth penetrated his skin.

Not a droplet of blood touched her lips. His flesh stayed as dry and rubbery as a mannequin. Or something far, far creepier. But that train of thought seemed absurd, impossible. Briana abandoned it.

She remembered, though, how he had warned her about questioning her sanity.

Sebastian waited until the last of the shudders had raked through her before tugging away. Briana pulled at him, her nerves unwilling, even unable, to let such intense gratification subside.

One thing nagged at her, though. "You didn't—" she began.

"It's all right." He brushed a finger over her lips to silence her. "I'm more than satisfied. Trust me."

"You seem to say that a lot," she pointed out.

"Probably because I can't quite believe you do."

He stepped away, and Briana sat up. Her back remained a bit sore from the desk, their nakedness more awkward now than in the throes of passion. Sebastian's thoughts again seemed one step ahead of hers. He went to the cot and retrieved the top blanket, which he wrapped around her. Grasping her hands, he helped her off the desk and led her to the tiny bed. He settled onto it and guided her on top of him, turning her at the last minute so her back nestled against his chest. His contented arms slid across her.

She drowsed a bit in the cot, soothed by his closeness, though the blanket lay between them. She savored the pressure of his fingers on her forearms and his thighs against the curve of her buttocks. Sebastian fell silent. Was he asleep? His breathing seemed so shallow she couldn't detect the rise of his chest at all.

What had he needed to tell her? Not letting him had been reckless. Could he be a wanted criminal? Dying of some exotic disease? His arctic physique and almost nonexistent circulation suggested a health issue, but he certainly wasn't impotent.

Still, he struck her as undeniably different, not just from any man she'd ever known, but from any human being at all. Belatedly she realized he hadn't even kissed her, or applied his mouth to her in any meaningful way. Was that also a European thing? Or maybe some strange private hang-up?

Most curious of all, she realized as she snuggled against him, he had no heartbeat.

The nervous sweat sprang up on her forehead and tingled its way down her body. Before long, the blanket seemed impossibly hot, his tight grip on her unnerving and claustrophobic.

Her mouth had turned to cotton. "Sebastian?"

Beside her, he stirred as if awakening. She still sensed nothing in the way of pulse or respiration.

"Yes?"

"Um…what did you want to tell me?"

He eased her off his chest and sat up. "Now you want to know," he surmised. "I told you this would happen. Lasting regret always outweighs a few moments of pleasure."

"I never mentioned regret. And my pleasure lasted more than a few moments, trust me."

A smile flickered at the corners of his mouth. Whatever his secret, she decided, she would find a way to handle it. Despite his oddities, or perhaps because of them, having Sebastian Morgan to herself was worth the sacrifice.

"Dine at my house tomorrow evening and we will discuss things further."

"What about Todd and Ruby?"

"I will arrange for them to be elsewhere. I must warn you again, though, that what you will learn will change your view of life forever. That is not an exaggeration or an attempt at self-aggrandizing melodrama. It is a simple fact."

Her stomach tensed. "All right."

"Come as soon as it gets dark." Sebastian tilted his head. "The storm's passed," he noted. It seemed fitting for him to announce its conclusion, since she now recalled that he had predicted it in the first place. "I can walk you home now."

The fact that he had no intention of staying the night disappointed her, but maybe it was for the best. "I think I'll stay here a while."

"That might be unwise, considering what happened earlier."

"That creep won't be back. Anyway, the door will be locked. Don't worry about me."

He rose and picked his rumpled clothes up from the floor. Briana considered offering him the use of the dryer in the back room but decided not to. She didn't want to reward him for taking off on her, and besides, their conversation had gone as far as it possibly could without veering off into presumably dangerous territory.

Soon he returned to her bedside, damp but dressed. "Until tomorrow," he said. "If you change your mind, I will understand."

"I told you—I'm stronger than you think."

"Be sure to lock the door behind me. Everyone will be safer."

She nodded. Her eyes narrowed as she watched him slip away. Still wrapped in the blanket, she got up and turned the bolt, testing the door as an extra precaution. She suspected it wasn't just the misguided young robber whose return he wished to prevent.

How typical, she thought as she returned to the cot and pulled her legs up into a fetal position. She'd finally found the man she'd dreamed of all her life,0 and instead of joy, or even relief, she felt only an impending sense of dread.

Waiting until tomorrow for answers would take patience beyond anything a normal person should have to endure.

Then again, if her instincts were on target about Sebastian, she might as well get used to such frustration.

* * * *

After he left Briana at the motel, Sebastian took up watch from a concealed position at the edge of the parking lot. Though the wind and rain, not to mention his soggy clothes, made his time there uncomfortable the elements also made his task easier. Not many humans, after all, would venture out in such a squall. If anyone did return to threaten Briana, however, he was prepared to act.

Part of him felt guilty for not guarding her in a more hands-on manner—as in spending the night with his hands roving over her willing body. The temptation burned strong. Many decades had passed since he had shared a bed with a woman who aroused him the way she did. Several lifetimes had passed since he had experienced such a powerful emotional response at all. But with passion came darker desires whose escape he dared not risk. Outside the circle of her intoxicating warmth, he could protect her from every perceived menace, including himself.

As he waited, the wind weakened and the sky began to soften and change. Daybreak loomed. Difficult as he found it to leave her, Sebastian had no choice now. By the time the sun rose, he had to be in his blocked-off bedroom, secured behind thick metal shutters and the sliding panels of his bed.

Walking at hyper speed, which humans would not be able to detect in the darkness, he reached Morgan House in a matter of minutes. The storm diminished to an annoying drizzle as heavy clouds scudded past Darkisle.

Just then, Ruby pulled up in the Maserati. She coasted up alongside him and rolled down the window as he trudged toward the front steps.

"You're out late," he remarked.

"I dropped Todd off at home. We had a delicious evening together." Ruby licked her lips. Sebastian knew the scarlet shimmer wasn't the result of cosmetics.

"I'm glad."

Ruby parked the car, jumped out, and followed him into the house.

"So what have you been doing? You went to her, I assume?" Ruby frowned at his tight-jawed silence. "Sebastian, you didn't kill her, did you? That would really mess up my plans for Todd."

"Of course not." He pushed inside the house and slung his dripping leather jacket on the brass rack. "She's asleep, as you and I need to be momentarily."

Her already-dilated eyes widened farther. "You took her, didn't you?" His silence provided the answer. "You did! Oh, I'm so happy for you! This is what you've wanted for so long."

Sebastian had placed his hand on the banister, newly polished by Todd, and had already started upstairs. He whirled on her in sudden anger. "I am not prepared to discuss this. Remember your place, young one."

"Okay, sorry!" Ruby flung her hands up, palms out, in a gesture of callow impertinence. "So kill me for being happy that you finally got laid!"

Her forwardness, along with her crude language, grated. Yet Sebastian couldn't help smiling. Who would have guessed that, age-wise, this nubile female was actually an elderly woman?

Sighing, he shook his head. "I am the one who should apologize. I forget sometimes that I am no longer responsible for you. I'm still adjusting to seeing you hunt on your own."

"Yeah, well, give me another sixty years and you should have it down pat."

"We'll discuss this later. When you rise tonight, I would like you and Todd to go out for a bit."

"She's coming here, isn't she?"

"Yes. I need to talk to her."

"You two seem to talk a lot more than Todd and I do." Shrugging, Ruby flipped her gelled hair back. "But to each his own."

"Thank you for your understanding."

He walked up and stood outside the door to his room until Ruby entered hers which was located at the other end of the hall.

Inside, he checked the shades and clicked the small locking tabs in place. When he closed the door he heard the lightproof seals kick in. Perfect pitch blackness swathed the room. His specially constructed bed awaited.

Sebastian shed his wet clothes with relief and crawled naked into the black silk sheets. Stretching out, he slid the cabinet door shut. Encased in two layers of protective screening he let himself relax. No fear of sunlight here.

He could still smell her on his skin. Fresh threads of human desire rippled through him. So many years had passed since he had felt anything similar.

In some ways, he envied Ruby. Born to a different time, and subject to very different expectations, she held attitudes far more progressive than his would ever be. She approached her interest in Todd so casually. He wondered what the two of them experienced together. So far he saw no need to intervene. Certainly she had kept better control over the situation than he had.

His interest in Briana had spelled trouble from the beginning. Even now, he winced when he remembered that evening on the beach. She'd drawn in close, too close. Her fingers had made contact with a part of him that had pleased many women over the last hundred years but should have remained off-limits to her. The pressure of her hand and the quick response of her own secret places to his intimate touch had almost proved too much. Shame washed over him like a cold splash of water when he recalled angling his head and drawing back his lips to expose his long-unused fangs.

One bite, and a succulent crimson thread would bathe his tongue in the fluids of life. Its effects would refresh both his body and spirit, not that he was convinced he still owned a spirit. That time, thankfully, he only got as far as resting his lips on her skin. When the moment came to force his head down, to tear his way through sinew and vein, Sebastian had shoved her away instead. He'd retained that much control.

What had happened tonight was in some ways far more dangerous. He could still feel the pleasurable sensation of her strong feminine muscles enveloping his cock, squeezing the last tendrils of resistance from him. That sweet, honey-filled crevice had been his to explore and plunder, and he had done so with relish. Meanwhile, her soft breasts had stroked against his own blunt nipples, pulling them to pert attention along with his erection, as their bodies scraped against one another in convulsions of pure bliss.

That same spasm of bliss could have ended in her death. He should never have gone so far. The same way his fangs had to remain in his mouth, his cock had to remain in his pants. Until tonight, he'd found that vow difficult, but not impossible, to keep.

Still, he couldn't give her up. He wanted her here with him now. For the moment, it remained impossible. Maybe it would always be.

Tension coiled in his body. His clenched fist slid down the taut muscles of his stomach, moved lower still. He had been alive so long. He had known, and enjoyed, simple human lust, followed by the more complex pleasures of bloodlust. Until now, the two had never mingled. Inevitably, they had.

Opening his fist, his fingers curled around that part of him that had pierced her mere hours before. What did hours matter to someone who had lived for centuries? Yet the memory of her burned like a hit iron on his flesh. His eyes filled with tears of frustration and fear.

His flesh hardened, strained, lengthened against his equally firm fingers. In days long past, the finest courtesans in London, Paris, Rome, and other exotic places had sought creative ways to please this most discerning part of his body. Tonight, all he needed was the memory of Briana's emotional and physical responses to him. He squeezed, and wrung, and soon felt a release he hadn't known since his human days.

Satiated for the moment, he drifted off to the temporary death that held him until the moon rose again.

Chapter 9

The office cot felt as uncomfortable as always, but Briana slept like the dead while the storm filtered from the sky and her discarded clothes dried on the floor. She woke at almost eight in the morning, which left her just enough time to clear out before Reggie and his grandmother showed up. After dressing, she tidied up the office and trudged up the hill toward the house. The air blew cool, but fresh, while saturated ground squished under her feet. Walking home took her a bit longer than normal, but she didn't mind. Her whole body still sang with the pleasures Sebastian had brought, and slogging barefoot through a snowstorm wouldn't have dampened her mood. The walk also gave her time to consider how much she should tell Todd.

When she got home, she found him sitting at the kitchen table with his back to her. Her heart stalled when she spotted a glass in front of him. She stole up behind him, relieved to catch him indulging in nothing stronger than orange juice.

He squinted at her. "Have a good night?"

Briana shrugged and got another glass from the cupboard. "It went okay."

"Yeah. Sure." Todd bit back a grin. Briana saw no point in lying; they knew each other too well. "Let me guess: Graham Smith?"

"No way. I'm done with him."

"You know, he was never good enough for you. You deserve someone special. Someone who treats you right."

"The way Ruby treats you?" She settled next to him and poured herself some juice.

"Ruby?" Todd's demeanor turned evasive. "Well, yeah, you know, she's okay."

"She must be. Won't Ami be jealous?"

"Ami?" His eyes glazed over, and he frowned. "What I had with her was nothing but the booze talking. I know that now. Hopefully she does too."

"Don't you think you're playing with fire where Ami is concerned? You ought to talk to her."

"You're at the motel most of the day. Why don't you?"

"Me? You've got to be kidding, Todd!"

In response, Todd shook his head. The light happened to strike him the right way, and Briana noticed the side of his neck. A huge wound marred the tender skin from his earlobe to his shoulder blade. When Todd saw her eyes widen in horror, he covered the gash with his hand. "Hurt myself working," he said. "Board swung around and caught me. It's nothing."

"Do you need stitches? That looks pretty deep."

"Fuck it. You know we can't afford a hospital bill right now. Speaking of which, you get any business at the motel last night?"

"In that storm? Fat chance." Briana considered telling him about the holdup and then decided not to. But she found it strange that he would ask that, considering what had happened. Almost as if he expected her to bring it up.

"I still think we ought to sell that useless money pit. Maybe we could get enough for it to pay off at least some of what we owe."

"In case you haven't noticed, offers aren't exactly flooding in. Anyway, things will get better when the tourist season starts."

"Place isn't worth the time you put into it." Todd picked up his orange juice, peered into the glass, and set it aside with a disgusted expression.

Briana noticed that he barely listened to her. Of course, she felt pretty distracted herself this morning. She got up from the table. "I need a shower. Want to go out for breakfast afterward?"

"Thanks, but I think I'll go back to sleep for a while. The thought of food makes me feel sick right now."

"Funny—I felt that way yesterday. Maybe we've both been bitten by the same bug."

"Hmmph."

As Briana walked upstairs to the bathroom, she reflected on the words she'd just used. Bitten, she'd said. Todd's neck wound didn't look like a scrape from a loose two-by-four. It really did look like he'd been bitten.

Cranking up the shower to full blast, she shed her clothes and leaned against the shower wall. The water tendrils teased her body like playful, inquisitive fingers. Again she found her mind overpowered by thoughts of Sebastian. She wanted him there with her so desperately that her most intimate muscles began to spasm and clench.

Tonight, she'd hear the dire secrets he'd hinted at, secrets he thought repulsive enough to derail her interest in him. However unlikely that possibility was, she couldn't help wondering how big a disappointment awaited her.

She thought again about his reluctance to please her with his tongue, never mind kiss her. Graham had never been so hesitant. Did his confession have something to do with that?

Well, she knew that plenty of guys had inhibitions, even if she had rather limited experience in that area. No doubt they could teach each other a few things over time. "Time" was, in fact, the operative word. Unless he needed to tell her that he was some kind of wanted criminal or serial killer, a possibility she couldn't rule out, she had no intention of letting Sebastian Morgan drive her away.

* * * *

Years had passed since Briana had shopped for anything besides bulky sweaters, flannel-lined chinos, and waterproof outerwear. After almost an hour of pointless wandering through the mall, she ventured into a boutique whose window promised attractive, yet modest evening wear priced within Briana's budget. Fortunately, a savvy saleswoman seemed to intuit what she was looking for.

"You want to give him an idea of what's in store, but you want to make him work for it?" she guessed. When Briana nodded, the woman gestured for her to follow. "This would be perfect for an evening out ...or in," she said, holding up a pewter-colored dress with a scooped neckline and a hem at mid-thigh. The fabric shimmered a little when she wriggled the hanger. "It reveals just enough to maintain a touch of class. I think the color would bring out the shine in your hair."

"Thanks. I'm going to need all the help I can get," Briana admitted.

"First date?"

"Well...not exactly. The situation is kind of, um, unusual."

Noting Briana's sudden blush, the woman nodded sympathetically. "Dating can be so complicated these days. I'm glad I got married before these computer match-ups became the rage. I wouldn't know how to impress someone I'd never met in person either."

Briana thought it best not to mention that although she and the gentleman in question had shared a night of wild sex in the middle of a gale, they hadn't even kissed. "Oh, it's nothing like that. I've seen him in person plenty of times. It's just that...well, he's sort of...stubborn."

"Ah, one of those fear-of-commitment types. Now that I can relate to. Online or in person, I suppose they're all the same when you get right down to it. Remember that men are visual creatures. You have to make them want what they see. And if you don't mind my saying so, I think this dress might do the trick."

"Maybe you're right. Why don't I try it on?"

"I can tell it's going to look wonderful on you. And if you like it, it just so happens I have matching shoes and jewelry in stock. A little metallic lip liner couldn't hurt, either."

As she stepped into the fitting room and peeled off her sweater, Briana remembered why she avoided dressing up whenever possible. On Graham's fishing boat, simply staying clean proved enough of a challenge. He'd never noticed or commented on anything she wore, except to suggest she let him take it off her.

Obviously, Sebastian was a different sort of man. His impeccable taste and European sophistication both intimidated and inspired her. She longed to prove herself his equal, a worthy companion in public as well as in private.

The dress, when she finally struggled into it, pleased her more than she'd expected. The fabric's subtle twinkle brought out the shine in her otherwise ordinary brown hair and eyes, while the neckline gave the suggestion, rather than a full view, of soft cleavage waiting to be admired and caressed. With a shudder, she imagined Sebastian's hands gliding along the sleek silver encasing her hips and his fingers drifting to the zipper and tugging it down while his warm mouth finally, lovingly, settled beside her ear. She could almost hear—and feel—his murmurs of pleasure ripple against her skin.

Quickly she stepped out of the dress, worried that she'd begun to sweat into it. Her fingers shook as she clumsily replaced it on the hanger.

"I like it a lot," she announced to the saleswoman, who was already heading toward the dressing room with a shoebox, a cosmetics color card, and a tray of jewelry. "It'll be perfect."

"I hope so," the woman agreed. "Now we need to pick out some accessories."

* * * *

She saw that Sebastian had prepared for her arrival as soon as she arrived at his house. The car was gone, and real flames burned in the sconces on either side of the front door. Guided by the twin flickers, Briana picked her way up the steps in her tight new shoes, holding the purse as if it could save her from taking an embarrassing tumble. She still felt a bit foolish carrying around something so impractical, but the lady in the shop had assured her that the outfit would be incomplete without it. Briana had decided to put her cell phone in it, along with her car keys and wallet. After all, she still had no real idea what Sebastian wanted to tell her. The possibilities she'd conjured in her mind unnerved her enough.

The moment he opened the door, she could tell that he approved of her new image. He had spent some time getting ready himself, donning a black suit with a Mandarin collar and tucking a loosely knotted ascot inside a crisp white shirt.

"You look wonderful," she said, unable to hide her pleasure at seeing him go to so much trouble for her. Her ordeal at the dress shop had been worth the grief after all.

"As do you," he said, in such a sincere tone that she found no further compliment necessary. His attention warmed Briana all the way down to her nylon-clad toes.

"I assume we're alone?"

He nodded. "Ruby is taking your brother out on the town tonight. Don't worry—she won't allow him to drink."

"I don't think he wants to drink any more. Anyway, he needs to take responsibility for himself. You and I are the topic tonight."

"Yes. We need to talk. About last night, obviously. But about a few other things as well."

"That's why I'm here. I told you I was strong enough to hear whatever you have to say."

"Let's dine first. I'm sure you're hungry."

Sebastian held out his hand. She took his cold fingers and followed him to a room at the end of the hall. He pushed open the door to reveal a formal dining room, beautifully adorned in high Victorian style. Briana marveled at the starched lace tablecloth, delicate China place settings, and polished silver tureens. A row of gleaming platters and bowls stretched across the table, each filled with fragrant seafood and buttery steamed vegetables. Best of all, he'd exchanged the electric lighting, at least temporarily, for tall white candles. Briana felt as if she had just stumbled into the film adaptation of a Jane Austen novel.

"Surely you and Ruby didn't cook all this," she said in amazement.

"I took a more expeditious route. I inquired around town for a suitable caterer and engaged her services. The tableware, however, is authentic. My great-grandparents dined on this very tablecloth, using these exact utensils. May I seat you?"

"How wonderful," she said as he pulled out a chair for her and settled her at one end of the table. A bit awkwardly, she set the clutch purse beside her. Why had she bothered to buy it?

A crystal carafe and matching tumbler sat beside her plate. He filled her glass with sparkling ice water before circling around to take the seat opposite her. He didn't bother to pour any for himself.

"I considered hiring a server as well, but I assumed we would prefer privacy."

"My thoughts exactly."

He fell silent, and Briana busied herself with the food for a few moments. Sebastian had cut no corners there, either. She ladled out generous helpings of warm lobster bisque, sautéed scallops, glazed baby carrots, and other treats. All had been cooked and spiced to perfection. She bet the original owners of these dishes and utensils had never tasted anything as magnificent.

When she looked up again, she saw that Sebastian had placed a few token items on his plate, but had tasted nothing.

"You aren't having any?"

"In good time. Meanwhile, I prefer to share your pleasure."

"I find it a lot more pleasurable not to be stared at while I'm eating. It makes me self-conscious."

"I don't see why. My object is to admire you. Don't most women enjoy that?"

"I can't speak for most women. If I could, I doubt you would find me interesting at all."

Smiling, Sebastian picked up his fork and pushed around the food on his plate for a while, mostly to humor her, she suspected. Maybe he didn't care for shellfish and had ordered the meal for her benefit alone, but she also noticed that he hadn't touched the water or even the bread.

At least he had stopped watching her eat. Though the conversation returned to more general matters, like the renovations to the house and the provenance of the glassware, Briana's nervousness grew as the meal went on. Each bite, she knew, took them closer to the inevitable serious talk that would change their relationship forever. As delicious as every morsel was, her stomach had begun to tighten and churn.

For dessert, Sebastian uncovered a domed platter containing two delicate sponge cakes and poured out twin cups of strong, rich-smelling coffee. Briana found a silver creamer and sugar bowl already within reach. She suspected that her host had no intention of using them.

"Are we going to spend the rest of the evening doing the dishes?" she joked. As she'd expected, Sebastian raised his cup and put it down a few times, but did not appear to sip from it as far as she could see.

"Certainly not. Someone will be along to do that later."

For one wild moment, Briana wished they could always stay as they were now, sitting quietly together, brimming with desires unsated and darker secrets untold. But as fervently as she wished it, she knew that could never happen. One way or another, they had to move forward.

"You know, I have a feeling this discussion you have planned is going to ruin a lovely evening."

His face grew serious. "Perhaps. Wouldn't you rather know the truth?"

"Not always." Briana laughed uneasily. "Still, I suppose honesty is best."

Sebastian got up, folded his unused napkin, and tucked it under his plate. He crossed the room and held the back of her chair as she stood.

"You may recall that I showed you only part of the house the last time you visited."

"Yes...."

"You will now see more of it. I've decided it would be best if we talked upstairs. Come with me."

Did he plan to discuss their relationship in bed? Maybe this wouldn't be so bad after all. Already, in spite of every doubt that had nagged at her mind throughout the day, his mere proximity intoxicated her. Though determined to stay firm and protect her heart, she'd have to struggle to hold her ground in this conversation. Already she envisioned sliding her hands around his back, tearing loose that sexy cravat, and working those tight-fitting dark pants down his muscular hips.

She shook her head, determined not to ruin the moment by stumbling on her way up the stairs. Not sure about the protocol in such situations, she grabbed the clutch purse off the chair beside her and carried it along with her. Sebastian led her to the second floor, where she assumed his bedroom was.

"You may find the decor a bit unusual," he said. "I will explain everything in good time."

Briana paused while he unlocked the door. Was he into whips and chains or something even kinkier? So much, she thought, for her concerns that sexual repression kept him from using his mouth on her.

Maybe he had such exotic tastes that nothing so pedestrian got him going.

Who kept his bedroom locked, anyway?

When he opened the door and showed her inside, she half expected to find an Iron Maiden in one corner and a medieval-style torture rack in the other. But no—when Sebastian lit a candle and secured it in the sconce on the wall, the amber glow illuminated a simple, almost painfully bare room featuring what looked like a bed in the center. Large sliding wood panels enclosed the frame. One of them opened toward a narrow stone terrace. The drapes had been pulled halfway back, allowing the moonlight to pool on the sheets like milk.

Was this his big secret? That he liked to sleep in some weird Victorian bed that looked like a coffin? She could almost have guessed that.

Of course, the coffin part brought up some strange associations, but she put those aside for the moment.

"Is this some kind of homemade tanning booth?" she asked, bewildered.

"In a sense. However, unlike most creatures that thrive by day, I do not draw my life force from the sun. Instead, I take my energy from the night air and the moon. For at least an hour every night after the moon has risen, I lie here and absorb the light. It's a bit like the photosynthesis that nurtures plants—in reverse."

"Oh." Briana had no idea what to make of his confession. So he'd set up an unusual place to relax. What was the big deal? "Is this some kind of tantric thing? I've read about that stuff in magazines."

"There's a bit more to it. I don't simply prefer to exist in darkness. In order to survive, I must."

A sudden, horrible thought struck her. "I think I get it now. You have some kind of... medical condition."

"You could say that."

She swallowed. "Is it...you know...terminal?"

He nodded slowly. "Quite so. In fact, I succumbed to my illness in the year 1899. For almost one hundred and ten years I have walked the earth as a dead man."

"What?" Briana paused, stunned. How typical, she thought. No sooner did she find a guy she liked than he turned out to be stark raving mad.

"I can see it's going to take you some time to accept this. That's all right. I expected as much."

"Accept it? What you're suggesting is impossible. Insane." There was that word again. No wonder he'd warned her. Next to Sebastian, Graham began to seem like the picture of stability.

"Perhaps I should try to explain it in more concrete terms. Think back to two nights ago. Do you remember walking on the beach with me?"

"Sort of. Not really." Frowning, she tried once again to reconnect the disjointed flashes that remained. Every time something seemed to blend into a comprehensible image, the whole thing disintegrated again. "My memory's a little spotty these days."

"I did that."

"You told me that before, I think, but I still can't quite figure out what you meant."

"Again, a deliberate act on my part. I wanted to protect you. I didn't want you to recall what you saw when we entered the house. Try now." He lifted his palms to her cheeks, tilted her head back, and stared into her eyes. Almost at once, a strange, hypnotic lull came over her. She began to shake as a sudden torrent of sensations, blurry like reflections in a misted-over mirror, flooded her mind.

"I do remember," she announced. "Todd was there—and Ruby. She—oh, my god, yes. She…fed on him somehow. Drank his blood."

"Yes. She did. And, I confess, I longed to feed on you in just the same way. I held back because I wanted to be sure there was more to it than hunger and proximity."

Her mind reeled. A gnawing sense of physical fear, even revulsion, warred with the more pleasant erotic sensations his proximity aroused in her.

Fortunately, being half numb with shock enabled her to feign an outwardly calm demeanor. She struggled to keep her voice low, almost nonchalant. "And...and you're sure now?" she managed to choke out.

"Yes. I think we are suited to each other in ways I have only begun to appreciate." His hands suddenly dropped. "There is so much I would like to share with you, Briana, but it's far too soon for that. Were I human, we would progress in small, tediously safe increments, sharing our secrets as we went. However, the usual rules of dating exclude those like me."

Human? What did that mean? For a long time, she stood completely still in the middle of the room, feeling as though she'd slipped into some kind of bizarre dream state. Sebastian paced the room, eyes averted and arms crossed.

"Believe it or not, I spent hours rehearsing everything I wanted to tell you. Now that the moment has arrived, the words are gone."

As she watched him struggle, her own turmoil waned, replaced by a peculiar sense of sympathy and a slowly dawning realization. Not just the scene involving Todd and Ruby, but so many other tiny details, unnoticed at the time, suddenly slipped into place. All at once, she understood wholly, perfectly. And, sane or not, she wasn't afraid of him.

"Wait." Stepping forward, she took both of his hands in hers. Their coldness now made perfect sense. "You can stop now. I know the words—or I should say the word—you're looking for."

"Do you?" Pain edged his voice. That touch of vulnerability made her desire him even more.

"Of course I do. It's all so simple and obvious." She took a deep, leveling breath and blurted out a sentence she never thought she'd say aloud. "You're a vampire."

Chapter 10

Sebastian gaped at her, incredulous. "You know?"

Briana swallowed. Okay, so it wasn't the instant denial she'd hoped for. She put on her best poker face and met his eyes. "Yes."

"How?"

"The signs were there." Her head started to spin. He still hadn't denied anything, but then again, he'd made no mention of either axes or murders—a good sign, she hoped. "I've seen…you know…movies and books and so forth."

He frowned. "So much nonsense has been written about those like me. I hope you have been influenced by at least marginally reputable sources."

"I don't really have any way of knowing at this point. I hoped you could…enlighten me."

She forced herself not to move, not to flinch as his hands tightened around hers. Their coldness seeped into her skin, drawing on her warmth. She imagined that his fingers began to soften against hers. His eyes, though, remained the color of a harsh winter sea. "That was why I invited you here this evening. Had you forgotten?"

"No. And I came because I wanted to know. I still do. So please, Sebastian—tell me."

He nodded and dropped her hands. Then he backed away, pacing back to the opposite side of the room.

"I should start with some general information, the kind so often exaggerated to the point of outright lies when outsiders attempt to describe our community. True, there are exceptions—even the vampire world has its criminal element. Those rare specimens become the models for the rampaging monsters that populate melodramatic novels and television shows. I won't even discuss the ridiculous exaggerations that turn up in movie theaters. I realize all mass entertainment is based on hyperbole, but there should be limits."

"I see."

"I suppose most of the blame should go to vampire screenwriters for selling out their own kind. However, I can do nothing about that. I can only try to correct the mistaken impressions that pervade mortal culture. It wouldn't be your fault if you had accidentally picked up some of them, maybe without realizing it."

Were they really having this conversation? Briana nodded, suppressing a giddy, and wholly inappropriate, nervous laugh. "I'll try to be open-minded."

"We are not mindless killing machines with appetites only slightly more sophisticated than those of the sharks in the bay. Rarely does a vampire drain some innocent young virgin of every last drop of blood."

"It's a little too late for me in that department," Briana joked in a hollow voice. "Does that mean you don't…?"

"I have not fed that way for many years," Sebastian told her. "Some vampires do feed on the life fluids of others. It need not kill the donor, the odd accident aside, but it can bond us. Many humans find the process quite erotic."

"And vampires?"

"*All* vampires, even those who voluntarily deprive themselves, find it erotic." He smiled, lifting his lips just enough that she could see the subtle points of his canine teeth. A deep shudder ran through her. How could she have missed that? Now she knew why he had never kissed her.

Suddenly, her mind raced to a topic she'd forgotten to consider. As usual, she'd been in total denial about the mess her brother had gotten himself into. "What about Ruby?" she whispered. "I saw what she did. She's like you."

He nodded. "Ruby is a vampire as well. I promise you she will not harm your brother. I will see to that personally."

"Does Todd know what she did to him?"

"He does. As I mentioned, many humans enjoy the experience." His forehead creased. "Briana, you should know something else about Ruby. She is not my sister. She is my granddaughter."

Briana's head snapped up. "What?"

"Edgar Morgan, the old man who inhabited this house for so long, was my son. Her father."

"That old man? Your son?"

"I am a good deal older than I look."

"Did you…" She swallowed hard. "Did you turn her into…what she is now?"

"I did not…though I admit I am indirectly responsible for her existence. I take no pride in that, though she has been an agreeable companion to me, on and off, these past sixty years."

She shook her head, bewildered. Sebastian had a granddaughter more than twice her own age, not to mention a son he'd fathered more than a century before. And that wasn't even the most bizarre part. The two of them had wandered the world, feasting on human blood, while they lived this strange lie. How could she even begin to make sense of such information?

"This is…insane!" It was the only word she could think of. As soon as she'd said it, his earlier warning echoed in her mind. And Todd…he'd known of this for…how long? He'd never given her the slightest hint beyond his unexpected changes in behavior. She'd chalked those up to sobriety. Wasn't that a kick in the pants? Or, more accurately, a bite in the throat?

"To me, such realities are all too normal," he said. "I live with the weight of the past on my shoulders every day. It can be a painful burden. Does hearing this disgust you? Frighten you?"

"I don't know what I feel. I'm not afraid of you—not exactly. And I'm definitely not disgusted." She forced herself to laugh. "A little freaked out, sure."

"Well—that's a start."

She exhaled deeply, trying to stop herself from shaking. She raised her hands, and he grasped them, sliding his fingers over hers and up along her arms. His strength flowed through her, carried in that light, simple touch. Briana found it oddly reassuring.

"Can I ask you something?"

"Of course."

"Sunlight. What happens if it touches you? Would you...would you spontaneously combust?"

"I would not." He laughed with genuine amusement. "Another exaggeration. I would, however, receive an injury akin to radiation burns. Not fatal but in some cases disfiguring. Having seen a few victims, I have decided not to risk it. Hence my specially designed bed and curtains. With those panels closed, I am safe from sunrise to dusk."

She looked over at his bed, imagining him enclosed in its presumably airless confines. It seemed to be almost like being in a coffin which was exactly the point, she supposed. "It must be claustrophobic."

"You can imagine the difficulty if you ever spent the night."

"So mixed relationships aren't possible?"

"Not impossible. Difficult. Compromises can, and have, been reached."

"By you?" This time, she sounded jealous. There was no denying it.

"Not yet. I realize that few mortal women would even consider participating in my existence. Therefore, I have never asked."

"You won't ask me, then, I suppose? In spite of all these confessions?"

"I will ask you nothing yet. You need time to process what I have told you. Time to consider the impact of this new knowledge on your world—and your life."

She was quiet for a while. "I do have a lot of questions," she ventured at last.

"Of course."

"I just…don't know if I can find the words to ask them now. I'm sorry."

He waved away her apology. "When you are ready, you will. We both will."

She swallowed again and raised a hand to his chest. Her fingers trembled as she rested them against his shirt. Still no heartbeat. Her own pulse raced with enough force for them both.

"I'm sure I want to stay with you, Sebastian. Tonight. Now. For however long I can."

He closed his eyes, drawing her toward him. She pressed her face against him, just above the spot where her palm still rested, losing herself in his presence. His strangeness itself intoxicated her. "I had hoped you would," he whispered.

Then he stepped away from her, crossed to the window, and took hold of the drapes. At first, she thought he intended to fling the curtains open. Instead, he pulled one of them free and spread it like a soft rug on the floor.

"We'll put it back later," he said, as if to remind himself.

Moonlight flooded the makeshift stage as Sebastian moved into its center, kicking off his shoes as he went. He held out his hand to her, and without hesitation she joined him in that pale blue circle.

"I like your dress," he murmured against her ear. His fingers stroked her back, toyed with her zipper. "The color reminds me of mist. I must confess, though, I prefer what lies underneath."

"It's yours," she told him, shuddering with pleasure as he began to slide fabric past hot flesh, freeing her of its confines with the grace of a cool wind over surging waves. "Everything."

"I'll remember that."

"Do." Before long, she really did feel the crisp ocean breeze on her skin…everywhere. Sebastian, too, was nude except for the ascot which was still rakishly tied around his throat. She ran her hands over the silky cloth and savored the unique sensations of both it and the velvety drape underneath their outstretched bodies.

Briana couldn't help studying him with fresh eyes now that she knew his secret. His paleness, of course, made perfect sense. Bathed in the hazy moonlight that filtered through the window his flesh took on an otherworldly, almost transparent glow. The smudges of charcoal fuzz that dappled his chest and groin stood out in stark relief. Most striking was his erection which stretched up from its murky cloud of curls.

He had no way of hiding his desire for her. The thick, ropey sinews that wrapped its considerable girth strained with need. Though part of Briana still wondered whether she should pull away in fear, gather her clothes, and flee Morgan House forever, a larger part felt mesmerized by the sight of him. She extended her hand slowly, letting her open palm hover over his fleshy helmet for just a moment. The dark gash of his slit seemed to pulse slowly, responding to her nearness like a moonflower opening under a summer sky. A magnetic current seemed to buzz between them.

Her hand fluttered over his shaft, her fingers closing around his rigid flesh like a butterfly folding warm wings over its perch. Sebastian's eyes narrowed to slits as she roved slowly down his length, pausing to caress his hefty sac. When her hand moved on and he opened them again, his pupils had expanded into deep, dark pools that transfixed her.

He began to mimic her gestures, sliding his gelid palms over the hot planes of her thighs until both his hands met in the crease between her legs. This time, unlike at the beach, his fingers moved boldly, taking quick possession of the object of his desire. He burrowed deeper, his left thumb parting the plump folds of her feminine cleft while his right, index, and middle fingers dipped inside.

"Apparently my confession didn't repulse you as I'd feared. You feel wet and ready for me."

"You know things have gone too far for me to stop now." Her words came out in a near gasp. "Whatever you are—I need you."

The pressure of his fingers increased. The clash of his cold skin and her warm liqueur made her jolt with pleasure. When his thumb pivoted to apply pressure to her swollen bud, her hips bucked in an involuntary spasm. She couldn't suppress a gasp. Her desperation seemed to amuse him. His thin lips curled in a smile.

"Not yet." His hands slid away with agonizing slowness. Her slippery folds flexed and clamped at his retreating fingers as if anxious to trap him there. She knew, however, that more satisfying diversions law ahead. Reluctantly, she let go of his cock. It would find its own way home soon enough.

Reaching higher, she burrowed her fingers in his hair and guided his face between her breasts. He nuzzled her with his cheek, and Briana imagined his fangs nudging her through his half-parted lips.

"I understand now why you wouldn't kiss me before."

His words came out in a groan. "Too risky. I needed to maintain control."

"That's not always a good thing, is it? I mean—sometimes it's healthier to let go."

"Not in my case. Had I harmed you, you might have excused my behavior. But I could never forgive myself."

"Why do you assume you would? You said it yourself—the act can bring pleasure to both partners."

He shook his head. "The connection you refer to is not one that can be entered into lightly. There must be full disclosure and consent on both sides. The intimacy is more intense than you can imagine."

"Does it feel more intimate than this?" Briana wrapped her legs around his waist and dragged him against her. His thickened tip brushed her moistening folds, arousing her so deeply she nearly convulsed with need. Yet, he held back just enough to torment her.

"Infinitely more." He bucked his hips—pressing, parting, and then drawing away. His brief contact ignited a dull throb in her, one that reached directly from the apex of her thighs to her dully thudding heart. "One day, perhaps, you'll experience what I am speaking of. You will know then that such a sensation cannot be described...only experienced. And you will never forget it."

She answered with a moan.

"The feeling will obsess you—consume you," he continued. "Your body will regenerate the blood I take from you. When that happens, though, its very chemistry will change. From that point on, I will be a part of you. Our essences will intertwine, never to be separated again. The joining of mere bodies"—again he stroked against her, and then pulled quickly back—"is nothing, nothing in comparison."

"I want to experience all of it. All of you," she gasped.

"Not yet." He swiveled his hips again.

"Yes. Now." Her palms encircled his buttocks, holding him in place. A simple, single thrust would bring him inside her. "Please."

His eyes met hers, and his mouth set in a determined line. With a twist of his body he pierced her willing flesh.

His cock seemed to set off a chain of sparks inside her as it glided swiftly into her fiery center. Once anchored, he made no effort to pull back or begin the usual pumping motion. Instead, he simply rested his full weight on top of her and let himself sink until nothing but a few tufts of trapped hair lay between them.

Her hands slipped downward, and her nails dug into the backs of his thighs, keeping him tight against her. Sebastian had pulled her so close to the edge with his protracted teasing that she felt herself go tumbling off it the moment they came together.

Though he had spoken of a sensation more transcendent than this, Briana couldn't imagine anything that could be. Flashes of pleasure bolted through her, arching her back and forcing a near-scream from her throat.

Even in the throes of abandon she could see that he was changing, too. His body started warming against hers. She sensed it both inside and out, but suddenly a flash of pure heat seemed to ignite between them, as if the friction of her skin on his had struck sparks. His expression tensed, went slack, and grew oddly distant. Briana watched his eyes glaze over and his mouth open to emit a drawn-out, primal moan. She could just see the points of his teeth glint behind his parted lips. The ferocity of his emotion made an unexpected thrill rush through her veins. She realized at once what she had just seen.

Putting it into words proved more difficult, though. "Was...was that...? Did you...?" she fumbled when they tugged apart again and lay back, limbs entwined, on the drape.

Sebastian blinked and shook his head. His expression suggested embarrassment. Briana suspected that he did not enjoy being vulnerable, even for a moment. "Yes," he murmured. "I must admit that even I am surprised. It's been a long time."

"I told you—it's good to let go once in a while." She smiled at him, which seemed to put him at ease. She lifted a finger to his face and stroked the sides of his lips. She could detect the slightest bump where his fangs lay concealed. "Sebastian, I saw your...well, your teeth. I wasn't afraid. Will you kiss me now?"

"I'd better not."

She heard the pain in his voice and decided not to pursue the matter. Instead, she rested her head against his chest and lay back, letting the moonlight caress her.

"I never thought I could recapture that human part of me again," Sebastian said after a while. "I owe you a debt of gratitude."

"I'll think of some way for you to repay me." She cuddled up against him. Before long, tendrils of cold air filtered through the drafty window and tickled at her skin. Sebastian's body offered no compensating warmth. "We'll have to get up soon, I suppose," Briana said with a sigh. "We can't spend the entire evening stretched out on a curtain."

"I suppose not."

"How about a shower—together?"

He smirked. "You wouldn't like my idea of a shower. Quick and cold."

"Not very romantic."

"I'm afraid not. Vampires have a natural aversion to water."

"Why?"

"Simply put, we don't float. Though we cannot drown, we are not exactly graceful swimmers. Imagine dropping a marble statue off a pier and you'll have a fairly accurate picture."

"I can see why you wouldn't enjoy that."

"Hot tubs are out, too. I warned you there would be inconveniences."

"I'll learn to cope with them."

He grew serious. "I hope you can."

She watched him stand, gather his clothes, and leave the room. Not sure what else to do, she reluctantly pulled her own garments back on. At least the metallic fabric of her new dress hadn't wrinkled too badly. The saleswoman had known what she was talking about.

While she struggled with the zipper at her back, Sebastian returned, himself fully clothed again. He smiled sympathetically and moved behind her, fastening the dress easily.

"If they can put a man on the moon, you'd think they could come up with a dress a woman could zip up by herself. Maybe it's a conspiracy to make sure we always have a man around to help us."

"You should have seen what women wore in my day. It's a wonder the human race continued, given what a chore it was to even initiate the mating process. Fortunately, the drive is strong enough to surmount any number of obstacles."

"I guess that's safe to assume," she said. Her eyes dropped to his right hand which was clutching what appeared to be a small, battered box tied up with a ribbon.

"That brings me to what I wanted to show you." When he brought the object forward Briana saw that it was not a box but an antique photo album. Sebastian pulled the dried ribbon away, releasing a cloud of dust. "I found this in the room that once belonged to my wife. I didn't think I could ever share its contents with anyone but Ruby."

Briana opened the album gingerly. The pages flapped loose, their edges crumbly. Inside lay a collection of grainy, brown-hued photographs mounted between layers of thick, stained cardboard. One of the first depicted a dark-suited gentleman on an overstuffed chair. He posed stiff and uncomfortable, his face stern above a high collar and ruffled cravat. Her pulse quickened as she realized what she was looking at.

"You haven't changed at all," she marveled.

He nodded sadly. "True enough. I am a human artifact, frozen in time. Well—almost human."

She turned the page with shaking fingers. In the next frame, the same man and a woman stood formally posed against a plain background. The woman held a parasol. The picture, along with their faces, had gone blurry over time. Briana could tell that neither smiled.

"My wife, Amelia, and I."

Briana felt a stab of jealousy which she knew was irrational. Amelia was long dead. Or was she? Maybe Briana shouldn't make assumptions given all she'd found out tonight

"You don't look happy."

Sebastian nodded. "Taking photographs was an ordeal in those days. We had to stand still for what seemed like hours. Try that in the summer, with three layers of wool clothing."

Briana looked up at him, trying to read his expression. Then she looked down at the picture again. "Did you love her?"

"We defined love differently in those days. Our parents, equal in social standing and brought together by a common understanding, placed us together. We did our duty, as expected. We embarked on a respectable marriage and created a healthy heir. But love? No. We suited one another as well as most Victorian couples. That is to say we spent as little time together as was socially acceptable."

"You make it sound like love is a modern invention! I can't believe that."

"I'm sure it existed—for some. I know I never found it. My search took me all over the world, even after I married. You see what happened to me. I deserved it, in a way, for my arrogance and my betrayal."

"Then…your wife never knew?"

"I let her believe that I had abandoned her for lack of interest. That wasn't entirely false. I couldn't tell her what I had become, and I couldn't face eternity with her."

"How sad." Secretly, Briana found herself relieved. She turned another brittle page and found a more modern type of photograph, this one clearly taken after the turn of the century. It featured an older man with wavy bangs and a handlebar moustache.

Sebastian confirmed her suspicions about his identity. "My son—Edgar."

"Yes, the last man to live in Morgan House. I see the resemblance. What was it like to have a son so much older than you?"

"I can't say, because I never knew him. I left to tour Europe when he was only a baby. I'm not proud of that, but my life had become a misery. Perhaps, in an odd way, I did him and my wife a favor. Despite or because of my absence during his formative years, my son grew up to be a fine, responsible man."

"And he had Ruby."

He nodded. "He married for the first time in middle age though I understand he eventually made up for his late start. Ruby was his only child, and he doted on her. He even sent her to college which was by no means a common practice in 1950. Then the trouble began. She took one of those European tours expensive schools offered to the daughters of the elite. The idea was to polish their manners and perhaps teach them a smattering of French and German. Ruby wasn't content to plod around museums and tour stately homes. She decided to trace her errant grandfather's path—which proved to be a mistake."

"I'm guessing that path led her to…vampires?" In spite of everything they'd discussed, she stumbled over the last word.

"The same clique who found me in 1899 found her equally delightful sixty years later. Truthfully, she has managed quite well. She thinks of me as a brother now. We are more alike than I would have suspected."

"They say Edgar became a recluse. No wonder he became despondent."

"He never knew the truth—about either of us." Sebastian's mouth tightened. "We did what we had to. It broke his heart to think her dead, but he faced a much worse hell had he even guessed at the facts. How could a father make that choice?"

Did he refer to Edgar or himself? Briana shivered.

"I'm sorry. The pain must have been intense."

"For a century I have tried not to feel it or anything else for that matter. Only you have changed that. And though it is a bit…uncomfortable to acknowledge my emotional shortcomings, overall I consider my enlightenment a positive development."

"I'm glad."

He leaned down and encircled her shoulders with his left arm. Briana tentatively reached up and rested her hand on his pale cheek. Sebastian half-closed his eyes and leaned against her in a silent but powerful acknowledgement of their bond.

A strange thumping noise exploded the moment. At first Briana thought it was her own heart hammering uncontrollably. Gradually, she realized it came from the clutch purse she'd left on the floor. Damn that thing! Why had she even bought it?

"I'm sorry," she fumbled as she crawled away and retrieved the purse. "My cell phone."

He sat back and watched with amusement as she pulled the offending device from the handbag.

"The nineteenth century must have been nice in a way—you didn't have all these distractions," she said as she flipped the phone open. The number looked unfamiliar, but the message bore an "urgent" icon.

He laughed, casually exposing his pointed teeth. "You would not have enjoyed living in my time."

The moment Briana pressed the "talk" button, she wished she hadn't.

"Hey, Bri. It's me, Graham."

She didn't suppress her irritated sigh. "Graham, this really isn't a good time."

"I didn't call to chat. I'm at The Chum Bucket. Just giving you a heads up. You'd better come down here before your brother gets arrested again."

"Why? What's going on?"

"Nothing yet. But give Ami another ten minutes and we might be telling a different story."

The phone chirped in protest as she slammed it shut. "Sebastian, I'm so sorry, but I have to go. It's Todd. Some kind of trouble in town."

His brows lifted. "Should I assume Ruby is also involved?"

"I don't know. Graham didn't say. Do you want to come with me?"

"Of course." Gently, he closed the photo album and set it aside. "My past isn't going anywhere. We can discuss it another time."

Moments later they were in her car and heading toward town a bit faster than seemed strictly legal. Sebastian rested one hand on Briana's thigh while she drove. He meant the gesture as one of comfort, she knew, but he probably had no inkling of how difficult she found it to concentrate on the road when she longed to reach for him too.

The whole time she fought back a blaze of anger at Todd. Would he ever stop ruining every promising thing that came into her life? She really could kill him sometimes. Then again, considering all that she'd learned tonight, that particular threat didn't really carry much weight any more.

* * * *

The Chum Bucket was relatively crowded, but Briana quickly spotted Graham by the bar. His eyes flicked to Sebastian, who had walked in right behind her. Then he gestured toward a booth in the corner. Todd sat nursing what appeared to be a ginger ale and lime. Though that pleased Briana, she grew less optimistic when she observed Ami and Ruby hovering on either side of him. Ami clutched a beer bottle like she intended to use it as a weapon. Ruby's head was thrown back as if she had just finished laughing long and hard at her rival.

Graham made his way through the crowd to stand next to Briana and Sebastian. "I'd say we're about five minutes away from a girl-on-girl smack down," he said. "They've been circling each other for a while."

"We'll see about that." Sebastian strode toward the booth. Briana followed, still trying to wrap her mind around the fact that her brother's new squeeze was really a sixty-year-old woman whose grandfather Briana had now slept with twice.

"Ruby, what's going on here?" Sebastian asked in a stern voice.

"Nothing," Ruby snapped. "Todd and I were trying to have a conversation when we were so rudely interrupted by this…mannerless creature." She and Ami glared at each other.

"I have a right to talk to anyone here I want," Ami shouted above the pounding music. Her voice was far from steady. A few patrons grinned and moved closer to them, clearly anticipating some live entertainment.

"Not when the man in question has no desire to talk to you!" Ruby started to get up, but Sebastian's grip on her arm held her in place.

"You little tramp!" Ami shouted. "Why don't you go back to the cathouse you came from?"

"What an odd accusation, coming from someone who lives in a motel. Isn't that just the kind of place where people like you prefer to conduct business?"

"Ruby," Sebastian growled.

"Ami, please." Briana positioned herself between the raging woman and her brother. "You're going to start some trouble here you won't want to finish. Let's not forget what happened last time you and Todd spent an evening together."

In response, Ami raised her arm above her head and flung the bottle at Ruby. It sailed past Briana's shoulder just as Sebastian reached up and tried to catch it in mid-arc. It slipped through his fingers and smashed on the floor between his and Ruby's feet. A spatter of glass shards flew up around them, and Briana felt some sting her shins. She hadn't bothered to put her pantyhose back on at Sebastian's house. Now she glanced down and saw fresh blood sprinkling her ankles. Looking up again, she found Ruby and Sebastian both staring at the same spot—completely mesmerized. Hastily, Sebastian averted his eyes.

"Okay, enough. Come on, Ami. Sebastian and I will drive you back to the motel."

She extended a hand, intending it as conciliatory gesture. Ami, still tense with anger, misconstrued her purpose.

"You self-righteous bitch! Get away from me!"

"I don't want to fight with you. I just want you to make the right decision and leave with us."

In response, Ami flew at her.

The two of them hit the table together, sending Todd's drink flying. As some of it splashed her face Briana noted with an absurd sense of relief that it was, in fact, soda.

She slid off the table and regained her footing just in time to see Ami's nails coming at her eyes.

She didn't need to look around to know that the crowd had closed in to watch. Determined to give them plenty to see, Ami began pummeling her with a series of blows. Raising both arms, Briana swung, slapped, and snatched at whatever she could. A sharp pain exploded in her mouth, and she heard the sound of cloth ripping. Ami's curses continued to assault her ears as someone grabbed her under the armpits and pulled her free. The blows to Briana's body ceased. A crush of people surged forward and blocked her view.

When everything settled down again she found herself in Graham's arms with her back against his broad chest. On the other side of the table Sebastian held Ami, whose arms continued to spin in an ineffective windmill movement. Briana blushed when she saw Ami's shirt torn down the middle. Her miniscule bra had been knocked askew, exposing most of her right breast to anyone who cared to look. Sebastian's restraining hand lay only inches from her tiny, pert nipple.

"Let go of me!" Ami shrieked, clawing backward at Sebastian. "Pervert!"

Briana watched with a mixture of horror and amusement as Sebastian handed his captive over to two of the bar's staff members. Pinning her arms to her side, they hustled the struggling woman toward the bar and dragged her through a rear door.

"Are you all right?" Graham asked her, slowly loosening his grip.

"I'm fine," she said without looking at him. Her attention focused on Sebastian, who stood watching them with an odd expression. Briana suddenly remembered the wounds on her legs. Her lip tasted of blood as well. "I just want to get out of here."

"You're right. We'd better go," Sebastian said, moving toward them. He pulled off his suit jacket and draped it around her. The fabric felt soft but cool to the touch. Nevertheless, Briana gratefully burrowed into its protective shell. When she turned to say goodnight to Graham, he was gone. Ruby and Todd had disappeared, as well. She didn't blame them.

"Do you think anyone called the police?" she asked as Sebastian escorted her toward the door.

"I doubt it. With any luck, that was the last of tonight's adventures."

"Are you sure?" Briana asked as they walked toward her car.

Sebastian paused with his hand on the driver's side door. Again he trained his eyes on the ground, away from her. "I think I should leave you now," he said suddenly.

"I wish you could stay with me," she said.

"No," he snapped. Then, in a softer voice, he added, "I want you to think about everything I told you. Not in the heat of passion, but on your own and in a cooler frame of mind."

"All right. If you insist." Again her tongue detected that distinctive metallic taste. Briana touched her mouth, and her fingers came away smeared with blood. She now understood Sebastian's need to distance himself from her. A ripple of fear edged its way up her neck when she saw his expression. Raw hunger contorted his features.

"I do," he said in a quiet voice.

Briana knew better than to argue. Sebastian stood motionless on the curb, watching as she climbed into the car and pulled quickly away. Nervously, she wondered what had become of Ruby and Todd. She hoped an unsettling scene didn't await her at the house.

At the end of the block she slowed for a red light and spotted Ami standing on the opposite side of the street. Briana hit the gas and sped through the light when Ami opened her mouth to yell some insult at her. In light of everything that had gone on that day, the risk of a traffic ticket seemed utterly insignificant.

No one except Ami witnessed her minor transgression. When Briana got home she headed up to her room and stretched out on the bed, drained and bewildered.

Sleeping wasn't an option. She tossed and turned, fully dressed, trying to make sense of the bizarre things Sebastian had told her.

Eventually she began to wonder if she had just imagined the whole thing. She sat up, looking around her room as if she'd never seen it before.

"This is crazy," she said aloud, rubbing both hands over her face. "I'm going crazy."

"I warned you this would happen."

Briana dropped her hands and looked up. At the foot of her bed, half-obscured by shadows, stood Sebastian.

Chapter 11

She blinked at him, still not sure how much of this she was hallucinating.

"Have you...have you come to bite me?" she asked.

His face twisted, and for a moment she thought he might lunge at her. She crawled toward the headboard, forcing herself not to fear him. This wasn't some corny horror movie after all. She'd just shared the most intimate evening of her life with this man.

But why had he come, after telling her they both needed time to process what had happened? And what had changed him in the meantime? He seemed so distant...his mood so dark.

"I no longer feed on the living," he finally replied in a strained voice. "I want you to know that you have nothing to fear from me in that respect."

"I believe you," she said. "Did you come back just to tell me that?"

"Yes." He seemed to choke out the word. "I had no time to explain before. I feared I had left you with a misapprehension."

Briana nodded, still bewildered. He hadn't moved from the spot in front of her bed. Slowly she made a space for him beside her and motioned him forward. He took a single, hesitant step in her direction.

She asked her next question cautiously. "You said you no longer feed that way. Does that mean you did suck people's blood...before?"

"Once," he agreed. He seemed to relax a little. Gingerly, he eased himself onto the edge of her bed. "But now, I consume no organic substances at all. Instead, each evening I prepare and administer an injection that keeps me—well, I hesitate to say alive. Nourished and functioning might be a more accurate description."

"A shot feeds you? Then why does Ruby...?" Briana paused. She couldn't bring herself to envision, much less refer to, Sebastian's granddaughter gorging herself on her brother.

"Ruby feeds because she wishes to. I may disagree with her choice, but I have trained myself to respect it. She is not alone. Many—even most—vampires prefer to feast in the traditional manner." The grim lines around his mouth tightened. "I do not and will not. The injections are the only way I can be a part of your world. And for your sake, I want to be."

Moved by his sudden vulnerability, Briana stretched her hand to him. His gaze grew distant as he traced the bones in her wrist with his fingertips, sending nerve-wracking tingles through her whole body. Briana knew he was thinking about past regrets and mistakes he would most likely never share with her.

He dropped her hand and cupped her chin, tilting her face to his. His eyes burned with intense emotion held in check. "Enough of my medical concerns. I've spent the entire evening relating two centuries' worth of my own problems, yet I know almost nothing of your past. Tell me."

"There isn't a lot to tell." She shrugged self-consciously. Her own history seemed incredibly dull compared to his, but she sensed genuine curiosity. Perhaps he took an almost anthropological interest in the details of growing up in the late twentieth century. "My parents divorced when Todd and I were kids. My father wasn't equipped to handle us alone, but he tried. Eventually my mother was killed in a car accident in California. She tried to get as far away from Darkisle as possible. After that, my father kept working at the motel while he slowly drank himself to death. I figure that's where Todd got his weakness. Some people think it's genetic."

"Where does Graham fit in?" Her shocked look amused him. "It's obvious something existed between you."

"We went to high school together. About a year ago, we had a...a thing, I guess, but it's over now. We're incompatible at the most basic level, and I think he knows that, too. I'm sure he can find someone who suits him much better...like I have."

"You seem sincere when you say that."

"I am. Sebastian...your past is over with. What I see in front of me is someone who has made mistakes, but is trying to do better. I'm not perfect, either. The exact chemical composition of your blood—or whatever you have running through your veins—can't change the way I feel when I'm with you."

"Vampires have that effect on people," he said sadly. "It has something to do with pheromones. Each human has a subliminal trigger—a scent that creates instant sexual arousal. Vampires exude a sort of universal stimulant. Possibly that is what you are reacting to."

She couldn't help smiling. "Really? Because I thought it was just regular run-of-the-mill hormones."

He stared at her, his scowl gradually fading. "I have waited two lifetimes to meet someone like you, Briana. It is hard enough for me to believe that I have actually found you, but to find that you have the courage to savor every moment seems little short of miraculous."

"I do want that," she said as he drew her closer. He murmured with pleasure as his hand left her face and moved lower to cup her breast. The other drifted lower, sliding under the wrinkled dress she hadn't gotten around to taking off. Briana grasped, too, as his palm brushed over the curve of her thigh and moved toward the moist curls tucked inside.

They shed their clothes wordlessly, efficiently. She didn't resist as he pulled her on top of him, turning her at the last moment so that her back settled against his chest and her rear end fitted into the curve of his torso. His skin felt cool, like the sheets. His hands were equally frosty when he slid them around her middle and spread his fingers on her abdomen.

He hugged her close. "I can feel your warmth," he whispered. "It's warming me, too."

Briana felt it as well. As they lay pressed together, his chill slowly melted into her. It was more than an exchange of body temperature. Her pulse, her heat, even her most deeply buried thoughts and desires flowed into his and grew stronger. More intense than any sexual joining, more enthralling than any fleeting rush of physical pleasure, their merged desire crackled through her like an electrical charge.

Briana closed her eyes and let her mind drift into hazy pleasure as he tweaked and rubbed her nipple with one hand, while the other slipped lower, touching and teasing her most sensitive spot. His caresses moved slowly, rhythmically, each pass of his hand gradually bearing down with more pressure. This methodical strategy seemed to go on for hours, yet at the same time it seemed to peak far too soon. When he abruptly pulled away, her shallow breath caught in her throat and her entire body bucked with need. She needed more, so much more than just the playful tickle of his fingers.

Fortunately, she had warmed him sufficiently to give his desire the substance they both craved. Sebastian turned her over and positioned himself over her, parting her thighs with a swift movement of his knee. Instantly her legs coiled around his waist, her heels driving into his buttocks to force him against her.

His prolonged teasing had left her so aroused that her body offered no resistance. Releasing a sound that sounded half lovesick moan, half feral snarl, Sebastian plowed his way into her.

They rocked together, so closely pinned together that Briana lost all sense of separateness from him. He was absorbing her warmth, she knew, filling himself with her essence as surely as he filled her with his stony flesh. Sharing her aura with Sebastian was anything but a loss though. Paradoxically, the more of herself she gave to him, the stronger and more complete she felt. His coldness ebbed away, yielding to a strength that built in him—and her—with the force of a summer storm. When that storm finished its crescendo their mutual climax exploded like thunder.

The most intense pleasure she'd ever known, pure and fresh and white-hot, tore a path through her middle that left her tingling from her toes to her eyebrows. Sebastian, too, seemed lost as the maelstrom swept him up in its all-powerful embrace. He clung to her, and she to him as some invisible force greater than the two of them lifted, rolled, and pummeled them into sweet, shuddering oblivion.

The hurricane soon deposited them back in the bed, their entwined limbs twisted in the rumpled sheets and their conjoined bodies still locked together. Briana had never felt so thoroughly, deliciously opened, both physically and emotionally. When Sebastian pressed her down on the pillows and extracted himself with a quick backward motion of his hips, she ached for him before he had even fully withdrawn.

He stretched out beside her, on top of the sheets, and propped one arm under his head. The casual gesture belied an attitude that was anything but relaxed. Once again, he stared at her with an intensity that made the sweat prickle along her spine. Already his body had begun to cool, returning to its usual waxy complexion. He resembled one of those impossibly white statues in museums or art books, she thought as she admired his nakedness. The only difference was the stark contrast of his pale skin and the dark hair trailing over his forehead and dusting his chest and abdomen.

As she lay gazing at him, he reached out and curled his fingers over her shoulders. Slowly his hands glided down the backs of her arms, dragging her back against him. She let out a ragged breath when his maleness, soft and tepid now, nestled between her legs, the gesture one of comfort rather than urgency. Still, as the perspiration on her breasts soaked slowly into the velvety mat on his chest, she knew that embers they had ignited still smoldered.

"Sleep now," he murmured. His lips hovered so close that she felt them brush her mouth when they moved. Instinctively she pursed hers in a kiss, but the attempted kiss landed on air. He had tilted his head just enough to avoid it.

Yes, she thought, sleep would be welcome. In one evening, it seemed she had lived several lifetimes, traveled through an entirely new world, and maybe even left her own body for a moment or two. A retreat into peaceful oblivion, with Sebastian watching over her, seemed the only sensible alternative.

An overwhelming sensation of peace, safety, and perfect satisfaction closed around her like a blanket. Dimly she realized that Sebastian really had drawn her blanket over them both.

Briana slept.

* * * *

She opened her eyes to find him awake, still lounging on the pillows he'd stacked underneath him. She lay gazing at him as she turned something over in her mind.

"Sebastian...I want you to kiss me."

His face turned to stone. "I don't think that would be a good idea."

"But I want you to. I've given it a lot of thought. Whatever happens, I can handle it."

He shook his head sadly. "I don't think you know what you're asking."

"I do. I want you to kiss me. I want to kiss you. Can't we just try it?"

"It's too dangerous. You're in close quarters here with me. If I lost control of myself...well, let's not even consider that possibility. It would be better to avoid the temptation altogether."

"Sebastian, I can't go on sleeping with you and never even know what it would be like to feel your lips on mine. Maybe it's different for men...or, at least men like you. But please understand that it's something I need. Without kissing...I don't know...it makes me feel cheap."

"It could never be that," he protested.

"What's the worst that could happen? You'd bite me? I thought you could control that now. Why couldn't it be wonderful—just one more way for us to be intimate?" She paused to scowl. "Unless that's the problem. Are you having second thoughts about us?"

"Of course not. I should hope I've made my feelings for you clear by now."

"Actually...no, you haven't. That's what I'm trying to get across to you."

He sighed and rubbed both hands through his hair, something she'd never seen him do before. In fact, this was the closest she'd ever seen to abject frustration in him. It offered a rare glimpse of the conflicted human he'd once been rather than the supremely controlled uber-being he'd become.

"You're still warm," she exclaimed with surprise when she placed a hand on his chest.

"I have you to thank for that. The drug tricks my metabolism into thinking it's been fed...you did the rest. For the next few hours, I doubt that even a trained medical specialist could distinguish me from any ordinary mortal."

Briana raised a hand to his cheek and rested her fingertips against smooth, living flesh. She could even feel a faint pulse underneath the ruddy surface.

"You like me this way," he surmised, leaning into her caress and half-closing his eyes in obvious pleasure.

"I like you any which way," she promised.

Briana's heart expanded with a surge of compassion for him and something more besides. Her fingers slid along the firm, masculine angle of his jaw and moved to cup the back of his neck, threading through his hair. Desire throbbed in her like a dull, heavy ache. It seemed as if some part of her had been removed, either by magic or more sinister means, and Sebastian alone had the power to make her whole again.

His face loomed close to hers now, too. Her lips parted in perfect sync with his, almost but not quite touching them. She jumped when he extended the tip of his tongue and skimmed her lower lip.

He drew back for a second, tilting her head backward while his shadowed gaze searched her expression. She met his eyes boldly, determined to show no trace of fear or uncertainty. A second later, his mouth covered hers.

Then he kissed her with the kind of passionate desperation she'd only seen in movies or imagined in her wildest and most secret fantasies. She met him with equal enthusiasm, darting her own tongue against his and sweeping her teeth over his lower lip.

"Many decades have passed since I last experienced anything like that," he told her when at last they broke apart. "Not even when I lived as a human. You continue to amaze me, Briana."

"A lot's changed since your human days. I think it's safe to assume that women are a bit more...aggressive...than what you got used to a hundred years ago."

Before he could react Briana settled both palms on his hips and licked her way down his body, starting with the dark skin of his pebbly nipples and ending up in an area where his sudden arousal emerged far more apparently.

"May I?" she asked in a hoarse whisper. Sebastian murmured his consent, reaching down to rest his own hands on her shoulders.

His erection surged as hard and swollen as any living man's while Briana deftly moved her mouth over him and gifted him with a different, and even more intimate, type of kiss. That, too, was something he hadn't enjoyed for many decades, to judge by the way he moaned and thrashed in response. . Driven by a frenzy of desire to possess him, Briana allowed herself free reign to act out all the fantasies she'd repressed while forbidden to use her mouth on any part of him.

Hungrily she circled his distended ridge with her lips, sliding her tongue along the resilient stem that arced beneath it. She followed that path slowly, savoring the rocky terrain of muscle and tense skin. Her chin brushed the rounded surface of the equally tense orbs that lay beneath. He held no seed that could fill her or generate new life, she assumed, but she believed she could give him the same rush of pleasure a human man enjoyed. She would be more than content to share his gratification in some less conventional way. Exactly how would require some experimentation.

Wild as a winter sea, she licked, bit, suckled, and stroked him until he began literally bellowing with pleasure. This, she decided, was his way of reaching orgasm. His powerful shudders made her imagine that she was clinging to him while an earthquake rocked the ground beneath them.

When she'd driven him to an apparent state of exhaustion, Briana tugged herself free and hoisted herself onto his chest. She was about to ask him how he'd enjoyed the fruits of twenty-first-century feminism when, to her astonishment, he sprang instantly back to life. She felt an entirely fresh erection snap up against her leg, hotter and larger than she'd ever seen it before.

Barking out a guttural laugh, Sebastian spun around on the bed, pinned her beneath him, and dipped demanding fingers between her legs.

"I wasn't completely honest with you before," he informed her in a silky voice that sent a brief stab of worry through her. "Taking my medication makes my physiology temporarily resemble that of a human. It never makes me less than what I really am, however."

"What—what do you mean by that?" she gasped, already shuddering as his thick pillar parted her soft center in a single, well-positioned thrust.

"What I mean is I can carry on like this for hours. Even the most virile human's stamina could never hope to match a vampire's. In other words, to put it in colloquial terms a person of your century can appreciate, I'm more than up for the challenge."

"I can definitely appreciate that," she said. But she knew by the glazed look of pure lust on his face that the time for talk had ended. Then, moving with a speed and grace—and yes, stamina—she could only marvel at, he gave her plenty to appreciate.

Chapter 12

She drove him home with a few hours to spare before dawn. Darkisle's narrow streets lay deserted, and the gravel road that led to Morgan House seemed even more gloomy and treacherous than normal.

"Everything looks so different at this time of night," Briana said with a touch of wonder. Even the familiar surroundings seemed completely transformed. Sebastian, Ruby, and the others like them really did live in a different world. "For all we know, civilization might have come to an end while we were...preoccupied."

"Well, that's simple enough to find out." Sebastian reached down and turned on her car radio, clicking through different stations. All blared the normal number of songs and commercials. He snapped it off again. "Apparently your theory is incorrect."

"I wasn't serious. I meant that this is like waking up from a strange dream. Did all of that really happen?"

"It did. You can trust me—as a matter of physiology, I do not dream."

"Oh." His assertion struck her as a bit sad, though his tone remained matter-of-fact.

"Sebastian...."

"Yes?"

"How did...this...happen to you? I mean...I have a general idea, but no details. I'd like to know more. I think I should...don't you?"

"If you like. Some of it might be difficult to hear."

"It's okay." She swallowed. "I can take it."

"Very well, then. I've already told you of my impatience, my irresponsibility, and my self-centeredness. A dutiful wife, a healthy son—none of that mattered to me in the least. Such arrogance wasn't uncommon for a man born to my social class in that time period. Neither, I must admit, was a taste for the kind of excitement only true decadence can bring. And where better to indulge that taste than the Continent?"

Briana thought back to what Graham had said about Amsterdam. She'd heard about the kinds of things that went on there, with so-called "working women" openly advertising their wares in huge windows. No doubt many of them might have found Sebastian a charming companion for an evening.

Not noticing the jealous frown that flashed across her face, Sebastian went on. "I took an interest in a woman whose name was well known around certain sectors of Paris. Many men sought her attentions and were willing and able to pay handsomely for them. She chose her companions cautiously though. I was fortunate enough, or so I thought at the time, to be one of them."

Briana kept her head turned to hide her flushed cheeks. "I see. And you paid her too?"

"Of course. Don't mistake me. I sought a purely professional relationship with her. Back then I wanted the best of everything, and she was the best. It should have been the perfect arrangement."

She was looking at him again. As much as she disliked imagining him with other women, even in another century, she couldn't hide her interest in the story of his transformation. "So what happened?"

"Put simply, she began to find my company as pleasurable as I found hers. One night she decided to do something for me that she'd never done with any of her other clients. She showed me her true identity. She turned me into what I am now, thinking I would stay with her. She realized her mistake too late. With eternity at my fingertips, I could never be content to loaf in a Parisian bordello, no matter how exclusive or comfortable."

"So you left her."

He nodded. "Once I became adjusted to my new abilities and confident enough to seek my own prey I struck out on my own."

"How did she take that?"

"A vampiress scorned is a sight I hope you never have to endure. However, a few centuries of dealing with the vagaries of human and vampire nature tends to toughen one's feelings to some extent. Eventually she accepted it, though I'm sorry to say we did not part on especially good terms."

"Where is she now?" The thought of a jealous vampire courtesan stalking Sebastian across the years didn't appeal to her.

"Unknown." He shrugged. "She may have perished by fire during World War II, as many Parisian vampires did. Then again, she may have escaped and taken a new identity. She's had many lovers since 1899, you can be sure. I am probably little more than a distant memory to her now. If not for the fact that I owe my current existence to her, she would be the same to me."

"I guess that's kind of a relief."

"You needn't worry—she isn't likely to show up in Darkisle and consider you a threat. I want you to understand one thing. I promise that I would sooner be destroyed than see you harmed."

He spoke the words fiercely, almost as if challenging her to contradict his statement.

"Seeing one another won't be easy. But I'm thinking of a compromise," he continued. "Half in your world, half in mine. No extremes. Just a kind of mutual respect and tolerance. We'll see where it goes from there."

"That might work," she said after a few moments' reflection. "I mean, things seem to be going okay for Todd and Ruby. They must have had this same conversation at some point."

"Don't be too sure. Ruby may be sixty years old, but she is still less concerned with consequences than I would prefer."

"And I don't have to tell you that Todd can be the same way." Briana sighed. Not having to deal with her brother's constant problems for the past twenty-four hours had been a relief, but she doubted things would stay that way for long. "Let's just hope they haven't gotten into too much trouble without us."

* * * *

Moaning with the effort, Todd rolled over in the big four-poster bed, slowly easing himself awake. He had an incredible kink in his neck, not to mention a weird star-shaped bruise on his groin. Both sites hurt, but the memory of the pleasurable way he'd obtained the wounds quickly dispelled any complaints.

The pain seemed even less important when Ruby herself slipped into the room. She'd showered, to judge by her damp hair and the loosely tied bathrobe she wore. She slid onto the bed beside him without a word, brushing her hand across the front of the sheet that had gathered at his waist. After few quick caresses another part of his body ached just as badly.

He sat up, rubbing both hands over his face. "I didn't mean to sleep away the whole night."

"Don't worry about it," Ruby said. "We got a little wild. I'm not surprised you needed some time to recover. In fact, I'm glad you rested."

Todd's eyes widened as she peeled the sheet off him in one bold move. Wriggling out of her bathrobe, she crawled on top of him and planted both hands on his shoulders. He sank back into the pillows, moaning as she ran her tongue over the tender spot on his neck. A moist, burning sensation spread down into his chest as her lapping opened the wound again, yielding fresh blood that she consumed greedily.

Her body grew steadily warmer as his life force filled her. Meanwhile, his own desire grew until he could hardly contain himself. He waited until her flesh became hot and supple against his, and then surrendered to his growing need. Wrapping his palms around her backside, he guided her over his straining middle and pushed his way in.

They rocked together for some time, each taking what was needed from the other. Finally, Todd's hips began to buck and jerk, sweet release sending him into a spasm of mind-wiping pleasure.

Ruby rode along with him, her swollen mouth clamped to his throat, her own frame shuddering as succulent nourishment coursed through her rapidly expanding veins. When she, too, felt sated, she rested on top of his chest, still licking fresh blood from the corners of her lips.

"I feel like going out again before it gets light," she told him. "Go take a quick shower and put your clothes back on."

"Do I have to? I'd just as soon stay here." His fingers trailed longingly over the slope of her breast. Ruby moved so that they skidded off the pert tip of her nipple.

"Yes, you do. I've made special plans, and besides, my brother will be home soon. He's already seen enough of your bare butt to last several lifetimes. I wouldn't advise tempting him to kick it again."

Todd sighed as she rolled off him. "Okay. I guess I don't need any more trouble with the cops."

He stood, picked up the rumpled garments he'd tossed across the room a few hours before, and padded off to the bathroom. When he came back, wearing jeans and a towel around his neck, he found Ruby beside the hall closet, slipping into a long leather jacket.

Todd stopped and stared, slack-jawed. "Is that all you're wearing?"

Ruby closed the coat and tied the leather sash in agonizingly slow movements. "Of course not, silly. I can't go outside without shoes."

He shook his head incredulously. "You're really amazing, Ruby, you know that?"

"Actually, I do." She winked and headed for the front door, twirling the car keys on her finger. "Now hurry up. I'm waiting."

Todd pulled on his t-shirt and jacket and returned to the guest room in search of his sneakers. He found one under the bed, and the other in the corner. Since his second sock had vanished, he pushed his bare feet into the shoes without bothering to untie them. He was about to leave the room when he noticed the half-full bottle of spring water he'd left on the antique dresser. He carried water with him most places lately, mostly as a substitute for the beer he still craved from time to time. Ruby had also suggested that he take in plenty of fluids after they'd been together. Somehow drinking vitamin-enriched water helped counteract the effects of the blood loss. At least the distant buzz in his head resembled the one he used to get from alcohol. Better than nothing, he supposed.

He took a long swig, trying to ignore the total lack of flavor and kick. He'd just have to find stimulation elsewhere from now on. Luckily, he had Ruby for that. As crazy as the whole blood-guzzling thing was, she excited him in a way no drink ever had.

When he lowered the bottle and replaced the cap, his gaze drifted to the room's only window, a unique portal-shaped structure that framed a dramatic view of Morgan Point's rocky shoreline. Though a scud of heavy rain clouds had driven the moon into hiding, he could still make out plenty of details: the white froth bubbling up over the rocks, a seabird wheeling carelessly through the mist, and what appeared to be the stark white figure of Ruby, stretched out on the ground, this time without the leather jacket. Her right hand was half-raised toward him, her elbow resting against the grey, wet sand.

Apparently she hadn't been kidding when she'd mentioned special plans for this evening or about waiting for him to join her. Dropping the water bottle on the dresser, Todd rushed for the front door.

When he stepped outside, he paused, stunned to see her beside the Maserati, the leather jacket once again securely tied.

"About time," she said, twirling the keys again. "Keep me waiting like that, and I might just take off on my own." Seeing his expression, she paused. "What's wrong?"

"I...I thought I saw someone down by the beach."

"Impossible. No one comes up here. Well, except fools like you, of course."

"I saw it with my own eyes, Ruby. I'm telling you, someone's down there."

She gave in with an impatient flip of her head. "You're probably imagining things. Human perception is just about useless in most situations, but I don't want you to keep bringing it up all night."

Pocketing her keys, she strode across the lawn and headed down the stone steps to the water with Todd following close behind. The moment she reached the sand, she stopped walking and simply stared.

"There," he said, pointing triumphantly. "I told you. She's right there."

His gloating vanished when Ruby looked up at him with an expression he'd never seen on her face before. A sudden sick feeling washed over him.

A woman's body lay splayed out in front of the rocks, her hand spread toward the sky not in a gesture of enticement, but in the stiffness of death. Though he'd mistaken her for nude from a distance, she actually still wore wet, skimpy clothing, twisted up around her hips and chest. Slimy tendrils of seaweed coiled over her legs and shoulders like eels.

"Oh, my god," Todd gasped. His fingers felt rubbery and limp as he fumbled to get his cell phone out of his jeans pocket.

Ruby grabbed his wrist, causing the phone to fall into the sand. "No! Don't call anyone."

"But we have to!" His voice cracked with panic. She bent and grabbed for his cell, but he scooped it up and hit 911.

"Todd! They'll blame you! Don't you see?"

Todd didn't listen. Hysterical, he ran down the beach away from her, sobbing into the phone for help.

Chapter 13

Briana's first thought as she and Sebastian came up the hill in her car was that Todd had gotten himself into some kind of trouble again. What other reason could there be for flashing police lights in Sebastian's driveway?

The she saw the ambulance.

"Something's happened to Todd," she cried. "I knew we shouldn't have left them alone so long!"

"Nonsense. They aren't children," Sebastian barked, though he sounded far from convinced. He swung the car into the middle of the tangle of police cars, uniformed officers, and paramedics that formed a loose perimeter around the flashing rescue vehicle. Briana jumped out before the car even came to a full stop. She spotted Will Garvey, who stood by the ambulance doors, and ran straight to him. To her horror, his men were loading a stretcher covered with an opaque plastic sheet.

"What happened?" She grabbed Will's arm. Sebastian had stopped the car and come up behind her. "That isn't Todd, is it?"

Garvey eyed them both and then shook his head. "Your brother's actually the one who found her. Looks like a drowning victim washed up on your beach, Mr. Morgan."

With relief, Briana glanced across the driveway and saw Todd and Ruby, both in perfect health, giving statements to Joel.

"Do we know who it is?" Sebastian asked.

Garvey reached down and flipped back a corner of the synthetic shroud. "Recognize her?"

"Of course we do," Briana said, shocked. "That's Ami—she rents a room from me at The Dunes Motel."

"Is this the same woman you had arrested for trespassing, Mr. Morgan?"

"It appears to be."

"Does anyone know what happened?" Briana asked.

Garvey replaced the sheet and then removed a small notepad from his uniform shirt pocket. "We'll wait for the coroner's report before we commit to anything on that front. Meanwhile, mind if I ask where the two of you were this evening?"

"Together," Sebastian said.

"I suppose you could prove that?"

Briana noted that Sebastian's face grew stony, and she suspected that Garvey noticed it too. "If necessary."

"Any reason the victim might have been up here tonight?"

"None I can think of. As you know, I do have the occasional problem with trespassers."

"Isn't it possible the current pulled her in from somewhere else?" Briana suggested. "I mean, she could have fallen in anywhere along the shore and drifted. Ami did have a habit of…partying a little too enthusiastically."

Garvey nodded and slid the notebook into his pocket. "We'll have the experts check it out. I guess this is going to sound odd, but try to put it out of your minds for now. I'll get back to you when I need more information. And, by the way, I'd appreciate your not talking to the press. They're sure to come knocking."

"My sister and I plan to be away all day tomorrow," Sebastian informed him. "We would be unavailable for comment in any case."

"Good. Thanks for your cooperation. I'll be in touch."

Sebastian and Briana exchanged a look as he walked back to confer with his deputies. Sebastian's expression cautioned her not to speak. They stood in the yard, not moving, until the last of the emergency vehicles and police cars had pulled out of sight, lights flashing but sirens silent. After all, there was no hurry to get Ami to her next destination.

Ruby and Todd crossed the lawn toward them. Todd looked dazed, Ruby simply exasperated.

"Everyone go inside," Sebastian ordered. "Now that the police have asked their questions, I have a few of my own."

The four of them turned and strode into the foyer. Sebastian made sure to lock the door before he faced the others.

"All right, Ruby. Explain yourself," he demanded.

"Me! You think I iced her?"

"You must admit, it's not a terribly farfetched assumption."

"Well, I didn't!" Ruby's full lips drew into a pout. Briana wondered if her brother—or grandfather—found that as endearing as she found it annoying. "I can't say I'm sorry the little tart's dead though."

Briana gasped in shock at her callousness.

"That is exactly the kind of reckless talk humans pick up on," Sebastian snapped. "Since this incident is bound to subject us to some unwelcome scrutiny, I suggest you make an effort to suppress such outbursts in the future. Todd, you tell me what happened."

"Just like we told the cops. We were just…just hanging out when I noticed something outside. We went to investigate and found her…like that." Tears sprang to his eyes the moment he finished speaking.

"No question, this looks strange," Briana ventured as everyone glared at each other. "But so far, I don't see any reason to assume we're dealing with anything but a terrible accident. We all know Ami drank too much and took chances. It could be a total coincidence that she ended up here."

"You'd best be right." Sebastian continued staring at Ruby, who met his gaze evenly, even defiantly. "If you do know what happened, accident or otherwise, you need to tell me now, so we can take the appropriate actions."

Ruby smirked. "I told you, I had nothing to do with it. Todd and I stayed together all evening. We can vouch for each other. In the most intimate detail, in fact."

Sebastian turned to Todd. "Is that true?"

"Yeah. It's true."

"Under the circumstances, we will suspend the work on the house," Sebastian said. "I will continue to pay you, of course."

"I don't want charity." The picture of misery, Todd jabbed his shaky hands in his pockets and walked back outside. Ruby stormed off, thudding up the stairs, leaving Sebastian and Briana alone in Morgan House's sparkling new foyer.

"I'm sure it was an accident," Briana said again. "Everything fits. She got drunk, fell in, and washed ashore where the currents brought her. Every year, we lose at least one tourist that way."

"Yes. Let us hope that is the case. The alternative would be...messy at best."

Briana considered his words and frowned. "Sebastian, what did you mean about taking 'appropriate actions' if Ruby were involved?"

"I meant that if Ami was killed by a vampire—my sister or someone else—we must do what we can to protect our own."

His tone troubled her. So he had no problem with a killer escaping if it proved to be a vampire? Strange, too, that he referred to Ruby as his sister again. Had he forgotten that she knew the truth? A slow knot formed in her stomach, along with the feeling that he had deliberately shut her out.

"I think I'd better take Todd home," she finally said. "He seems pretty upset."

Sebastian sighed, but didn't try to dissuade her. "Very well. I will contact you later. Meanwhile, I have a few more questions to ask Ruby."

* * * *

Todd hunched in the passenger seat of her car, resting his head against the window. "I can't believe it," he said, blinking away another onslaught of grief. "Poor Ami. I just can't believe she's gone."

As Briana climbed behind the wheel, she hated herself for thinking that now, with Ami out of the picture, all their lives would be easier. Had someone else, Ruby, for example, realized the same thing and then made it happen?

She started the car, but didn't immediately pull out of the driveway.

"Todd...you told the truth before, didn't you? I mean, this is just us talking. Sebastian can't hear us."

His eyes widened in horror. "Yeah, of course."

"What's wrong then? I mean, I know it's upsetting that you and Ami were friends, but you seem to be freaking out a lot more than I would have expected. The way you ran out of there—what's going on?"

His gaze started sliding to the left, a sure sign that he was getting ready to evade her question. She'd seen it hundreds of times over the years. She grabbed his arm and forced him to look up at her.

"Todd, I need you to answer. Do you think there's any possibility that Ruby did that to Ami? Some kind of jealousy thing? Or it might even have been self-defense. Tell me. And more importantly, tell me you aren't implicated somehow."

His lower lip quivered. A fresh volley of tears streamed into the razor stubble that peppered his chin. "It's Ruby," he finally choked out. "The look on her face when we found Ami. She was—I don't know. Wild. I'd never seen anything like that. I thought I knew her."

"I'd say there's a lot we don't know about those two." How foolish to pretend otherwise, she thought. When she glanced back at Todd, the tears still streamed down his face. She hoped they were for Ami. She didn't dare to ask.

Chapter 14

Briana spent a sleepless night, endlessly replaying imaginary scenes in her head. Most involved recreations of Ami's last minutes, some far wilder than others, while the rest featured Sebastian grilling Ruby at Morgan House—or the other way around. Finally, when the sun came up and she knew she wouldn't hear from Sebastian for the next eight hours or so, she dressed and headed over to the motel to assist with the housekeeping chores.

Instead of finding Reggie and his grandmother, she found Joel Tanner unrolling yellow tape across the door to Ami's room.

She pulled her car straight up to the curb and jumped out to confront Joel. "What's this?"

"Hey, Bri." He greeted her with an unhappy look. "Don't worry, it's just routine. Have to preserve anything that could be part of a crime scene."

"Crime scene? That's nuts! Do you know what this will do to me? Business is bad enough as it is!" She rubbed her forehead, which was already beginning to throb. "Look, we can do this more discreetly. I'll lock up the room and make sure no one goes near it. Just…pull down the tape. Please."

"You'll have to take that up with Sheriff Garvey. Sorry."

"You bet I will!" Bad as she felt about Ami's death, and as much as she wanted to find out what happened, she saw nothing noble, or necessary, about bankrupting herself in the process. She marched into the office and got Will Garvey on the line. To her intense frustration, he confirmed what Joel had said.

"Until we hear back from the coroner about the cause of death, we have to treat the incident as suspicious. Can't take a chance on destroying evidence. Anyway, having the cops out front might be good for The Dunes. People want to come and see stuff like that going on. Free publicity."

"That kind of publicity I don't need. Your guys are making it look like this place is a hotbed of crime! No one will want to stay here thinking the guests are being murdered in their rooms!" She paused, suddenly remembering the knife attack she'd endured a few days ago. Could that have been related to Ami's death somehow? Maybe she should mention it to Will. But no. There couldn't be any connection. Getting the police involved in that little episode could only bring more unwanted attention to The Dunes and to Sebastian.

Still, she couldn't ignore one fact. A lot of strange things, to put it mildly, had started to happen ever since Sebastian and Ruby had shown up.

"I'm asking you to take it down," she started anew, aware that her mind had wandered.

"Sorry, Bri, no can do," Will continued. "Actually, though, I'm glad you called. I want to come up and take a more detailed statement from you. It might as well be at The Dunes."

She didn't miss the hint in his voice that suggested he would prefer to talk to her without Sebastian present. If only he knew how little chance there'd be of Darkisle's newest resident walking in on their conversation anytime during daylight hours.

"Of course," she agreed. "I'll be at the front desk."

"See you in a few minutes then."

True to his word, Will showed up almost immediately, in full uniform and driving a marked police car. Great, she thought as she watched him approach the glass door. More free publicity.

"Did you want me to walk you down to her room?" Briana asked, standing.

He shook his head. "Just a few questions at this point. Can we can talk privately?"

"Sure. Come into the back office." Briana motioned for him to follow and showed him to the seat opposite hers at the metal desk. She blushed a little when she remembered leading Sebastian into that same concealed area—with intentions far removed from conversation. "There's not much I can tell you."

"We'll take what we can get at this point. Every piece of information is equally valuable until we know what we're looking for," Will said.

She spread her hands in front of her. "Okay, ask away."

"Just want to get a few facts on the record. You and Ami had a run-in, from what I hear, at The Chum Bucket last night. Want to tell me about that?"

"She got drunk and argued with my brother. It was nothing."

Briana didn't like the way he wrote that down in his little book. "Because he showed up with Ruby Morgan?" he prompted.

"I guess. I didn't see the whole thing."

"Sebastian Morgan was also present, I understand."

"Yes, we went in together," Briana stated. Will seemed to be waiting for her to say more, but she wasn't about to fall into that trap. Talking too much always led to trouble on TV cop shows.

"You know anything about Ami's relationship with Sebastian Morgan?"

"Relationship?" In spite of her vow not to give him any extraneous information, she bristled. Will noticed. She cursed herself under her breath. "There wasn't one that I know of."

"I meant in a general sense. After all, he'd had her arrested. That must have led to some animosity on her part."

"She shouted at him in The Chum Bucket that night, but like I said, she was drunk and yelling at everyone."

"And you know Sebastian Morgan pretty well yourself, I guess?"

Her blush, which returned with a vengeance, said it all. "I'd call us good friends. He gave my brother a job, and I appreciate that."

"Sure. Any idea when I can talk to him? He mentioned he'd be away today. I stopped by his place earlier, but they must have left early."

"He'll be back in the evening. I mean, I think that's what he said."

Will wasn't buying a word of her naïve act, and she knew it. "Tell him I want to talk to him, just like we're talking now, for a few minutes when he gets in. Anytime today is okay. Looks like we'll be working this case until late."

"I'm sorry, but...um, case? It was an accident, wasn't it? Ami fell in the water, I'm sure."

His eyes slid away from hers. "We'll go over this again," he said. "Meanwhile, give Mr. Morgan the message."

By the time she left The Dunes later that afternoon, every scrap of laundry was clean and put away, the floors were mopped, and every room, with the exception of Ami's, gleamed spotless. Even the glass doors to the office were polished. Too bad she had no guests to appreciate her hard work. Before she left, the sheriff called twice. Once was to remind her to keep Ami's room undisturbed so the experts could process the evidence as soon as they arrived. The second call reiterated that Sebastian should come in and make a statement as quickly as possible. No doubt he assumed she spoke to Sebastian at will during daylight hours.

Back at the house, Todd plodded through the day with a good deal less energy. He didn't look healthy either. He had grey skin and hollow, miserable eyes, as if he were suffering from the flu.

"How much blood did she take anyway?" Briana asked him. He leaned against kitchen counter, sorting through a box of mixed tea bags with agonizing slowness. "Are you going to be all right?"

"A little too much, I guess. It's okay though. She says I just need rest and vitamins, and my natural supply will replenish."

"How lucky for her."

"Isn't it the same when Sebastian bites you? Maybe you're stronger. You never look run down at all."

"That's because Sebastian doesn't bite me."

Todd's eyes widened in astonishment. "Seriously? Never?"

"Never." She shook her head. "Todd, let me ask you something. You said last night that Ruby frightened you when she reacted to Ami's death the way she did. Can you tell me more about that?"

A long, uncomfortable silence passed between them. Todd licked his pale lips and brought a hand to the back of his neck. He kneaded his skin compulsively.

"I've been going over it in my mind," he admitted. "I wasn't with her every minute. After she…you know, after we did our thing, I passed out for a while. I always do. Ruby says I'll get stronger over time, and I won't need as much rest. Anyway, she had time to do it, but I don't think she had the motive. You probably think she hated Ami. She didn't. That is, she didn't feel anything toward her. Or any human. Not really."

"Including you?" Briana asked, surprised.

"Yeah. I can't deny it. You shouldn't either. At some level, we don't really count as far as they're concerned. Ami, me, you…we're expendable to them."

"Sebastian isn't like that," she retorted. "If anything, he's too protective of me."

"Ruby seemed that way to me at first too. Now I'm not so sure."

Briana stepped away and left him to his teabag selection. She wandered out of the kitchen with her arms crossed over her chest. She'd asked about Ruby, but instead found herself engaging in unwelcome speculation about Sebastian. She couldn't deny that part of what Todd said made sense. Sebastian himself had reminded her plenty of times how different they were, and how short and meaningless human lifespans seemed to immortals. She also considered the way he had treated his own wife and child, even if a hundred years had passed since he'd abandoned them. Could becoming a vampire have made him more compassionate and responsible? Unlikely.

For all she knew, he and Ruby had fled Darkisle before sunrise. They could be back in Amsterdam by now.

Her answer came soon after her last glimpse of the sun through the curtains. Her scalp prickled as an odd sensation crept over her. As if someone were staring at her.

She turned to find Ruby's face framed in the front door's tiny window.

"You didn't ring the bell," she said as she turned the knob.

"Why bother? You knew I was here." Ruby stormed into the house, glancing from side to side. She was hungry. Briana could see the lines around her mouth and hear the stress in her voice. "Where's Todd? I want to talk to him."

"Um...I'm not sure if he's here. He said something about going out."

"Don't bother lying to me. Do you think I can't find him on my own?" Ruby started toward the kitchen. Todd stepped out to meet her, a cup of tea in one hand. "That's more like it. Briana, you can leave us alone now."

Briana ignored Ruby's icy look and the dismissive wave of her hand. "You forget this is my house."

"Fine, stay. Todd, come with me. We have a lot to discuss."

"You don't have to go if you don't want to, Todd," Briana reminded him.

Todd looked from one woman to the other. The hand holding the mug trembled. He set it on the table. "It's okay, Bri. I'll go."

"Are you sure?" Instinctively Briana moved in front of the door as her brother pulled his jacket off the wall peg. Ruby's entire body looked tense, and her expression smoldered with rage at Briana's interference.

"Yeah. I'm sure." Todd shrugged into his coat. "I know what I'm doing."

"I hope you do." Briana followed them outside as far as the front step. Briana couldn't resist glancing at the Maserati's windows to see if, by some chance, Sebastian waited inside. She saw no one.

After they drove away, she realized that she faced her first evening alone since Todd had begun working on Morgan House. "No big deal," she said aloud as she went back inside and locked the door behind her. She'd found ways to occupy herself every night of her life before Sebastian Morgan came along. Tonight would be no different, and she wasn't about to waste even one minute of her time wondering about his activities and whereabouts.

She decided to start off with a long, hot shower, after which she would brew herself a pot of flavored decaf and stretch out in front of the TV. If nothing on the air pleased her, she could always choose a book from among the many she'd bought and never gotten around to reading over the years. She'd be sure to pick one without any vampires or supernatural themes—or one with a lot of sexy parts, for that matter. No use in scraping open that particular wound.

The shower flowed over her like liquid fire. She stayed in until her skin glowed red and tender and the tension began to melt from her muscles. Closing her eyes, she tilted her head into the blistering spray and washed her mind clean of any intrusive thoughts involving cops, motels, or seductive, silky-voiced creatures of the night.

When she felt as thoroughly boiled as one of the lobsters they served on the wharf, she turned off the water and slid open the shower door. Eyes half-closed, she reached for a towel.

Instantly her arm snapped back in shock. Sebastian stood only inches away.

He stood watching her calmly, and obviously had been for a while. Without turning, he reached to his left, lifted a towel from the rack, and held it open for her. She stepped into the soft cocoon and felt his arms close around her. The warm towel did little to counteract the chill that radiated from beneath his clothes. Her skin remained so hot, though, that a visible cloud of steam floated between them, misting the bathroom as well as his pale skin.

"I thought you hated water," she said, arching her back with pleasure as he moved his hands over the towel. Starting with her shoulders, he began drying her in slow, circular motions.

"That's why I waited for you to come out. Trust me, I considered joining you, but vampiric instinct is not easily overcome."

"So I've heard." The pressure of the towel on her shoulders eased and moved lower, sweeping down her breasts, sliding over her nipples, and drifting along the undercurve. So much for a solitary night on the sofa. How could she ever pretend that any substitute could replace the myriad pleasures Sebastian brought her?

The slightest flick of his fingers sent the towel crumpling to the floor. His arms slid around her bare skin, drawing her tight against his body. Briana undid the buttons of his shirt and reached for his belt buckle as he ran his lips along the wet strands of hair that clung to her neck.

She peeled him out of his clothes while they stumbled, totally entwined in one another, out of the steam-filled bathroom to her bed. By the time her back hit the mattress, he had stripped away the rest of his clothes. Parting her legs, Briana opened herself to him, pulling him into her own shell of warmth as he settled on top of her.

Sebastian wasted no time coaxing her desires to a peak or teasing her swelling folds into full ripeness. He fitted himself against her, grinding his flesh against hers, merging his coldness with her pulsating heat.

Briana gasped as he drove himself deep inside her in a single thrust. The sudden burst of pleasure knocked the breath from her lungs and every thought from her mind except one: the certainty that she wanted, needed this man—this vampire—above any other she had ever known or even dreamed of. She wanted to be part of his body and dwell in his mind, to be his lifeblood and the pulse that pushed it through his frozen veins.

She bucked her hips up to meet him, forcing him even deeper inside her. Another surprise awaited her when he thrust his face against her shoulder blade and parted his lips. His tongue curled out, dragging along her breastbone, dipping into the hollow of her throat. He seemed to hesitate for a moment, and the part of Briana that could still think wondered if he'd finally lost the battle with his primal urge to feast on her. Then the moment passed, and his moist kiss continued its slow, painstaking journey to her mouth. Their tongues brushed each other as they fed together, not on blood but on the pure emotion that fueled their lust.

Suddenly, Sebastian tensed his grip on her shoulders and rocked himself sharply to the left. His powerful grip swung her up and over so that she ended up lying on top of him, his massive erection still straining inside her.

His palms slid down her thighs, leaving her to balance on her own. She reveled in the feel of holding him captive underneath her, her thighs pinning his, her supple aperture holding his cock like a commanding fist.

The expression on his face was one of contentment, but she spotted something else in his narrowed eyes. A hint of challenge, perhaps? She'd insisted so many times that she refused to fear him. Perhaps he wanted proof.

Without a moment's hesitation, Briana took control, raising herself above him so far that his cockhead snagged in her wet shallows. Then she waited, tantalizing him by hovering there completely still, leaving him neither fully anchored nor fully outside her body. She felt his abdomen flex, his muscles instinctively trying to pull her back down on him, but she resolved to hold her ground. Briana braced her hands on his chest and held herself aloft until her arms began to tremble with strain.

Sweet resistance inflamed them both, heating even his icy core. By the time she loosened her hold and let herself slide back down onto his upthrust groin, his erection seemed to have doubled in size. He filled her completely, deliciously.

His hands sought the curve of her buttocks, his thumbs sliding inside the hot crease and pressing down in the exact center of her perineum. This time, he orchestrated her long, enjoyable expedition up his staff, his hands pushing her from below in agonizingly brief increments. Once again, his bloated crown stopped just short of re-emerging from its sheath. Briana took over from there, making her return journey in a sudden, impulsive plummet. From there, the sequence began anew, over and over. A long, painstaking climb followed a reckless drop into a maelstrom of pure enchantment. Before long, every nerve between her legs burned with need, the slippery passage rubbed raw as they slammed together.

Her climax tore through her with enough force to knock her backward. Unwilling to let go, she grasped his hips between her knees and shuddered her way through a series of bone-wrenching tremors that nearly drove her insane with pleasure. For a few delicious minutes, everything in the room, in Darkisle, in the entire world's past and future ceased to matter to her. She cared only about Sebastian and the dizzy ecstasy of feeling him burst into glorious life inside her. A dark red haze descended over her eyes, blocking everything else from view, the only sound the throb of their mingled pulse and heaving breaths.

With one, last turbulent twist, her body shook itself loose of the spell he'd sent roaring through her. His cock finally softened inside her, and she would have fallen all the way back if not for the way her knees had locked her into place on top of him. As her senses cleared, she realized that he still gripped her wrists, clinging with such force that her own fingers had gone numb. Briefly she remembered the way he had broken the intruder's hand and breathed a quick sigh of relief for whatever self-control he had mustered this time. Then he pulled gently on her arms and she slumped forward, drained and awash in contentment.

For a while she lay stretched out on top of him, threading her hands through his hair, massaging the length of his body with hers.

"I wish we could stay like this all night."

"You wouldn't like the way I looked in the morning." He sat up, rolling her into his arms. "Still, we have a few hours of darkness left. I see no reason we can't make the most of them."

"That would be wonderful." Tucked against him, she nuzzled his chest with her cheek. Suddenly, reality intruded on her thoughts, shattering the peaceful moment. "But Sebastian, we can't. The sheriff has been calling me all afternoon. He wants you to come into town and talk to him."

She felt his muscles tense. "I thought he might," he admitted.

"Is that a problem?"

"Anyone looking into my private life is a potential problem. However, avoiding him would look even more suspicious. I'll meet with him and answer his questions—to the extent I feel comfortable doing so." Shifting her to one side of the bed, he stood and gathered up his clothing. "We'll go into town now. Unfortunately, we will have to take your car—my sister has commandeered the Maserati." He sighed. "I really must look into buying her a car of her own."

"I don't mind." Briana sat up herself, pushing the hair from her eyes. She watched him stride back into the bathroom and heard the water running—ice cold, she assumed with a shudder. He emerged fully dressed again, his damp hair combed back from his pale forehead. The slight flush his skin had taken on during their romp in her sheets had disappeared, presumably chased away by the frigid water.

"Get ready, and I'll take you to dinner in town. I sometimes overlook your probable desire for an evening meal. Please excuse my shortsightedness."

"That would be nice," she said as he left the room and plodded downstairs to wait for her. She showered again, more briskly and efficiently this time, dressed and followed him down to the living room. He sat by the window, staring out into her darkened front yard, motionless and expressionless. For a moment, his complete stillness unnerved her. He reminded her of a wax figure in a museum—or a corpse. Then he turned, suddenly aware of her, and left behind whatever labyrinthine thought process he'd immersed himself in. What had consumed his mind so thoroughly she couldn't begin to guess at. Was he thinking about Ami? Preparing a believable story to tell Will, perhaps?

They walked out to her car, saying little. Sebastian looked a bit surprised when she slid into the driver's seat. He got in without protest and rode in silence as she pulled onto the road and headed toward town.

She parked on the wharf, within easy walking distance of both The Chum Bucket and the police station. "Where to first?"

He held out his hand to her. "Let's walk for a moment."

"All right."

His icy fingers closed around hers, and the two of them drifted down the length of the pier. They walked alone, without even the company of stars in the overcast sky. Briana shivered as a clammy sea wind blasted them, making her exposed skin feel raw and chapped. Sebastian, in contrast, seemed invigorated by the onslaught. He probably hated summer as much as she looked forward to it.

Beneath them, the water churned, dark and angry. Had Ami slipped and fallen into a similar abyss?

"How do you bear it?" she asked suddenly, thinking out loud. "Having everyone in your life die first, I mean?"

"Two ways. One is by getting close to almost no one. The second is by turning them into vampires."

"Not much of a choice."

He stopped walking and leaned on the rail. "I convinced myself I could live without love."

"I can see why it would be difficult," Briana said.

"Of course, I'm not totally alone. I have Ruby, who will always remain young, but as I've pointed out, at sixty she is still immature by immortal standards. And, like most of the young ones, eventually she'll go off on her own, for a few decades at least."

"Like a teenager leaving the nest."

"Except that in some cases, the teenagers can be hundreds of years old."

She shook her head in wonder. "What was our town like, back when you were...ah...?"

"Alive. You can say it." He slid his arms around her waist and rested his cheek on her shoulder.

"We had quiet without cars, radios, televisions, cell phones. No tourists. No vulgar t-shirts in store windows. Just the ocean and the fishermen working—and cursing—on the dock."

"Must have been peaceful."

"'Boring would be more accurate. Another point to consider is that women didn't venture down here much. It wasn't considered proper."

"That seems pretty sexist."

"We were very smug about gender differences then. Men and women weren't even thought to have equal sex drives. Women of good breeding tolerated intimacy to please their husbands." As he spoke, his hand strayed up toward the front of her jacket. She tensed with pleasure as his fingers dipped inside, sliding sideways past the buttons to tweak the hem of her bra. "Of course, my wife didn't even pretend to most of the time."

Briana couldn't stifle a nervous laugh. "No wonder you ran away."

His touch strayed lightly across her breast. "I couldn't wait to leave Darkisle. Then I sought professional assistance in that area. We know how that turned out." He sighed. "I won't even mention those tight clothes we wore—layer upon layer, even in the summer. Talk about frustrated."

"A little frustration can be a good thing."

"I'm talking about a lot of frustration." His fingertips strayed lower, deeper. Her nipples stood at attention. His touch strayed across the peak, kneading and then retreating. "If it lasts too long, it can become dangerous. Men and women alike have died from it."

"But you can't."

Abruptly, his mood darkened. He pulled away his hand, dragging her breath along with it, and turned her around so their eyes met.

"There have been times when I wished to," he admitted.

"I believe you."

"Imagine knowing that you will live for hundreds, maybe thousands, of years, the one guarantee being that you will always be alone. I know Ami's death has affected you. Unfortunately—or fortunately, depending on one's perspective—it cannot possibly affect me the same way. Death is a companion that walks beside me every night, from the moment I rise until I hide myself away again."

She shuddered. The relaxed sexual reverie she'd drifted into dropped away, replaced by a dread that felt uncomfortably like fear. Of him. Of them. She forced herself to ask the question she most dreaded the answer to. "Have you ever…killed anyone?"

"Never directly. But my kind has an effect on our surroundings that we can't always control or anticipate. Ami is simply the most recent in a long line of collateral deaths."

She cast her eyes downward. "I'm a peaceful person, Sebastian. I'm the type who pulls flies off flypaper and sets them free. You're describing a mindset I can't even comprehend."

"You have always known that I am not like other men."

"Maybe the fact that you're a little mysterious, even dangerous, excited me. And, I don't think of your body as that of a dead man."

"If you want to be technical, it isn't. My metabolism is slow, so slow that physicians in the nineteenth century found it imperceptible, hence a certain degree of medical confusion that became more distorted with time. Yet I did undergo a metaphorical death, if you will. My fate proved a fitting end to my profligate ways as a human and my utter failure as a husband, but I was, and am, determined to do better in this incarnation."

"You'll succeed. I know you will. Despite everything, I believe that you're a good man, and you do have a soul, whatever the legends may say. As you've pointed out so many times, they're wildly inaccurate."

He nodded, and for a moment he seemed genuinely at a loss for words. Finally he swallowed and slipped his hands over hers again. "Briana," he said at last, "I've never asked this of anyone, mortal or not, since the change. But I'm asking you now. Stay with me."

Briana blinked, astonished. "What?"

"You say I have a soul. I do—it is yours. Vampires call it a blood bond. It's more than a marriage. Love is too weak a word. We will literally sustain each other in every sense of the word."

"You mean like Todd sustains Ruby?" Tears sprang to her eyes. "With blood?"

"No. Their relationship is nothing like ours. Todd does not—I'm sorry—does not have your strength. What I am suggesting is far more serious than anything they could even comprehend."

He moved closer, and Briana forgot about the wind, the ocean, even Ami. Her mind spun, her composure unraveled. "Sebastian—I don't know. Of all the things I imagined you might want to talk to me about tonight, this wasn't one of them. I've worked very hard to build a life of my own—it isn't something I ever seriously thought about changing. And yes, I know Todd isn't a strong person. He needs me. I can't ignore that."

"Have you considered the possibility that I need you, too?"

"I...I always perceived you as totally self-sufficient."

"There are plenty of things you don't know. Still, take as much time as you want to think this over." He gave her a wry smile. "I have plenty of it."

He seemed about to say more when they heard a loud blip and saw a police car heading up the wharf toward them, lights flashing, Joel in the driver's seat. He rolled down the window as he pulled up alongside them.

"Sheriff wants you both to come with me," he said. "Get in the back of my car."

Chapter 15

"This is an outrage," Sebastian roared as they stepped into the police station with Joel right behind them. "We were on our way to dinner. What right do you have to detain us?"

"Relax." Will Garvey came around the counter to meet them. "I told Joel to give you a ride over as a courtesy. I'd been trying to contact you today, and since he saw you together, I figured this would be more convenient. We'll give you a lift to the restaurant of your choice later."

"Back to the wharf will be fine," Sebastian replied in a frosty tone. "We can find our way from there."

"Whatever you like. Meanwhile, if you'll both have a seat in my office, we can get this over with in a few minutes."

His expression guarded, Sebastian followed Will to his desk. He and Briana sat down in mismatched chairs in front of it.

"Just a few loose ends to clear up." Will flipped open his little notebook. "Briana and I went over most of this information already, but I wanted to get your perspective, too, Mr. Morgan. Why don't you start by telling me how well you knew Ami?"

Sebastian's eyes narrowed. Briana suspected that he wasn't buying Will's casual act, either. "I had her removed from my property, as you know. Aside from that, I scarcely exchanged five words with her."

Will tapped his pen on the blotter. "You had Miss Dempsey's brother arrested at the same time. Seems like everyone got over that pretty fast. The four of you seem to be out socializing quite a bit these days."

"The trespassing incident turned out to be a misunderstanding. Miss Dempsey's brother apologized, and as a gentleman, I felt obligated to accept."

"Sure, I can see that. It's a small town. We all have to get along." Will paused. "So what happened in The Chum Bucket last night?"

"Your question suggests that you already have a description of the event," Sebastian said.

"It really amounted to nothing," she cut in. "Sebastian and I came in just as Ami was leaving."

"But you both stayed long enough to hear her threaten Mr. Morgan's sister. Then she turned on Miss Dempsey, according to several witnesses. Is it safe to say that might have piqued a little gentlemanly outrage?"

"Don't twist Sebastian's words around like that!" Briana burst out. "Ami was drunk and rude. True, the scene wasn't pretty. But I think we all stayed very restrained, considering the circumstances."

"Briana," Sebastian cautioned in a stern voice.

She hurtled on, ignoring him. "We know Ami's state last night. She went staggering along the docks, slipped, and fell in. It's obvious."

"Is it? Only one problem there: the coroner doesn't think she drowned. She was in the water, all right, but the cause of death seems to be strangulation. That doesn't happen by accident."

"No—I don't believe it. That's impossible."

"Why? Because things like that don't happen in Darkisle?" Will sighed. "I wish you could see half of what I see in the course of my duties, Miss Dempsey. I know it seems like we don't have much crime here, but that's been changing lately. We get the occasional assault with a deadly weapon...not to mention a few rapes, both attempted and accomplished."

Briana felt her ears go red. She refused to look at Sebastian, knowing they both remembered the boy with the knife. Not reporting that incident was a mistake she wished she could undo. Telling Will about it now would look suspicious—assuming he even believed them.

"So you see my dilemma," Will continued. "I have to ask myself—who had a conflict with the deceased? Only four names have come up so far. Two end in Dempsey and two in Morgan."

Sebastian got to his feet. "Briana and I want to help keep our island safe. And we both want justice for Ami. But the tone of these questions suggests to me that we should say nothing until we've engaged the services of an attorney." He stood and reached out his hand to Briana. She took his clammy fingers and got up as well. "I hope you don't think us abrupt, but as we have already discussed, it's dinnertime."

Garvey's eyes narrowed as he stood too. "I understand. And I can assure you both that I'll be doing everything in my power to solve this case. Ami's killer will be brought to justice—whoever he or she might be."

"We would expect nothing less."

They started to turn for the door, but Will held up his hand to stop them. "Oh, one more thing. I'm in the process of collecting DNA and hair samples to assist in the investigation. This is strictly voluntary, of course, but could I get a strand of hair and a saliva swab from both of you?"

Sebastian never flinched. "I told you—I intend to consult my attorney. You may deliver any and all warrants to him."

Will turned to Briana. "I hoped I wouldn't have to go that route. Easier if we can eliminate both of you as suspects right away."

"Well, I'm willing to help," Briana said.

"I appreciate that," Will said. "Come with me. Mr. Morgan, you can wait here."

"Briana, I ask you to reconsider," Sebastian said. His tone was as controlled as always, but the note of desperation clawing at the edges concerned her.

"We won't be long," Will informed him in a clear dismissal. He had taken Briana's elbow. Briana watched Sebastian struggle to suppress a flash of rage.

Garvey led her into a smaller room lined with metal shelves and file cabinets, though apparently it doubled as a lab in a pinch. Removing a test kit from one of the shelves, Will swabbed the inside of her lower lip with a cotton swab, which he deposited in a jar. He then plucked a couple of hairs from her head with tweezers and put the samples in an envelope. "Appreciate it," he said.

She felt a lot less positive about her decision to cooperate now. "No problem," she answered in a shaky voice.

"Briana, I considered your father a friend of mine."

"I know. You've reminded me plenty of times."

"Because I think it bears repeating. Truth is...I hope you know what you're getting into with this fellow."

"I can see how people around here would find him strange. He's lived most of his life in Europe. They do things differently over there."

"They sure do. Police work, for one."

"Excuse me?"

"Did you know your friend was under investigation there? Could that be why he left?"

The words had barely left Will's lips when Briana felt as if he'd lashed out and slugged her in the gut. Every muscle in her body clenched in dread, and the floor seemed to tilt under her. Desperately she tried to hide her reaction from Will, but she could see from his expression that she hadn't been successful.

If anything, Will seemed pleased. "I can see that you didn't know. Maybe he hasn't been as forthright with you as you thought."

Briana struggled to mask her roiling emotions. What Will had said couldn't possibly be true. Either he was making things up to rattle her, or he'd stumbled upon some huge misunderstanding. "Under investigation for what?" she asked in as calm a voice as she could muster.

Will crossed his arms and leaned against the file cabinet. "Believe it or not, the murder of a young woman."

"As a matter of fact, I don't believe it. Where did you get that information?"

"Amsterdam police. Background check came in this morning by fax. Seems they found a body in one of their canals. She'd been in the water a while. Hard to say what happened, but they did say the neck area showed...well, some kind of strange damage. Could have been strangulation."

"That sounds like a lot of innuendo without many facts to back it up." Gruesome as the details were, Briana found their vagueness reassuring...except for the part about the victim's neck. Still, there could be many explanations.

"Agreed...but we've got a few too many similarities for my comfort...right down to the killer thinking that putting her in cold water would throw off our calculations."

"I also don't see how any of this is connected to Sebastian."

"According to the Amsterdam cops, he and the victim knew each other. How well, I don't know."

"Apparently he wasn't charged. So all of that means nothing."

"True, but just because you can't prove something doesn't mean it didn't happen. Do me a favor and think about it, Briana. For your dad's sake."

Briana fidgeted closer to the door. She kept her eyes on the shelves around her, unable to look directly at Will. "Can I go now? You've got your samples."

"Yeah. Go on and enjoy your dinner. I'll be in touch if I have any other questions."

Joel waited for her out in the lobby. Sebastian stood by the front door, clearly impatient to leave. "Sheriff says I should drive you back to your car," Joel said, holding up his keys.

Sebastian quickly stepped between the deputy and Briana. "No thank you. We would prefer to walk."

"Suit yourself." Joel shrugged.

"You did a foolish thing," Sebastian said under his breath when they stepped onto the sidewalk. "Never give your enemies information to use against you. It will come back to haunt you every time."

"Not if you have nothing to hide," she shot back defensively.

"We all have things to hide, Briana."

"I don't think I ever did—until I met up with you."

He grimaced. The jagged tips of his canines flashed in the darkness. "My point exactly."

She said nothing more about the interlude with Will until they entered a tiny restaurant at the far end of town. Sebastian chose a corner booth, away from the windows and out of the view of the entrance. Fortunately, the only other customers were an elderly couple and a gaunt-faced man who studied a racing form while he ate. Until she smelled the aroma of baked fish and roast chicken wafting through the dining room, Briana hadn't realized how famished she felt. By the time the waitress brought the clam chowder and rolls, her stomach was in knots...though hunger didn't entirely account for her queasiness.

"I'm sorry you can't try the food," Briana said.

He winced. "To me, human cuisine is at best bitter, at worst repellent. Imagine yourself trying to eat fodder meant for some other species."

"I guess that makes sense. Can I ask you what exactly you do live on?"

He looked from side to side before answering. "The injection I take was developed by an American, but perfected by vampire physicians in Europe. As you know, blood-borne diseases have increased in recent decades. Like human doctors, we did research to protect our own. Some of the results proved unexpectedly advantageous." He paused when the waitress returned to refill Briana's water glass. When she moved on, Sebastian picked up his explanation where he had left off. "The defining characteristic of a vampire is not what he feeds on, but the fact that he cannot die. Therefore, the usual biological imperative to obtain constant nourishment can be overcome. The injection treatments are based on that deceptively simple premise. The serum eliminates the need to ingest blood by introducing the necessary nutrients in a compressed form."

"Sort of like a nutritional supplement?"

"More of a substitute. I suppose it also resembles the insulin some humans take."

"Oh." She tore into a buttered roll with a touch more enthusiasm than she considered strictly ladylike. Taking advantage of the privacy their table offered, Sebastian didn't bother to feign any interest in food or soup. Instead, he watched her with such intensity that her skin prickled.

Finally, she raised her eyes to meet his directly. "Sebastian...I need to ask you about Amsterdam."

"So that's Garvey's game." His facial muscles stiffened. "I assumed this was coming."

"You know what he's talking about?"

He steepled his fingers and nodded. "I thought I'd heard the last of that particular scandal when I left Europe."

"Is that why you left?"

"No. I had to go for many reasons. The unfortunate death of a casual acquaintance could never be a factor."

"And was her death an accident, too?"

"I don't know. I had nothing to do with it, whatever my detractors—both human and not—may insinuate. Though a large city, Amsterdam is in many ways a closed society. Rumors tended to drift like bad odors."

"The sheriff thinks that case resembled Ami's—right down to the body being in the water to obscure the time and cause of death."

"Of course he would like to believe that. A ready-made scapegoat would make his job easier. My people are used to becoming the targets of shortsighted bureaucrats like William Garvey. I don't take his ramblings seriously, and neither should you."

He stopped talking as the waitress approached to take their order. Her renewed appetite began to ebb again, so she settled for a bland-looking tuna salad and another plate of rolls. Sebastian waved her off altogether.

"Who was she?" Briana asked when they were alone again. "The woman who died in Amsterdam, I mean?"

"Her name would hold no significance for you, so I assume you want to know her relationship to me."

"Okay, fair enough. So tell me."

"I considered her a friend. Nothing more. A troubled woman who insisted on dabbling in things she could not possibly understand or control. I was sorry to hear of her demise—but, I must admit, not surprised."

"Will mentioned something about her neck."

"I can believe she suffered trauma to that part of her anatomy. Beyond that, I prefer not to comment."

As she watched his expression turn cold and impassive, Briana felt her heart sink. His answer told her nothing and everything all at once. Vampires had killed the woman in Amsterdam. Collateral victims, Sebastian had called them. They were humans who had gotten too close and paid the ultimate price. That might include Ami, too.

Would she and Todd soon find themselves part of that unfortunate group?

When the food arrived, she picked at it in silence, suddenly no more interested in it than Sebastian was. Eventually, hesitant to waste a perfectly good meal, she sent it back to the kitchen to be wrapped up as takeout. The waitress flashed her a sympathetic smile when she returned with the white Styrofoam box. Between Sebastian's refusing to eat, and Briana's inability to enjoy her meal, she'd clearly pegged them as a quarreling couple. If only she knew the half of it, Briana thought.

"I'd like to go home now," she told Sebastian as he settled the bill. "I have a lot to think about."

"Understood." The briefest flash of sadness tightened his face. For a split second, Briana considered changing course, throwing her misgivings out to sea, and inviting him back to her bed until dawn's approach forced them apart. Then, like an icy wind sweeping in past the cliffs, reality chilled her to the marrow.

What if the last woman Sebastian offered a future to had been the one in Amsterdam?

* * * *

The hours between bedtime and dawn had never crawled by so slowly, and her bed had never seemed less comforting. The prospect of leaving it unnerved her even more. For the first time, the shadows drifting outside her window felt ominous and threatening, as if some toxic agent infected the dark mist. She slept in fits, her mind and heart in turmoil. Over and over she ran through the events of Ami's demise, alternately finding no evidence to support Sebastian's involvement and seeing no logical way to exonerate him. When she did sleep, she became the woman in Amsterdam—trusting Sebastian, loving the feel of his hands on her body and his teeth in her throat, only to find his protection torn away from her in one bewildering instant. The cold hard surface of the canal rushed up to meet her.

When morning finally came, she got up much earlier than usual and headed to the motel.

Everything at The Dunes was more or less as she'd left it, and the sign-in book's blank pages showed that no one had registered while

Reggie did desk duty. With the police tape up, she didn't expect better results today. How long could a motel go without guests and still call itself a motel? She had the uneasy feeling she'd soon find out.

Settling herself at the desk inside the office, she retrieved the ledger book from the locked drawer. Paging through it gave her a whole new set of worries that had nothing to do with Sebastian, which proved something of a relief. On the other hand, The Dunes was now seriously in the red.

After toting up the numbers a few different ways and finding no way to interpret them favorably, she called Will Garvey.

"Any chance of getting this crime tape down soon? I'm not kidding, Will, I'm about to go bankrupt here."

"Word is the DNA experts will be there sometime tomorrow. Meanwhile, we have to keep everything secure. I'm sorry, Briana."

Disgruntled, she banged down the phone without responding to him. It immediately rang again, and she picked it up expecting a stern reprimand for her behavior. Instead, she found herself talking to a reporter from one of the larger newspapers in the area, seeking details about Ami's affiliation with the motel and her own reaction to the recent tragedy.

"I'm afraid I have no comment," she said, hanging up quickly. To her surprise, a similar call followed the first only minutes later, and after that came an inquiry from a television station seeking permission to film her parking lot and front entrance for the evening news. "Under no circumstances," she retorted, suspecting they would find a way to include the desired shots anyway.

When she put down the phone and glanced up, she saw Reggie by the desk. He pretended to ferry an armload of towels to the laundry room, but Briana knew he'd been listening to her take the calls. One of the towels dragged, unnoticed, along the ground.

"You were talking about the murder, weren't you?" Reggie asked.

"It wasn't a murder," Briana informed him. "Ami fell into the water and washed up on the rocks. I know how the gossip mill works in this town, but what happened was a tragic accident and nothing more." She bent and picked up one of the towels, heading toward the washroom. Reggie followed.

"Sometimes there's truth in gossip, you know."

She clenched her jaw. Might as well hear it now, since she expected it to be juicy and involve either her or Todd. "All right, tell me. What have you heard?"

Reggie grinned. "Word is those two weirdos up at Morgan House killed her in some kind of ritual. They threw the body in the ocean, but they didn't weigh it down right and it washed back up on their own beach."

Ugh. Worse than she'd thought. "I can't imagine where you heard that, but I hope you won't repeat it. It's ridiculous."

"Is it? You have to admit that they're a little strange. And that Morgan guy is incredibly strong I heard. Like he's got powers or something."

"Oh? What makes you say that?" Briana's eyes narrowed. It sounded almost as if Reggie referred to the way Sebastian had disarmed the burglar. How could he have known? Now that she thought about it, though, maybe it wasn't so farfetched to think that her clerk had inside knowledge. He and the robber seemed about the same age, and the whole incident had seemed a bit suspicious at the time. It couldn't have been Reggie himself, since his hand was clearly not broken, but she had to wonder about other possible connections.

Reggie suddenly backtracked. "Well, you know, just heard it around town. No one's ever seen 'em during the day either."

"They're probably still unpacking. It's a big house for two people."

"If you say so. People talk is all I'm saying."

"People should talk less." Briana took the load of towels from his arms and shoved them into the washer.

"I'd sure like to see what the cops find in her room when they toss it."

"Why? What do you expect to see?"

"That's just it—could be anything. Could be blackmail photographs of half the guys in town. Or maybe even—you know—stuff in the drawers."

"What do you know about Ami's room? Have you been in there?"

"Well, sure—I mean, I let her in a couple times when she locked herself out, stuff like that. She did that a lot. No pockets in those tight jeans, you know." His nervous grin faltered. "I guess I shouldn't talk like that. I'm sorry she's dead and all. That part just doesn't seem too real to me somehow."

"It doesn't seem real to me either. Listen, Reggie. Do not go in that room. Let the cops do whatever they're doing. We have to stay out of it."

He turned away, scooping up another load of towels. "Okay, I promise. Besides, I don't want my fingerprints on any of her stuff. I don't need to get involved with a murder investigation."

"For the last time, there's not going to be any murder investigation. Ami died by accident. This isn't some cop show on TV." Or some horror movie. Briana found herself amazed at her own hypocrisy.

"Reggie's got a point," came a voice from the doorway. Graham's voice. He sauntered into the laundry room and leaned against the door jamb, muscular arms folded across the front of his faded sweatshirt. "There could very well be more going on than we know. We all have to watch what we say and do until this blows over, one way or the other."

"Guess I'd better get to the front desk in case anyone shows up," Reggie said, slipping past Graham. He and Briana faced each other awkwardly.

"How did everyone hear about it so fast?" she asked him. "They only found her last night and already half the town has a theory about what happened."

Graham snickered. "More like three quarters. You underestimate the number of people plastered to their police scanners when it's cold and rainy outside. As for the rest...well, Joel stopped at the diner this morning for a take-out breakfast, and let's just say Reggie's tight-lipped compared to him. If it's any consolation, most people don't think you were involved."

"Well, that's comforting. Does that include you?"

"Come on. I know you, Bri. You'd never hurt anyone."

"Thanks for the vote of confidence."

"Anyway...I have my own theories as to who's responsible."

She could guess whom he meant. "Graham..."

"Don't defend him." He held up a calloused hand. "Maybe he does things for you, in or out of bed, —and I'm sure he's convinced you he's the man of your dreams. He's rich, good-looking, or at least you think so—what's not to like? But I know things you might not."

His foreboding tone worried her. No way could he know the truth about Sebastian and Ruby—could he? "Like what?" she asked cautiously.

"Well, I know he was sleeping with Ami at your motel."

It took all her self-control not to laugh. "Are you kidding me?"

"Nope. I saw him hanging around there. Then he went into her room. I was in the parking lot when it happened. He'd deny it, I'm sure, but I know what I saw. I'm not saying she meant anything to him—for all I know, she was charging him by the hour. But he betrayed you all the same."

"Graham, please. I appreciate the fact that you're trying to look out for me, but in this case, you're mistaken."

"I knew you wouldn't want to hear it." Graham expelled a frustrated breath. "Maybe it isn't in the cards for me to be anything but a friend to you, but I take that role seriously. I'll always be around to look after you, Briana, and I hope you know that."

"Thanks, though I don't think I need looking after. I never did. That was part of our problem...remember?"

"Whatever you say. But listen. They'll search Ami's room and find evidence that Sebastian went there. DNA, fingerprints, whatever. You'll see then."

"I guess time will tell."

He took the hint and slouched off, presumably back to his fishing boat and out of her business for the time being. Briana watched him go, recalling all the times she'd lamented her dull and lonely existence. What she wouldn't give to have a little of that tedium back now.

* * * *

Back at the house, Briana heated up the food she'd saved from her last, ill-fated date with Sebastian and switched on the TV to distract herself while she ate. The evening news was just coming on, and all the local channels were reporting Ami's death. Some even mentioned the word "suspicious" and a newly identified "person of interest," though no details emerged. Whether that referred to Sebastian, she wasn't sure. She had no doubt he'd be furious when he found out. At least The Dunes itself wasn't specifically mentioned in any of the reports, though there were a few generic clips of her parking lot and the sign marking the narrow road that led into town.

Eventually Todd came in to join her. He'd slept away most of the day again, and the purple bruising had spread above his collar.

"Is Ruby coming to pick you up again tonight?" she asked warily.

"I don't think so. We kind of reached an agreement last night."

"What kind of agreement?"

"I told her I needed some time to think. Besides, we shouldn't be seen together until this whole Ami thing blows over. There's definitely some heat coming down."

"You don't look very happy about it."

His hands, previously resting flat on his thighs, snapped into fists. "I keep thinking of her going out and finding someone else, and I...I get so freaked out I want to run right to her. It's not just the blood, though she told me it can work kind of like a drug for both people. You get addicted, you know. There's more to it with us."

"Like what? Try to explain it to me." Maybe she could get a grip on her own feelings that way. "What does Ruby have that makes you want to risk your life to be with her?"

Todd tipped his head back against the sofa and sighed. "It's hard to put into words. To her, I was never just a source of blood. It's like she saw something in me that I didn't know I had. She made me feel...I don't know, valuable. Like she cared about what I thought. What I had to say."

"Yeah?" Funny—to her, Ruby had always seemed just the opposite of considerate and sensitive. But, admittedly, she hadn't taken much time to get to know Sebastian's granddaughter.

"I wish I could say the same for Sebastian. I suspect I always came a distant second to his own needs."

Todd straightened in his seat, looking thoughtful. "You know, it's none of my business, but don't you think you're being a little hard on him? I mean, he's really tried not to hurt you. I asked Ruby about him never biting you because I didn't think it could be true. She told me about his injections—and what the hunger is like for them. She says it's like a constant burning in their stomachs, a pounding in their heads. She says it would drive her insane if she didn't give in to it. But Sebastian won't. He goes on taking those injections, in spite of what they do to him, mostly because of you."

She stared, almost forgetting to swallow the last bit of her tuna salad. "Ruby told you that?"

"Yup. He's a little scary, I'll definitely grant you that, but I do think he cares about you."

She shook her head. "My own brother is trying to convince me to stay with a vampire. If it wasn't so grotesque, I'd laugh."

"Well, you know, I'm just trying to help. You weren't this down when you broke up with Graham," Todd reminded her.

"That was different."

"No kidding!"

"Besides, you're still overlooking the larger issue here. Are you one hundred percent sure that he and Ruby didn't kill Ami? Even accidentally or in self-defense?" When Todd looked away, she pressed on. "Will said it himself. None of us have alibis. You told me yourself that you didn't watch Ruby every minute that night."

"I know." His voice quivered. "Poor Ami. I shouldn't have blown her off like that. I should have made sure she got back to the motel or somewhere safe."

"Todd, she got drunk and made a fool of herself. You didn't do anything wrong."

"But maybe Ruby or Sebastian did. Isn't that what you're saying?"

"I don't know what to think. I just know that Sebastian got cagey with Will. And Will says something in Amsterdam didn't look right. What did Ruby tell you about their time there?"

"Nothing, really. She hated it there, and they wanted to move back here. Once her father died, there was nothing to stop them. They put in their claim for the house and came back."

"All I know is that we shouldn't be involved in something like this. Drinking blood is bad enough—but murders, cover-ups, secret societies? No, I'm done. As much as I…love Sebastian, I can't."

There—she'd said it aloud. The one thing she'd been fighting against ever since this strange four-way friendship began. She could no longer deny or avoid it. She loved him, and in the current hell-on-earth in which they were both trapped there was no way they could be together. Todd looked on helplessly as she tried, and failed, to hold back tears.

"Listen, the weather's getting warmer soon. How about I start on that sundeck you've been after me to build?"

She paused and sniffled. "Really?" For years, she'd tried to get him to install one in the back, off the kitchen. He'd never gotten any further than a rough sketch on a paper napkin.

"Yeah. You'll be able to put your plants out there when it gets warm. Maybe even do some container gardening."

She couldn't help laughing. "Container gardening? You don't eat vegetables."

"Maybe I'd like them better if we grew them ourselves."

"I guess it's worth a try." The image of the two of them pruning tomato plants in plastic pails lightened her mood, but only for a moment. Soon Sebastian intruded on her thoughts again. What a mess her life had become.

"I'm serious about doing better," he said. "I've been sponging off you all my life. It's time I stepped up a little. Dad would have wanted that."

"You haven't mentioned Dad in years."

"I know." He saw that she had finished her food, and stood to take her empty plate back into the kitchen. While he was gone, she heard a car crunching onto their gravel driveway.

For one wild moment, she thought it might be Sebastian. He'd come to explain Amsterdam, or produce an official document from the coroner proving that Ami had died in a simple drowning accident after all. Everything would be normal again.

But Todd came back quiet and worried.

"Will's here," he said. "Looks like something's up. Stay there. I'll get the door."

Will came in, his expression as unhappy as her brother's. Joel and a female deputy she'd never seen before accompanied him. The emblem on her uniform sleeve revealed that she worked for the next county over. Surely there hadn't been bodies washing up there, too?

"Can we help you?" Briana asked.

"In a manner of speaking. We did some tests on those hair samples you gave us. Turns out they match some other ones found on the victim's clothes." Will shook his head regretfully. "I'm sorry, Briana. Gonna have to arrest you. Suspicion of murder."

On cue, the female deputy came around to raise Briana off the couch and pat her down. The cuffs clicked smoothly into place around her wrists.

Todd watched, ashen. "I'll get a lawyer," he vowed. "The best I can find."

He followed Briana to the police car waiting outside the house.

"Tell Reggie to keep the motel open," she called as the female deputy pushed her head down and guided her into the car. "We've got to try and keep the business."

Will and Joel got into the front, and the uniformed woman climbed into the back with Briana. Procedure, she supposed. Lights flashing, the car began a slow roll down the hill toward town. As they passed rows of houses, shops, and docked boats, people—neighbors she'd known all her life—gathered at windows and street corners to point and stare.

Chapter 16

Todd arrived at Morgan House a few minutes before dusk and banged on the door until it opened. Ruby stood blinking at him in surprise. Todd's eyes widened to find her dressed to go out—spiky hair, boots, and a short leather jacket over a purple midriff shirt.

"I thought we weren't seeing each other tonight," she said in an irritated tone. "I told you not to bother changing your mind."

"That's not why I'm here," he shot back. "It's your brother I want to talk to. I mean, your grandfather. Or whatever he is. Where is he?"

Ruby lifted her head to peer over his shoulder. "Briana's not with you? How did you get here?"

"How do you think? I took the car. Now where the hell is Sebastian?"

"You shouldn't be driving without a license," Ruby said. "You could have gotten pulled over!"

"Yeah? By whom? The whole damn police force just showed up at my house to bust my sister!"

This time Ruby's eyes widened. "What?"

"Explain yourself," Sebastian demanded. He loomed up behind Ruby as if he had suddenly materialized from the shadows.

"You heard me. She's been arrested. The cops think she killed Ami."

Though Sebastian stood perfectly still, his hands snapped into fists and his face became a storm cloud. "I feared something like this would happen," he said. "Fortunately, our community retains specialists who handle these kinds of things."

"What kinds of things? People killed by vampires?"

"When necessary. I don't think that's what happened in this case, though obviously the resulting investigation could have wider implications. In any event, Briana will need expert legal counsel. I will see to that personally."

"I don't understand why we need some vampire lawyer. Briana didn't do anything wrong!"

"That, unfortunately, is irrelevant. And technically speaking, the lawyer will not be a vampire. Though some of us do pursue that profession, they find it impractical to spend their days in courthouses."

"I'm glad you think this is amusing." Todd flared in rage. "Now I'll tell you something. My sister had better not be in this mess because of something you did, Morgan."

"Something I did? What a perfectly ridiculous suggestion. Why would I kill Ami?"

"Who knows? You might have had reasons. Ami wasn't stupid—and she knew how to manipulate guys. Maybe she found out the truth about you. Maybe you weren't feeding off my sister because you were feeding off her. Maybe you did it for kicks. What does it matter? You'd never admit it anyway. Survival for the two of you—that's all you care about. Briana and I don't matter one bit to either one of you! I bet you'd kill us both to stop us from revealing what we know!"

Like a strike of winter lightning, Sebastian flew across the foyer. His icy fingers curled into the collar of Todd's shirt.

"You dare to question my motives toward your sister after you've humiliated and lived off her for years?"

"I admit I haven't always done the right thing." Todd's voice came out a bit more strained than usual, owing to the bunched fabric compressing his windpipe. "But things are different now. Better."

"I see little evidence to support that conclusion. What progress you have made is the result of my, and my sister's, —intervention. And now that I think about it, you had more motive to kill Ami than I did. Did Ruby demand that you put an end to her following you two everywhere you went? You'd do almost anything to please her, I think."

"Not that. Never."

His rage fading, Sebastian relaxed his grip on Todd's shirt and pushed him away. "Forgive me if I find that hard to accept. I have lived a long time, and I know mortals are capable of violent acts that would disgust many vampires. I've seen humans tear each other to bits over petty mortal jealousies they don't even remember the following day."

"So I guess we should all follow your example. Sucking people's blood until they pass out is one way to build character, I'll grant you that."

Sebastian's body tensed, visible rage boiling up in him. Hastily, Ruby stepped between them and placed one hand on each man's chest.

"That's enough! Both of you need to get a freaking grip! None of us wants the whole truth to come out, and I'm pretty sure that includes you, Todd. Besides, if you fight with Sebastian, you'll lose—big time. So cut the crap, and let's find a way to work together."

"Frankly, I'd prefer to handle this on my own," Sebastian said. "The two of you can help me best by staying out of the situation."

"Like I'd trust you to help my sister," Todd exploded. "Just like I said before. Neither of you gives a damn." He brushed Ruby's hand off his chest and tore from the house.

* * * *

Sebastian and Ruby exchanged grim looks when they heard the engine of Briana's car start and then roar off down the long driveway.

"He didn't seem drunk," Ruby said hopefully after a moment's reflection. "A little angry, maybe."

"Drunk or not, we've got problems." Sebastian sighed. "Ruby, I'm only going to ask this one more time. Tell me one or both of you didn't get out of control that night."

"No. You can trust me this time. I like living here much better than I liked Amsterdam. I'm not planning to cause any trouble. I don't want to leave right away."

"Really?" Sebastian's brows rose. "And here I thought Darkisle bored you."

"Turns out I found more things to keep my interest than I expected." Her eyes drifted toward the door Todd had stormed through. Her full lips curved in a wicked smile. "He'll come back. They always do. And we'll get past the rest of it."

"True enough." She had a point, and he knew that when she wanted them to, her lovers always did return. And unfortunate events like Ami's death usually faded from public consciousness soon enough, leaving them free to slip back into their shadowy existence.

This time, though, Todd and Ami, and whatever connection existed between them, weren't the most pressing problem Sebastian faced.

He now knew that he was in love with Briana. And she had decided that he was a monster.

* * * *

Briana's grey, sparsely furnished cell turned out more comfortable than she'd expected, if that was the appropriate word. She had heat, a narrow but adequate cot with a clean mattress, and a TV bolted to the wall outside the bars. She could reach through to change the channel or adjust the volume.

On the downside, the toilet sat in the middle of the cell. Men had definitely designed jails, she thought, though at least a door separated the detention area and the front desk.

"There's cable," Joel said hopefully, sounding more like a real estate agent than a cop locking her up for the night. "I can get you something to read too."

He looked genuinely sorry, Briana thought, as if he'd rather be anywhere else and doing anything else at that moment. No doubt he remembered her goody-goody image in high school and wondered how she'd managed to sink so low in less than ten short years.

She sat on the cot and waited while Joel locked the cell and ducked into the next room. He soon returned with a cardboard box containing magazines and paperbacks discarded by the public library.

"Thanks," she said, taking the box to the cot so she could rummage through it. "Thoughtful of you." Most of the magazines were outdated celebrity gossip rags, though she found a book of crossword puzzles. A few of the grids hadn't been filled in, but Briana had nothing to write with. "Can I have a pencil?"

Joel blushed. "Uh...I'll have to ask Will if that's okay."

Briana looked up, eyes narrowed. "I'm not planning to use it as a weapon or a lock pick."

"I know, but jail rules are kinda strange. I gotta follow them, even though it's you."

"Well, go and ask him then."

Joel nodded, but paused to test the cell door before leaving her alone. When he'd gone, a sudden rush of hot rage boiled up inside her. Hurling the magazine to the floor, she huddled up on the cot, hugging her knees to her chest and fighting off a wave of pure despair.

Sebastian had been right about the hair sample. The cops planned to frame her, or someone did. Had Ruby or Sebastian himself killed Ami and then set her up to take the fall? She hoped he didn't hear about her arrest and come rushing up here. He was the last person she wanted to talk to right now. At the same time, his were the only arms she wanted to dissolve into while she bawled out her frustration and fear.

In spite of herself, she perked up when she heard footsteps approaching from the outside room. Quickly she wiped her face and composed herself. No one walking in to visit her would ever know how truly nervous, even frightened, she felt.

The door opened a second later, and Will came though it holding a tiny yellow nub with no eraser. It was the kind of pencil they handed out at Bingo halls and miniature golf courses.

Briana took it from him without bothering to hide her irritation. "Thanks."

"Doing okay?" Will asked.

"Just peachy. How long do you think it will be before I can arrange bail?" she asked.

"That could be tricky. No judge on call until Monday morning," Will told her. "Looks like you'll spend the weekend in jail."

Briana cursed small-town justice. "Why are you doing this to me, Will? You know I didn't kill Ami."

He leaned against the brick wall, not looking directly at her. "I think it's possible you did. Maybe it was an accident, or maybe the two of you started fighting over Morgan. Luckily, I don't have to prove anything one way or the other. All I have to do is act on the evidence the coroner's found so far."

"Meaning a couple of hairs stuck to her jacket? You've got to be kidding me. There could be any number of explanations for that, assuming it's even my hair."

To her surprise, Will's voice took on an almost pleading tone. "Briana, please. Don't push this. You're safe where you are. Can't we just leave it at that for the time being?"

"Safe? What's that supposed to mean?" She frowned. "Are you telling me I'm in here for my own protection?"

"I'll deny I ever said this, but there's no getting around the fact that you're better off with me. It's possible you killed Ami, sure, but to my mind there's an even better suspect. Now that Morgan knows we're on to him, who's to say he won't do something crazy? I don't want you caught in the crossfire."

"Because my dad wouldn't have wanted that. I know." Briana sighed. "But you're wrong about Sebastian, Will. He wouldn't hurt me."

"You might be comfortable with those odds, but I'm not. Anyway, the issue right now isn't what he might do to you, but what someone did to Ami. According to the M.E.'s preliminary report, you're the most plausible suspect so far. That's good enough to keep you here for a while. Try to make the best of it."

She spent the next few hours alternating between the crossword puzzle and a battered novel from the library box, one of those old-fashioned blockbusters filled with corporate intrigue and crude sex scenes, neither of which held her attention. The puzzles seemed more promising, until the lack of a fine point and an eraser began to stymie her attempts to distract herself. Relief came in the form of Joel, who showed up with a take-out box and a Styrofoam cup of coffee from the diner.

"It's decaf," he told her as he passed the cup through the bars. "I figured you wouldn't want to be up all night."

"Thanks, but I think that's inevitable. I've never slept in a cage before."

"Yeah, I know."

Inside the box she found a roast beef and cheddar sandwich that smelled as delicious as it looked. She bit into the soft roll while Joel watched with satisfaction. Weird how she always ended up with someone watching her eat these days.

"I've seen you order that before," he said with a grin. "I figured it was something you liked."

Her face grew serious. She put down the sandwich. "I didn't do this, you know, Joel."

His cheeks reddened. "That isn't for me to decide. All I'm supposed to do is keep you safe while you're in here."

"Will said the same thing. To tell you the truth, I'd just as soon take my chances out on the street."

"I'm sorry, Bri. I'll tell you, I never thought it would come to this. Back in high school, heck, I got in trouble a lot more than you."

She couldn't hide the smile that tugged at her mouth, though the memories proved bittersweet. Her father had been alive, Todd was a fresh-faced teenager, and the alcohol-fueled conflicts that rocked their household still loomed years away. "Times have changed since then, all right."

"We go back a long way," Joel agreed. "You know what people say—if we only knew then what we knew now."

"I'll bet we'd still make the same mistakes. So, for fun, tell me...where did you imagine me ending up, if not here?"

"Oh, I don't know." His blush deepened. "To me, it seemed like you could have gone anywhere. You were always the smartest one in the class. And even then, you did such a good job helping your dad run The Dunes. I guess I could see you maybe running a big hotel in Halifax, or managing a yacht club somewhere. And I thought you and Graham would get married."

Her chin snapped up. "Graham and I, married? What made you think that?"

Joel shrugged, clearly uncomfortable now. "I don't know. To me, it always looked like you were crazy about each other. I thought for sure it would last."

"Well, things can change."

"Yeah. I guess I should get back out front now. You need anything, just holler."

"I will. Joel...if anyone comes to visit me, can you tell them I'm not up to it tonight? Really. I need time to think."

"Sure thing. I'm pretty sure Will doesn't want anyone back here this late anyway."

"That suits me fine." She meant it. The last thing she needed was Sebastian coming in here and getting her all confused again. Whatever his game, she couldn't afford to play it right now...literally.

At least The Dunes hadn't gone bankrupt yet. If worse came to worst, Todd might be able to use it as collateral to get bond for her. She refused to take any money from Sebastian, though he'd surely offer some. Getting her out of here was probably his biggest priority right now. She wished she could be sure that was because he worried about her well-being and not just about what she might spill to the cops. She could never betray him, even if she couldn't convince anyone except Todd of her innocence.

* * * *

With no customers or management on the premises, the motel seemed quiet, creepy, and even a little dingier than usual. Fortunately, Reggie liked it that way. He stretched out on the little cot in the back office, an open beer on the floor beside him and a magazine open on his lap. If his grandmother had caught sight of either one, she'd skin him alive. Though he felt sorry about Briana being in jail he definitely saw some advantages. Not having to fold the towels was the least of them.

He took a swig of beer and felt his senses tilt pleasantly. His fingers ruffled through the worn pages of the magazine, where entire choruses of beckoning beauties jostled for a role in his swelling fantasies.

His pulse quickened as he browsed, counteracting the sedative effects of the beer. The physical sensations mimicked the war between frustration and satisfaction that played out in his mind. Sometimes it seemed like the entire world teemed with beautiful, sensual, and willing women—all of them inaccessible to him. Briana was hot, though maybe not in the way a centerfold magazine would appreciate, but she was his boss. Most of the other women around town seemed coarse, both in appearance and behavior, and Sebastian Morgan's sister just plain scared him. The only promising prospect to alight in Darkisle in years had been Ami Sheridan. Sure, like most of the tourists she had looked down on him as some kind of servant, demanding fresh towels and any number of replacement keys to her room. Each of her appearances in the office triggered a lecture from his grandmother, who claimed to know all about "girls like that." Too bad Reggie wanted to know too. Desperately.

The sudden click of metal on glass interrupted his reverie. He froze, realizing that someone had come into the lobby. From his position on the cot, he couldn't see who—which meant that the person couldn't see him either.

Reggie remained as rigid as a statue, hardly daring to breathe as the unseen intruder crashed into the middle office and flung open the desk drawers, one at a time. Next, Reggie heard the scrape of a key being hastily jammed into another lock. Any moment, he expected to be confronted, even attacked, when the thief moved to the back room.

Instead, the whole incident came to an end with a light clang he recognized as the petty cash box being slapped shut and dropped on the desk. The heavy footsteps turned not toward his hiding place, but back to the lobby desk. The bell jingled as the front door closed again.

Reggie's relief felt so intense that he almost forgot to start breathing again, but when he did, an unfamiliar bitter taste tickled his nose and throat. Rolling up the magazine and chucking it under the cot, he got up and crept toward the door. He cautiously peered around the doorjamb at the front desk.

A silhouetted figure raced past the closed glass door, followed by odd shadow drifting along the concrete walkway. It took him a moment to realize that he wasn't looking at a shadow, but a huge cloud of thick black smoke, rolling like a storm cloud across the parking lot. When he came around the front desk and opened the front door, an enormous surge of heat pushed him back inside.

Curses, rather than real words, rose to his fear-numbed lips. Then he covered his face with both arms and made a break for it. He could smell and hear the fire all around him now. Vicious flames grabbed at his clothes and licked at his hair. A terrible roar filled his ears.

By the time he reached the far side of the parking lot, the entire motel had become engulfed. Still shielding his face, he glanced back at the room Ami had once occupied. The door stood open, the window shattered. Reggie could see the flames leaping inside, devouring the bedspread, consuming the furniture, peeling the paper off the walls. A few bits of melted yellow police tape fluttered past his face, propelled by the giant plumes of fetid smog.

Finally, he found his voice. "Help!" he screamed. "Fire! Fire!"

In the distance, he heard the blare of sirens and knew that Darkisle's only fire truck and assorted gang of volunteers would soon assemble in an effort to save The Dunes. Their second act, he felt sure, would involve pinning the disaster on him.

The only thing left to do was turn and run.

When he did, he crashed into something solid. Powerful hands gripped Reggie's shoulders, stopping him in mid-stride.

Sebastian Morgan stood glowering down at him.

"Reggie—what have you done?"

Chapter 17

No sooner had Briana found a TV show she could tolerate than a cacophony of sirens erupted outside, drowning out the soundtrack. Since the cell had no window, she could only listen for clues about the emergency vehicles' direction. She assumed a boat engine had exploded, not unusual along the public moorings, or a grease fire had broken out at one of the seafood restaurants downtown.

Not long after, Will came in wearing an odd expression.

"What's going on?" she asked. When he didn't answer directly, she knew something was wrong.

"Any idea where your brother might be right now?"

"That's pretty funny, considering you dragged me out of my own house in irons. I assume he stayed behind."

"Before we got there, did he mention any plans? Any place he usually goes in the evening?"

Briana's eyes narrowed. She could see where Will meant to take this. "I think it's safe to say he's not out with Ami. Whether he had a date with anyone else, I couldn't say."

"That kind of attitude won't help any of us, Briana, least of all Todd. Try to think back and give me some ideas. We really need to find him."

She frowned. "May I ask why?"

"Bri, those sirens you just heard were for you. Your motel just burned to the ground. Arson."

Briana felt as if she'd taken a blow to the stomach. Weakly, she sagged to the bed. "Oh, no. Was anyone hurt?"

"We're still sifting through the rubble, but for now, no one's reported any injuries. The kid at the desk called for help first. He's fine."

"What does this have to do with looking for Todd? You don't think he's inside, do you?"

"There's no evidence of that. But we do want to talk to him. Reggie saw someone slip in and then run out of the office. The person had a key and knew where you kept the cash box. We're pretty sure it was Todd. Everything fits."

"But why would Todd burn down our own motel? It doesn't make any sense."

"Simple. To destroy evidence. To protect you, maybe. Or himself."

"No! That's impossible." Though she tried valiantly to hold them back, angry tears spilled down her cheeks. "You're always talking about what a good friend my father was to you. How do you think he'd feel if he knew you wanted to throw both of his children in prison?"

Will shook his head. "I don't have the power to put anyone in prison, Briana. That'll be for a jury to decide. But I can promise you that I'm going to find out exactly what happened to Ami and to The Dunes. That motel belonged to your father long before it belonged to you, don't forget." His stubborn expression softened briefly. "Look, Briana. For your dad's sake, I'm advising you to hurry up and get a lawyer. A lot of people will be wanting to talk to you soon."

"I'm working on that," she murmured.

"All right, then," Will conceded. He turned to go. "We'll leave it there for now."

She remained huddled on the cot as he walked away, not looking up as he closed the connecting door between the cell and the lobby. She wasn't sure how much time passed before she heard it open again.

"What's the matter, Will?" she growled without looking up. "Did you think of some other crime to charge me with?"

When Will didn't respond, she lifted her head and gasped in surprise. Sebastian stood in the exact spot the sheriff had occupied moments before.

"I-I thought I couldn't have visitors tonight," she blurted.

"They don't know I'm here." Sebastian's gaze traveled along the ceiling and corners. "There's no surveillance. I'd be able to tell." A slight smell of smoke followed him into the room. "You've been to The Dunes," she said.

"Yes."

"Sebastian, Todd is missing. The police think he emptied the petty cash box and set the fire. I was afraid he got trapped inside, but I couldn't be sure until now."

"Todd did not perish in the flames. No one did. I sensed no aura of death."

He stepped closer. The same magnetism that had drawn her from the beginning still hummed between them, even though she had decided she could no longer trust him. Her hands itched to reach through the bars and pull him to her. Somehow, she managed to hold back.

"I've made a few calls," he told her. "A lawyer will be here for you tomorrow morning. Needless to say, I won't be able to accompany him, but I want you to know that I am doing my best to help you."

"You don't have to."

"I do. I know you think this is somehow my doing. I promise you it isn't, but I still consider you my responsibility."

She blinked away a fresh stream of tears, hoping he couldn't see them. She knew that would be futile though. Sebastian always knew everything. "What about those things Will Garvey told me? About Amsterdam? I thought I knew you."

"You do know me, better than anyone. Briana, that woman was a troubled soul who tried to infiltrate our community. She wanted to be one of us. That wouldn't be impossible, or unheard of, but she wasn't an ideal candidate. She approached a number of us and asked us to turn her. Each of us refused. Not long after, she disappeared. Eventually, I learned of her death. I did know her, but nothing existed between us except my advising her to drop her idea and find another means of fulfillment."

"Who killed her then?"

He shrugged. "The list of suspects is longer than the Amsterdam police could ever be allowed to know. Perhaps she eventually connected with the wrong people. Perhaps she foolishly attempted to blackmail someone into meeting her demands. Unfortunately, I can offer no more than speculation. The authorities in Amsterdam were not content with that, but they were forced to accept it. I'm afraid you must as well."

"I believe you didn't kill her yourself. But like you said—death follows your kind. That woman became one of the casualties. Ami turned into another. And it's looking more and more like my brother and I will be next."

"Not on my watch." The cords in his neck stiffened visibly. He seemed to grind his teeth in frustration. "Perhaps I was to blame for some of this, but I intend to repair the damage. If we cannot resolve the issue legally, there are always...alternatives."

Briana scowled. "Like what?"

He slid his hands through the bars and snapped his grip tight. She had no doubt that the slightest flick of his wrists would twist the metal into an unrecognizable wreck. "If you leave with me, I can make sure we are never found."

"I can't do that. I'm sorry. I'll try to beat this case as best I can, but I'm going to do it the regular way."

"I suspected that would be your answer. However, the offer will stand. You need only ask. I'll handle the rest."

Slowly, Briana rose to her feet and joined him at the cell door. She could feel the tension radiating from him. Every fiber of his body poised to erupt in violence. She had no fear that he would turn such force on her; however, being near him in such a state unnerved her.

"Last night, you asked me to join my life to yours. Funny thing about jail is that it's the perfect place to think things over. And I have thought about it, Sebastian."

Her tone made his eyes narrow. His attitude became instantly wary. She felt him pull back from her a little. "Very well," he said after a pause. "Tell me."

"The more I considered a future with you, the more questions I had. How could it ever work? You don't age, and I can't be like you." Her voice caught in her throat, and a painful weight settled in the middle of her chest. She forced herself to continue. "In forty years, will I start masquerading as your mother? Then, in sixty years, your grandmother? Just like your granddaughter has now become your younger sister? How will that be possible?"

"I cannot answer that. I do know that most problems can be solved, given sufficient time and motivation. I have plenty of both."

"I never doubted that. It's me I'm not so sure of. As much as you've shown me about your world, you've shown me a lot about myself too. And as intense as my feelings for you have become, I'm afraid I can't go any further."

He turned his head so that a shadow fell across his face, momentarily obscuring his features. He cleared his throat before he spoke.

"I won't beg you to reconsider," he informed her without a trace of emotion. "I understand."

She grasped at his fingers as they slid from the bars. "Sebastian...this isn't the way I saw things working out between us. But so much has happened. This is in your best interest too. The less the sheriff connects you and Ruby to the crime I supposedly committed, the safer you'll be. Trust me, he already suspects you."

"I care nothing for what he knows or suspects," he snarled. Then the mask slipped back into place. "However, I respect your decision. I will continue to protect you...but from afar."

"You don't have to do that. I do all right on my own."

He shook his head in mock irritation. "Blasted modern women. In my day, things were simple and clear-cut."

She managed a rueful smile. "But so much more boring. You told me so yourself."

"True enough. Fortunately, stubborn though you are, I cannot think of a way for you to stop me."

"All right, I accept that. But Sebastian...will you do one thing for me?"

"Of course."

"Find my brother before Will Garvey does."

He nodded once. "Consider it done."

Briana remained silent as she watched him turn and leave the room. She wished she could summon the words to tell him how much their parting hurt her, and how much she knew it would cost her. But strong enough words did not exist.

At least this way, all four of them had a shot at staying alive. Her own misery seemed a small enough price to pay for that.

* * * *

Moving at a speed most humans would find difficult to detect, even if they might be temporarily conscious of a flash of motion, Sebastian slipped past the deputies' station and back through a side exit. Ruby waited for him in a parking lot down the street.

"I see you didn't bring Briana with you," Ruby observed. "I knew she'd turn down your offer of escape. Stupid humans. Their whole business of right and wrong never fails to blow my mind."

"You forget that you were human once."

"Luckily, I wasn't bothered by silly concepts of morality even then."

Sebastian suppressed an amused smile. She was so much like him or the way he had been. Perhaps intemperance, like insanity, skipped a generation.

"I made Briana a promise. Apparently Todd has managed to lose himself amid all the confusion. Our task is to locate him."

Ruby's grin widened. "Normally, I'd give you hell for promising her anything after the way she's treated you. Still, that particular assignment has a certain appeal. I don't suppose you made any promises about what we get to do with him after we find him."

"I didn't, but I'm going to remind you again that this isn't a game, Ruby. There could be lives at stake here."

"Human lives." She rolled her eyes.

"Yes. But one of them could be Briana's. That means something to me, and for that reason, I hope it means something to you. I'm willing to proceed alone, but I would welcome your help. After all, you know him better than anyone. His scent...his aura."

She sighed. "Grow a sense of humor, will you? You know I'll help you." She shifted the car into drive and eased onto the road. When they got back in the vicinity of the motel, though far enough away that they wouldn't be spotted by the lingering emergency workers, she pulled off onto the shoulder and rolled down the window. Tilting her face into the night air, she opened her mouth and drew a deep breath into her flared nostrils.

"Nothing," she said a moment's reflection. "Nothing but the smell of smoke."

"Could he be dead after all?"

"That would be one explanation, though I think I'd still pick something up. More likely he's far away."

"In Briana's car. All right—let's try this the human way."

They drove back into town. Sebastian pointed to a liquor store across the street from The Chum Bucket. "He wouldn't go to the bar with everyone looking for him, but you saw the state he was in. The temptation to go back to a familiar source of comfort is going to be strong. I should know that better than anyone."

At his direction, Ruby pulled up in front of the shop. He got out of the car and strode purposefully inside. Ruby lagged a few steps behind him.

The older man behind the counter smiled, thinking he had a customer, but his enthusiasm faded when he saw the gravity of Sebastian's expression.

"Todd Dempsey," Sebastian announced without preamble. "Has he been around here tonight?"

"Todd? Why would he come here?"

"You know the answer to that as well as I do. I need to speak to him. You heard that The Dunes burned down a few hours ago. I need to find out if Todd was involved."

The clerk's eyes narrowed. "You a cop?"

"Let's just say I fall somewhere between cop and concerned citizen."

The man pointedly turned to a supply catalog that lay open beside him. "Sorry, buddy. My customers deserve privacy."

"Not in this case."

In a flash, Sebastian leaned over the counter to grasp the man by the shoulders. Raw fear leapt into the clerk's eyes as Sebastian pulled him forward and trained a murderous glare on him. Soon the emotion drained from the man's face, and his head bobbed lightly, as if losing consciousness. "He wasn't here," he managed to murmur before drifting off into a hypnotic daze. "Sorry."

With a grunt of disgust, Sebastian pushed him backward into a chair behind the counter.

"Well, it was worth a try," Ruby comforted him. Her own pupils gleamed with anticipation. "Where now—The Chum Bucket?"

Ignoring her, Sebastian swung around to survey the store, as if he might spot Todd cowering behind one of the cardboard displays.

"Do you sense him? Was he here?" he demanded of Ruby.

She shook her head. "I'm not picking up anything. Maybe Todd really did manage to stay on the wagon."

"The cops don't know he has Briana's car. That will buy us some time. We need to figure out where he is before they start looking for it."

"My money's still on The Chum Bucket. Come on, Sebastian, you know I need to feed. I'll be a more productive assistant if I can concentrate on something else besides my hunger."

"There'll be time for that later," he grumbled. "Let's keep searching."

* * * *

Briana stirred from a troubled half-sleep when Graham showed up outside the bars of her cell.

"Good news. You're being released," Graham said. He held up the keys to the cell and jingled them.

"Where are Joel and Will? How did you get those?"

"The cops are all out working on the fire," he said as he proceeded to unlock the door. "I went down to volunteer, and Joel told me that all charges against you have been dropped. He temporarily deputized me so I could come and let you out."

Briana remembered Joel's sentimental attitude toward her lost relationship with Graham and winced. The two had always been good friends. Still, his explanation struck her as peculiar.

The barred door swung open. All that lay between herself and freedom was Graham himself. He leaned casually against the wall, twirling the keys on his right index finger, apparently in no particular hurry.

"Are you sure this is okay with Will?" she asked suspiciously.

"Of course it is. In a way, the motel burning down worked out in your favor. Since you were in here when the fire started, it's obvious you couldn't have done it. Will didn't share all the details, but he says he found proof that the two are connected."

She nodded, stepping out with relief. "I told Will that from the beginning. It's about time he started taking me seriously." She'd only been locked up for a few hours, but release tasted sweeter than the richest chocolate sundae on earth. Never again would she take her freedom for granted. "What changed his mind?"

"Well...you're not going to like it, actually. The fact is that Sebastian Morgan committed the murder. Will knows that now."

Briana started through the connecting door into the station lobby when Graham's words registered. She paused and swung around to face him. "What?"

Graham shrugged. "Yup. Turns out he and Ami had been sleeping together all along. I guess he's quite the sugar daddy. Ami threatened to tell you unless Morgan kept the affair, and the money, coming. She confronted him after you left The Chum Bucket, and he strangled her. Still, I'll give him this: he really does care about you. He got so desperate to keep you that he was actually willing to kill for you."

"That's—that's just insane. Sebastian didn't even know Ami! What proof does Will have?"

"Believe it or not, the information came from Todd. Ami told him the truth a while ago. He knew how you felt about Morgan, and he didn't want to hurt you."

Briana stared, incredulous. "Todd? Are you sure?"

He shrugged again. "Ask him yourself. I can take you to him right now."

"You know where Todd is?"

"I took him to my boat as soon as he got done spilling the beans to Will. Morgan threatened to kill him too. That's the main reason they want you out of here. You're a sitting duck once Morgan finds out everyone's onto him."

"Is Todd all right? Who set the fire?"

"Morgan. Obviously he left something in that room he didn't want found. Todd apparently saw him light the place up, and that's why Morgan is after him. Face it, Briana. The guy is practically a serial killer. You made a big mistake this time."

Briana smacked her own forehead in frustration. "And I sent Sebastian to look for him!"

"Well, luckily I found him first. Morgan won't think to keep an eye on me. We'll be safe."

Briana frowned, recalling the odor of smoke on Sebastian's clothes when he'd come to the jail earlier. Had his offer to help her escape only been a ruse to get her under his control?

No, there had to be some mistake. She found it impossible to accept that Sebastian had been involved with Ami. If he had said anything remotely like what was being ascribed to him, he had most likely been covering up for Ruby or some other member of his "community," as he called it.

They'd just have to sort that out later. Right now, she had to get to Todd. Seeing their motel go up in flames, whether or not Sebastian bore any responsibility, seemed like the kind of thing that could drive him back to the bottle.

"We've got to go to my boat," Graham reminded her. "Morgan's already burned down your motel. The police station could be next. Will wants you as far away from here as I can get you. Come on."

She noticed the lights on in the lobby of the station as they hurried through, but the front desk sat unmanned. It seemed odd for Joel to desert his post that way, but there was a fire, a manhunt, and a murder investigation that had all happened at once. Darkisle had never seen so much excitement, and none of it was good.

They ran to the docks and jumped into Graham's boat under cover of darkness. He didn't switch on the lights as he revved the engine. "Go to the cabin," he told Briana. "Don't want anyone to see you."

She went down and then came back up. "Where's Todd? I thought you said he'd be here."

"He's actually up the coast a bit in an old fishing shack I rented to store my gear. Morgan will never find him. We'll go right up there."

He pulled away from the wharf and off they went, the boat's prop cutting a deep furrow in the inky water. Briana had an uneasy feeling as they pulled away from the dock. She'd trusted Sebastian once too often. He'd almost gotten her to believe black was white, and day was night, and living forever by feasting on human blood could be the most normal thing in the world. Under his strange, drug-like influence, she'd lost not just her motel, but nearly her brother and her entire sense of self as well. If that was love, she'd be better off without it.

Chapter 18

"What's wrong with you?" Graham demanded. She huddled in the corner of the bow, watching the colored reflections in the water as the long row of waterfront buildings flashed by. They'd put a few hundred yards between them and the shore now, moving parallel with the coast. Graham traveled at a deliberately slow clip, his lights on the lowest possible setting. He didn't want to be seen.

"I was just thinking," she said, looking up at him. "I still can't believe Sebastian would do any of those things, never mind all of them. Why would he strangle Ami? And burn my motel? He knew how much that place meant to me."

"Because he's a creep, that's why. Psychotic. Not getting caught is what matters to him—not your feelings. Sorry to be so harsh, Bri, but it's time you faced facts."

Briana shook her head, still trying to sort things out. In one way, knowing what she did, everything Graham said made sense—Sebastian might well have fed on Ami in a weak moment and then had to come up with a quick plan to silence her. Perhaps some sort of evidence in the motel would lead either to him or some other vampire he desperately wanted to protect.

Then she'd remind herself that they were talking about Sebastian—the man she knew better than any other living soul ever could. The man she had grown to love. Was every good thing she sensed in him a product of her hormone-saturated fantasies, or had he perhaps brainwashed her in some way? The more she tried to analyze the situation, the more confused she became. Between that and the bobbing motion of Graham's boat on the choppy night surf, she actually grew dizzy.

"And another thing. If Sebastian killed Ami, how do you think my hair got on her body?"

"Isn't it obvious? He either planted some hair or it was just coincidence. He probably had sex with you and then with her on the same night. Bet they'll find his DNA on her too."

Briana wondered about vampire DNA. What would it look like under a microscope? Different enough from a human's that it would likely tip off the wrong people. Another plausible motive for Sebastian to lose control, she had to admit.

"But my whole motel," she lamented. "Couldn't he have just torched the one room?"

"Maybe that's what he intended to do, but the fire got out of control. In a way, it's a good thing you stayed in jail while the place went up in smoke. I could see you running in there trying to play hero and getting yourself killed. Anyway, let it go. I told you to sell that old fleatrap years ago. It's never been anything but a headache for you. Now you're free of it and him."

Briana's discomfort grew as the motor continued churning and Darkisle's grungy landmarks steadily faded from view.

"Where did you say this fishing shack was?" she asked. It dawned on her how little sense it made for Graham to keep his equipment so far from town when Darkisle had plenty of off-season warehouses he could have rented for pocket change.

"Right up here a little ways. Hard to see it in the dark. That was the whole purpose."

"Did Todd seem comfortable when you left him?" She hugged her arms together as a sudden chill pierced her skin. "It's really cold out here this time of night."

"That's the wind blowing in from Canada." He turned the engine even lower and propped the wheel against the dashboard with a metal rod. "Come on down to the cabin. I'll make us some coffee. Got fresh half-and-half and everything. I remember how you hate that powdered crap."

"What about the boat?"

"Told you, I had it all outfitted like new. I can monitor our speed and course from down below now. We'll be fine."

Still shivering, Briana got up and plodded down the four steps that led to the cabin. Graham followed, but paused to set up the drip coffeepot he kept on a table in the corner. "I've got graham crackers in the top drawer too," he announced.

"That was the only good thing about jail," she said, trying to keep her tone light despite the sinking feeling in her stomach. "Not much in the way of snacks there. I might have been able to lose some weight."

Graham snorted without glancing back at her. "You look fine the way you are. Did Morgan tell you that you were too fat?"

She looked up, taken aback by his gruffness. "No, not at all. He made me feel very…attractive."

"All part of his game. He didn't care about anyone but himself. Thought he'd found a bunch of small town hicks who'd let him take all our women and trash our buildings without saying a word. Stuck-up piece of Eurotrash."

The coffee began bubbling, and the comforting aroma of dark French roast filled the tight space. Graham turned toward her. The anger she'd heard in his voice thankfully didn't appear on his face. Instead, he wore a relaxed, almost dreamy smile. He motioned for her to sit on his bed, where he clearly intended to join her.

Pointedly, Briana shifted to the other side of the room.

"Graham, we should get something clear right away. I'm grateful for you helping Todd, and now me. You know I'll always care about you. But as far as there being anything between us again—we're as wrong for each other as ever. More so now."

The blissful expression vanished from his face. "You're still thinking of Morgan, aren't you?"

"Of course I am. He's the whole reason we're here, isn't he? If it weren't for him, Ami wouldn't be dead, I wouldn't have been in jail, and Todd wouldn't be in hiding right now. I think he has a lot to answer for. And believe me, I intend to confront him."

"Don't be stupid, Briana. The man's violent. He'll snap your neck the same way he snapped Ami's."

"Well, you know, that has me puzzled. If he really did kill Ami, why would he leave her on his own property? Or if he couldn't think of another place, why not hide her way down inside the caves and cover her with rocks? He didn't do a very good job of covering his tracks."

Graham opened his mouth as if to shout at her, but then he seemed to think better of it. With an overly casual shrug, he returned to the coffeepot and began preparing two mugs.

"I'll bet the body washed up by accident. He probably tried to get it into the caves, but the tide came in and he couldn't weigh her down right. Most criminals get caught because they make one small mistake that sends the whole house of cards tumbling."

He handed her the coffee and moved to stand in the corner. "Go on, sit on the bed," he told her. He punctuated the invitation with a brief, bitter laugh. "You don't have to worry about me. I'm good over here."

Moving cautiously, making sure Graham wasn't going to follow her, Briana edged back over to the bed and sank down on the edge. She was all too aware of Graham's eyes following her every move as she sipped from her mug. Despite the warm and filling coffee, Briana still felt a chill sweep through her core.

"Too hot?" he asked. "Enough milk?"

"It's fine, thank you."

To delay further conversation, she lifted the mug and pretended to take a long, slow draught from it. Though she desperately tried to push the memory aside, she couldn't help thinking back to the last time she'd been in this cabin…in this bed. How foolish and desperate she'd felt before Sebastian had become part of her life. Graham couldn't even begin to guess the enormity of the gap between the affection she'd entertained for him and the fever she had for Sebastian. His touch, cold as it was, had branded her soul and burned a hole in her heart. It still pulsed, raw and empty, and could never be filled by any other man. She knew there would be no point in even trying.

Her cheeks reddened with embarrassment as her gaze fell on the pillow she'd used when she'd given in to Graham that last time. She remembered how she'd thrashed her head from side to side, her primal physical needs blotting out any semblance of common sense.

Suddenly, comprehension struck her with the force of a slap in the face. The tiny dark strand against a plane of pale linen spelled out the truth more clearly than bold lettering on a ten-foot billboard.

"Graham," she blurted, dropping her cup to her lap so abruptly that it almost slipped from her fingers, "the hair on Ami—the hair the cops found."

He sounded unconcerned. "Your hair. Yeah, I remember."

"They did find my hair. Will was right. And I know now where it came from." She ran her hand over the pillow and found another hair—clearly hers, clearly left there the morning she'd met Sebastian Morgan for the first time. The last morning she'd spent with Graham. "Ami came down here. She slept in your bed. After I did. Didn't she?"

The moment Graham's eyes dropped from hers to his coffee cup and slid off to his left, Briana knew. "That's crazy," he said. "I didn't even know her."

"Not true. You went to The Chum Bucket that night, too, along with the rest of us. You two hooked up after we left. She was upset—she'd have gone with you. Maybe it started off as some kind of misguided revenge against Todd and me."

Graham's expression darkened. Moving in what seemed like slow motion, he put down his cup and came toward her. "Why would you say that, Briana? Why would I want revenge against you? We're friends now. Aren't we?"

His fingers curled into his coarse palms. Hastily she tried another tactic. "Graham, we have to be honest with each other. If we're going to start fresh, I mean. No secrets. No deception."

To her astonishment, her strategy worked. Graham's shoulders slumped, and his fists relaxed. "Okay, yeah. She came here that night. I screwed her. It didn't mean anything. It was just…you know, like you said. Blowing off stream."

"That's what Ami thought. Being with you would be a way to get back at Todd, and at me, at the same time. On top of that, she probably liked you. I know how charming you can be when you want to."

Mistaking her comment for praise, Graham straightened and grinned. "I always did have a way with the ladies. Not that anyone would consider Ami a lady. But you know what I mean."

"You slept with her right here—you let her use the same pillow I used. Then you killed her and took her to Morgan Point to frame Sebastian. You torched my motel. Not because Sebastian's DNA was in there but because it wasn't. This way, there would be no proof either way. Plus you've wanted me to be free from The Dunes for a while. How long had you been plotting to destroy it? Because of the police tape, I had no guests—and you knew you'd found the perfect time."

He nodded as if they were discussing something of no consequence at all. "You needed to ditch that motel and Todd. They were like chains around your neck, dragging you right down to the bottom. Now, thanks to me, you're free."

Though her mind was reeling, and her heart slammed inside her chest with such fury she thought it might actually break through her chest, Briana fought to appear calm, even unconcerned. Her survival depended on appearing to be on Graham's side, maybe even grateful for the crimes he had committed on her behalf.

Belatedly, another piece of the puzzle fell into place in her mind. Stifling a wave of nausea, she flipped her hair back and looked at him with a nonchalant expression she struggled to maintain.

"Graham...you didn't have anything to do with the robbery at The Dunes, did you? You know...trying to scare me into giving the place up? Did you hire that kid who threatened me with the knife?" When he looked away again, she pressed on. "Come on, you can tell me. No secrets, remember?"

"Kid came around the docks one day, looking for odd jobs," he finally blurted. "Just so happened I had one for him. He wouldn't have hurt you." His cheeks flushed a dark, angry red. "I didn't count on Morgan showing up."

Her next realization proved the most horrible of them all. Tears sprang to her eyes, and her throat closed up until she could hardly speak. But she had to ask him. She forced out the words. "Did you...did you also kill Todd? Are we going out to where you dumped his body?"

"Never mind Todd. It's just us now. You can't go back to Darkisle. They'll be looking for you as a jailbreak. Will didn't really drop the charges against you, you know. I bailed you out in my own private way."

She exhaled sharply. Will and his colleagues would be searching everywhere for her, she knew, but not in order to rescue her. They'd see her apparent escape as a guilty plea in the murder of Ami as well. "Why, Graham? Why would you do that to me?"

"Isn't it obvious? I did it so we could be together. A few hours and we'll be in Fundy Bay. We can start over in Canada. Just the two of us. Truly free. We can change our names and follow the currents. No one will ever know who we really are."

He stood in front of her now, his hands stretched out toward her, his eyes aglow with lust.

Every muscle shaking, Briana forced herself to stand. With a low moan of pleasure, Graham drew her body against his. His arms slid around her middle, his lips grazing the tender flesh below her ear. She felt the harsh scrape of his stubbly whiskers on his skin and forced herself to suck in a deep, calming breath.

Then she brought her coffee mug down on his head with all the force she could muster.

* * * *

On their third pass through town, Sebastian and Ruby drove slowly past the sheriff's station. Sebastian stared at the drawn shade of the front window with an almost longing expression.

"Forget it," Ruby warned him. "She won't want to see you. Didn't she already tell you to buzz off once tonight?"

"Yes, but she wants me to look for her brother. Since we have had no success so far, perhaps we should go back to gather more information. Perhaps he's even been here since we left."

"Whatever you say." Ruby pulled the Maserati into a space marked *Sheriff's Vehicle Only*.

As soon as the two of them stepped out, they paused in unison. Their eyes met across the top of the car.

"You smell that, don't you?" Sebastian asked her.

She nodded. Her lips already felt moist. "It's fresh."

"Inside, quickly."

They dashed up the steps and into the lobby. The source of the odor that had assailed them with such force was immediately apparent: Joel Tanner lay sprawled behind the front desk, his scalp and shirt drenched in crimson. A quick check of the back room revealed that Briana had vanished along with her brother.

"Is he dead?" Ruby's tongue circled her mouth as Sebastian knelt beside him. His fingers shook slightly as he turned Joel's head to the side, exposing a vicious wound above his left temple.

"No. Knocked unconscious, I would say."

"Wow! Way to go, Briana! I didn't think she had that kind of nerve! I'm liking her more already."

"Don't be ridiculous. Briana couldn't have done this. It must have been Todd." Sebastian tapped Joel's face with his open palm. "Hey! What happened here? Where is Briana?"

"Do you have to wake him up yet?" Ruby swiped a finger along the wooden stool that had apparently served as the bludgeon and licked up the droplet of blood she collected. "I haven't fed yet, you know."

Sebastian ignored her and continued trying to rouse Joel, who eventually stirred and moaned.

"Tell me what happened," he demanded again. "Where is Briana Dempsey?"

"Hit me," Joel moaned. "Took her."

"Who hit you? Todd?"

"No," Joel wheezed. A fresh stream of blood trickled past his ear, causing Ruby to gasp. "Not Todd. Graham Smith."

Sebastian stood. "Smith—it fits. His boat would be a logical place to start." He reached for the desk phone. Ruby covered his hand with hers and looked up at him with a pleading expression.

"Can't you wait just a few minutes before you call for help? It won't hurt anything—and it would help me more than you know."

"Ruby—"

"Look at him! He's not going to remember a thing. Whatever he does mention will get written off as a hallucination. How often do we catch a break like that?"

Sebastian sighed. "Very well—but make it fast. I'm going to dial for help in exactly thirty seconds."

"Deal." She paused to smirk. "Seems kind of funny to be calling for help from the police station, doesn't it? Gotta love these small towns."

"Just get on with it."

Sinking to her knees, Ruby cradled Joel's head in her lap and bent down to feed. Sebastian turned away discreetly, the phone still in his hand. He studied the opposite wall until the sounds of giddy feasting ceased.

Thirty seconds later, they were back in the car and heading for the docks. Inside the sheriff's office, the phone lay in Joel's outstretched hand, the emergency operator asking over and over again if anyone could hear.

* * * *

As Graham slumped to the cabin floor, Briana raced from the cabin and back onto the deck.

To her horror, she saw that they no longer putted alongside the shore. The boat was heading straight out into open water.

Fortunately, she could still see the lights of town.

"I can do this," she said, getting into the pilot's position and grasping the wheel. She turned it sharply, making the boat tilt so violently that she nearly flew from her seat. Still she hung on and managed to turn the boat back around so it again pointed toward shore. Groping in the near-darkness, she found the throttle and pushed it down, gunning the engine to a higher gear. They began to move steadily in the direction of home.

They drew closer to shore, so Briana looked for the control to raise the lights. One dial seemed promising, so she reached down to twist it. Before she could, she felt something knock her hand away roughly. A moment later she sprawled facedown on the deck.

Graham stood over her, clutching the back of his head with one hand and holding her wrist in the other. His face contorted in fury and pain.

"You ungrateful bitch! After all the risks I took for you! What are you going to do, head back to shore so we can both get arrested?"

"I'll take my chances with Will!" she shouted back.

"Morgan's got you so brainwashed you don't even know what you're saying. This is for your own good, Bri! You're coming with me!"

Stepping over her, he climbed back into the pilot's seat and jerked the wheel back around. Again the boat pivoted with such force that Briana felt herself sliding across the tilting deck. Desperately she grabbed at the gritty boards under her and somehow hoisted herself to her feet. Then she launched herself directly at him and grabbed for the wheel. Gripping it with one hand, Graham roughly pushed her back with the other.

Though she fought desperately, Briana knew she didn't have his strength. Years of seamanship had hardened his muscles, and his manic determination supplied an extra burst of sheer force. Still, she refused to let go, no matter how low the boat dipped or how many icy waves crested the bow and hit her face and shoulders.

* * * *

Ruby pointed to the nearly empty parking lot across the street from the docks. "There's Briana's car. How did we miss seeing it before?"

"Probably because it wasn't here yet." They rushed over to look inside. Sebastian saw nothing unusual in the empty front seats, but right away he smelled blood in the back.

"It's Todd's," Ruby said without hesitation. "Trust me on that."

"I do. Let's look for the boat."

Neither of them expressed surprise at finding Graham's usual berth empty. The dinghy Todd had once stolen bobbed quietly in a spot much too large for it.

Sebastian walked to the edge of the public pier and scanned the darkness. The harbor lay quiet except for the steady shriek of the sea wind across the bay and the corresponding groan of the jostled surf.

Out farther, much farther, his sharp eyes picked out a boat with its lights on low, moving erratically. No human could have seen it.

The next gust of wind carried its scent toward them. Blood. The same blood they'd found in the car.

Sebastian looked at Ruby, who nodded. "That's it," she said in a near-whisper.

He couldn't suppress the tremor that ran through his body as he gazed back out at the sea.

He looked at the water—something every vampire hated almost as ferociously as they hated sunlight. He couldn't drown, of course—his breathing was so shallow it hardly counted as breathing at all, but the claustrophobia and the inevitable, immediate sinking of his body to the slimy ocean floor stirred an even more primal fear.

"We could steal a boat," Ruby suggested. Sebastian barked out a sardonic laugh.

"You and I have no boating skills. They'd be across the bay before we even cleared the pier."

"Then we're stuck, I guess."

His expression hardened. "Not quite. I'll have to swim out to them."

Panic rose in her so strong that he, too, felt its reverberations. In truth, he shared her anxiety. But he couldn't afford to dwell on that now. It would only make what he had to do that much more difficult. He had to maintain his focus: Briana.

Ruby seemed to read his thoughts. "There's no proof Briana's out there. It's Todd's blood we smelled."

"She is. I'm sure of it."

Ruby's long fingernails dug into his sleeve. "You can't do this!" she protested.

Gently, he brushed her hand off his arm. "Watch me," he said. "Or better yet, don't. I am your grandfather, after all. We have to maintain some semblance of propriety."

Walking away from her, he began to strip off his clothes with brisk efficiency.

"Sebastian, stop! What if someone sees you?" Ignoring his effort to preserve modesty, she grabbed each garment as he shed it: dark wool overcoat, tailored shirt, and expensive leather boots. When he went for his belt buckle, she finally turned her back on him.

"Then whoever it is will get an eyeful," he growled.

Within moments, the cold air enveloped his naked skin. Sebastian tilted his head back and stretched out his arms, letting the frosty blast invigorate and refresh him. He concentrated on summoning every ounce of energy and courage his body contained, knowing how much the task ahead would drain him.

Then, in a single powerful motion, he plunged off the pier and torpedoed into the water below.

As expected, his first sensation was that of sinking deep and then deeper into what seemed like an endless well of suffocating pitch. The water's weight felt like piles of stones flattening him; for the first few minutes he drifted downward, unable to flinch a single muscle to right himself.

Then, gradually, he adjusted to the pressure and the darkness. The welcome cold seeped into his pores, solidifying his resolve even as it hardened his flesh. Soon he could stretch out his arms and glide along with the speed and grace of a merman—or, more accurately, he thought, a predatory shark.

In the distance, he could hear the steady whirr of the boat's motor.

He could hear other sounds, too, amplified by the water and his own razor-edged hearing. He heard Briana screaming. Pumping his arms and legs in short, potent thrusts, he propelled himself onward.

* * * *

Briana fought for control of the boat with everything she had: her fists, her feet, and her voice. Finally, though, Graham lost his tolerance for her ineffective pummeling and her screaming in his face. Shoving her back one last time, he rose from his seat and wrestled her to the deck.

"Stop fighting me!" he snarled, wedging her hips between his thighs and capturing her flailing hands in his. "You'll thank me when we get to Canada."

"No, I won't! I'll turn you in, Graham! You're going to pay for what you did to Ami and to Todd!"

His face had changed—she saw it clearly now. Their struggle was no longer about her giving in to his desire to control her. It was all about survival now, and only one of them could prevail. He planned to kill her, just like he already had killed Todd and Ami. How could she have ever pegged Sebastian as some kind of serial killer? That title belonged to Graham now, and Graham alone.

Poor Todd, she thought as Graham's calloused hands closed around her throat. Sebastian and Ruby had finally given him a chance to thrive and her own poor judgment had cut that promise short. And Ami.—What Briana experienced now was the same thing Ami had endured before she died. Perhaps her punishment for what she'd done awaited her in the next life. One way or the other, she suspected she would find out soon.

Then Graham's fingers tightened, and she began to black out.

Chapter 19

As Graham's rough hands steadily wrung the life from her, Briana watched the world tilt and go blurry around her. With each futile gasp, her will to live lost ground to hopelessness and surrender. Even her anger at Graham's cruel betrayal began to feel dulled and distant. She only regretted that his face, contorted by evil, would be the last thing she saw.

"You couldn't leave well enough alone, could you?" He kept banging her head on the deck, timing the blows to the cadence of his voice. And still he kept squeezing. Her fingernails embedded in his wrists seemed not to inconvenience him at all. "You had to keep going on and on about Ami. We could have left all of this behind us. Started fresh."

"You didn't have to kill her. Or me." She wasn't sure if she spoke the words out loud or only thought them. All she could hear was the desperate throb of her pulse in her ears, punctuated by the thud of her skull against glossy wood. But he did, of course. She saw that now. She knew the truth about him. He couldn't let her go. He couldn't let her look at him with the disgust she felt. She would never be able to hide it.

Then, just as she sucked in a shallow breath she expected would be her last, she heard a different kind of thump, loud and sharp, not beneath her head but from somewhere above.

Graham fell back, his limp fingers sliding from around her neck. She was vaguely aware of his body slumping down alongside hers.

Half-conscious and disoriented, she lay back until a welcome blast of air refilled her lungs and her vision cleared. When her eyes could focus again, she saw what, or who, had curtailed Graham's attack.

Todd hovered above them, none too steady on his feet, holding a long wooden oar in both hands. Briana shuddered when she saw the front of his shirt spattered with blood, both dried and fresh.

"Oh my God... Oh God, Todd... you're alive!" Her voice dissolved into a painful, gasping sob. "I thought, I thought...Graham told me he'd killed you!"

She struggled to sit up, but failed. Dropping the oar beside him, Todd crouched down and pulled her into his arms. "He sure as hell tried, and that goes for both of us. You okay?"

"Everything hurts," she confessed. "What happened? How did you get here?"

"I was on board the whole time. Luckily, the bastard thought he'd finished me off. I think he planned to take me out in the bay and throw me in the water. That must be what he did to Ami." Todd's own voice began to quiver. "Bri, the motel's gone. I'm so sorry."

"I know. Did Graham do that too?"

He nodded tearfully. "It was my fault, though. I asked him to help me get you out of jail. We drove to The Dunes, and I went into the office to get the petty cash. I had this crazy idea that we could convince Joel to take the money for your bail. When I came out and showed it to Graham, I saw the smoke. Then he clobbered me. I guess he put me in your car and drove me to the boat. Next thing I knew, I woke up in the cargo hold. I heard your voice and found my way up here."

Briana reached up and pushed Todd's hair aside, examining the nasty gash that Graham had put there in the course of overpowering him. Curiously, it had already begun to dry out and scab over. Anyone would have sworn it he had received the wound days, rather than mere hours, ago.

Seeing her confusion, he grinned. "Yep, it's already healing. I guess I have Ruby to thank for that. Must be something she put in my blood. Maybe that's what kept me alive, too. I'm pretty sure Graham thought he killed me. He didn't bother to tie me up or anything."

"Obviously, I made a mistake," a low voice interrupted. Both of them looked up to see Graham getting to his feet again. He'd retrieved the oar and now used it to steady himself as the deck bobbed and rocked in the powerful currents sweeping them toward the bay. "On the other hand, this is perfect," he continued, staring straight at Briana. "Everything fits. I tried to get you to safety, but your brother attacked you or maybe vice versa. It doesn't matter. Will already thinks you snuffed Ami. Anyhow, the two of you killed each other in self-defense."

"Graham, don't," Briana pleaded. "Stop this now. Todd and I are all right. You're just making things worse."

"Thanks for the advice, but I don't see it that way," Graham said. "I admit that bringing you here might have been a mistake. Sometimes, though, it's best to erase mistakes and move on."

Graham raised the oar above his head like a long-handled axe. Had it been outfitted with a blade, the sharp edge would have pointed straight at their heads.

Then he took a deep breath and swung it at them.

Briana closed her eyes and braced herself for what she knew would be a crushing blow. Instinctively, she spread her hands over Todd's back as if the simple gesture could protect him. She heard and felt the rush of cold air as the tear-shaped paddle came whistling toward their heads. The sound of shattering wood that filled her ears would, she suspected, be followed either by searing pain or numbing oblivion.

When neither proved to be the case, she tentatively opened her eyes again. She gasped.

Sebastian had caught the oar in mid-descent, stopping it mere inches from their huddled forms. What remained of its lower section was wedged between his fingers and splintered into jagged shards. His face was the picture of smoldering fury, while water streamed from his body. Most shocking of all, he'd attacked completely naked.

Graham staggered away still gripping the top half of the oar. The end had broken off, forming a tapered point. A perfect stake, Briana realized in horror, though fortunately Graham didn't see the significance of his weapon of choice. He slung a clumsy blow Sebastian's way, but Sebastian easily fended it off and delivered a rock-like fist to Graham's face. He followed that up with another and sent his opponent sprawling against the starboard rail and onto the deck. The oar handle flew off into the darkness and landed with a clatter a few feet away.

Sebastian flung aside the broken bits of oar and advanced. His stance and expression suggested to Briana that the next blow he struck would be the last.

"Sebastian, don't kill him, please! We should turn him over to Will—make him pay for what he's done."

At first, Sebastian seemed not to hear her. He continued to move toward Graham, his fists churning at his sides as if gathering strength to lash out with sudden, murderous force. Graham cringed against the deck, shaking his head to clear it, while Briana and Todd watched, frozen in place. When he reached striking distance, though, Sebastian slowed his pace and finally stopped. His arms relaxed at his sides.

"As little confidence as I have in Darkisle's justice system, keeping him alive is no doubt the most expeditious means to clearing your name. Find something to tie him up with."

"That shouldn't be a problem," Todd said, scrambling to his feet. "This is a fishing boat—got to be rope around here somewhere."

He moved off in search of some, while Briana stared at Sebastian in amazement. His body gleamed like polished stone in the cloud-filtered moonlight. Every muscle stood at attention under his bloodless skin, rippling with barely-contained strength.

"You swam all the way out here?" she asked incredulously.

"Against my better judgment." He gritted his teeth. "I don't suppose you have any way to call for help? I'm afraid I had nowhere to stash my cell phone."

"I'm pretty sure there are flares on deck. Every fishing boat keeps some on hand. If we shoot them off, we'll have plenty of company in no time flat." Briana also crawled into a kneeling position. She then stood gingerly and began to look around. "I suggest you find something to wear before the Coast Guard shows up."

"That will have to wait. First, let's secure him."

Todd returned, carrying a length of rope. He walked a bit unsteadily, rubbing the back of his head. "Found this," he said, holding it out toward Sebastian. "Seems pretty strong. It should do the trick."

Sebastian half-turned at the waist, extending his right hand to accept it. For the briefest fraction of a second, he let his gaze drift from Graham to Todd. Briana instantly recognized the movement as an uncharacteristic mistake.

Graham did too. In a single movement, he rolled across the deck and snatched back the oar. Then he came up on his knees and thrust the spiky tip squarely into Sebastian's chest. Briana heard his bark of surprise, followed by the dull, cracking noise as the pole split his ribcage and wedged deep inside his body. Graham leapt into a crouching position and, still gripping his makeshift spear, drove Sebastian backward. Somehow, Sebastian remained standing until the small of his back slammed against the opposite rail. There, Graham continued to push at him, determined to force him overboard.

Sebastian's moment of weakness passed as quickly as his expression of surprise. Planting his feet, he wrapped both hands around the protruding wooden shaft and drove it back toward Graham. The tip soon re-emerged from his chest, as clean and dry as before. The wound itself was equally bloodless.

"What the—" Graham's face contorted in open-mouthed shock. Then Sebastian jerked the oar free, flung it overboard, and lunged forward. Even before Sebastian delivered the inevitable knockout blow, Graham's entire body seemed to slump in defeat.

He hit the deck, limp arms and legs outstretched, as harmless as the puffy clouds above them. Todd didn't wait for Sebastian to direct him this time. Quickly he pulled Graham's wrists behind his back and lashed them together with the rope. For good measure, he sat down on their captive's back and hooked his feet around Graham's knees.

Briana ran to Sebastian just as he, too, crashed the deck. His hands covered his still-open wound, and his face looked even greyer than usual.

"Shouldn't...shouldn't have let my guard down," he said, stammering as he took deep breaths. She'd never seen him do that before. "Guess I'm not...not as comfortable with public nudity as I expected. I may not be human any longer, but...but apparently I'm still a Victorian through and through."

"I can relate, man," Todd piped up.

Briana knelt beside him, brushing his wet hair from his forehead. "Sebastian, you're hurt."

He shook his head roughly, dismissing her concern. "Nothing to worry about. He missed my heart."

"Let me see." She covered his hands with her own, gently attempting to push them aside. She felt him tense up with resistance.

"No. You've already witnessed many things never meant for human eyes. Don't concern yourself with this. I'll heal...in time."

Briana frowned. She stopped tugging at his hands, but left hers resting on his. "How much time, Sebastian?"

His expression tightened. She knew he was in pain. "I don't know."

"That isn't normal for you, is it? I mean, you would usually heal right away. What's changed?"

"It...depends on the wound." He averted his eyes. "I can assure you that nothing irreversible has taken place. Now leave it, please.

Perhaps you could find me something to wear. As you pointed out earlier, I am not exactly in any state to greet our rescuers."

"Can you make it down to the cabin with me? There should be clothes there."

"Yes, I believe I can."

Keeping one palm flat over the gash in his chest, Sebastian leaned against her and hoisted himself up. As he did, his hand briefly slipped out of place and Briana caught a glimpse of his wound. The jagged perforation gaped just enough to reveal desiccated tissue, a few rubbery strands of muscle, even a hint of bone. Everything beneath the outermost layer of flesh puckered ash-black.

She said nothing until they entered the cabin below. She rooted through Graham's things, tossing Sebastian a pair of jeans and a sweatshirt without looking around. When she did, he had dressed again, looking for all the world like any tourist who had booked an evening cruise around the bay, albeit a seasick one. His only concession to his obvious discomfort was the way he leaned in the doorway instead of supporting his own weight and the way his fingers still lightly massaged the spot of his injury, this time through the concealing shirt. He glanced down at the colorful logo with obvious distaste.

"When I returned to the States, I vowed I would never wear a garment featuring a decal. It didn't take me long to break that promise."

"I'm sure you've done a lot of things you didn't expect to since you met me."

"I can't deny that."

"Why aren't you healing? It's those injections, isn't it? The medication does something else besides stopping your hunger. It takes away your…powers."

"That is an overly dramatic way of putting it," he scoffed, "though not entirely inaccurate."

"Tell me."

"Very well. The treatment's most serious disadvantage, the one that has led most vampires to spurn it, is that, ultimately, it robs us of our immortality. Already, as you can see, I must live with wounds that would once have healed within minutes. My strength is still considerably more than that of any human, but by vampire standards, it has begun to decline. In the years to come, it will decline further."

"What are you saying, exactly?"

"Probably no more than you've already guessed: I came back to Darkisle to die. Not even Ruby knows that part of it. She is only aware that the serum has changed me—in her opinion, not for the better. Don't look so shocked, Briana. I don't mean that I'm going to waste away and turn into a shriveled corpse before your very eyes. I mean that I'm going to age gradually and naturally—at least, at a rate that is natural for me. It may take me twice as long as a human man, or even longer, which would still give me another century or so. At some point, though, the process will become apparent."

He paused, waiting for her to react, and Briana exhaled sharply. Her heart had frozen in fear when he'd mentioned the word "die." It had begun to beat again, cautiously, as his explanation had unfolded. What he'd said made sense. It fit in with the few bits of evidence she'd managed to gather on her own. Most importantly, it neutralized one of her biggest fears regarding a continued association with him—remaining human and aging beyond the point of desirability, while he remained young and virile, and eventually impossible to satisfy.

In other words, they could grow old together after all.

"Why didn't you tell me any of this before? Back at the jail, I brought up the age difference, and you didn't contradict me."

"That was hardly the time. Besides, there is a much larger issue. You don't trust me. You considered me a murder suspect twice over. Perhaps that is not as significant to you, but to me, it is of much greater concern than whose hair goes white first."

Her face flushed. "I can never apologize enough to you for the things I said. I know that you had nothing to do with Ami's death. I always knew, but I let Will and then Graham sway me in a moment of confusion. That will never happen again. I swear."

"And Amsterdam?"

"I believe what you told me before. A troubled woman fell in with the wrong people. You probably did try to help her. She didn't listen—just like I almost didn't."

He lowered his head for a moment, his expression unreadable. "Speaking of that, we need to get back on deck. Todd won't be able to hold him down forever."

"You're right. There's just one thing."

"Yes?"

"Can wounds like...like that speed up the aging process you talked about earlier?"

"I don't know. I suppose they can. No one really knows. It's not as though there are archives of scientific studies documenting all possibilities."

"Then...would some blood help you to heal faster? My blood, specifically?"

The vulnerability that had slowly crept into his tone and body language vanished abruptly. Briana saw the old stubbornness return. He spoke firmly, as if the subject were not open to debate whatsoever. "It might, but we will never know, Briana."

"Well, I think we should find out. You said it yourself—there's insufficient research. I suggest we start an informal investigation of our own."

"No. I will keep the wound hidden as long as I have to."

"That might not be as easy as you think. Trust me, we can't always predict every situation we end up in. We're about to be boarded by the sheriff's department, the Coast Guard, and the National Guard, for all I know. There's bound to be a medical technician at some point. Do you really want to take that chance?"

"You know I don't."

"Then take my blood. See if it helps you. Who knows? We might even be benefiting some other serum-dependent vampire down the road. Don't be so selfish all the time, Sebastian."

He fell silent, bowing his head again, forcing himself not to look at her. She knew, though, that this particular battle was hers to win.

When he replied, his voice came out in a growl. "I told you—maintaining control when using a donor is difficult, even impossible in some cases. I can't deny that I am in agony, and not just because of this hole in my chest. Taking only as much as I need would prove no threat to your well-being...but taking as much as I want would kill you."

The ferocity in his face unnerved her, but she fought back her doubts with a courage, or a foolhardiness, she hadn't known she possessed until tonight. Holding her breath, she moved closer. He didn't flinch when she pushed down the neckline of her shirt.

"Earlier, when I thought I'd thrown it all away between us, I almost couldn't bear it. And when I thought I might die before I could tell you that I was wrong...well, to me that felt worse than being kidnapped." She stroked her fingertips along her neck, feeling her own pulse beat madly beneath her touch. She knew he sensed every tremor in her veins. "Let me do this for you. I trust you enough to know you'll be able to stop."

Slowly, his hand slid up alongside hers, pushing it away from her neck. His fingertips settled into the same groove hers had just left, caressing and plumping her flesh. Trembling, she tilted her head and closed her eyes as he leaned over her. The frosty moisture of his excited breath tickled her for a moment. She heard a distant moan of pleasure, unsure whether it had come from her own lips or from his. Perhaps, in a sense, it belonged to them both.

Then came the bite. In some ways, it was nothing like she had expected. In others, it seemed as though she had dreamed of this moment over and over, and the reality only confirmed what her fantasies had promised her. Sharper than a needle, sweeter than an orgasm, the sensation of his teeth—and his hunger—tearing through her flesh seemed to melt her bones and intoxicate her spirit all at once. The sting of arousal swept through her with such force that all she could do was lean against him, surrendering both physically and mentally to the power of his need.

He drank from her passionately, desperately. At one point, she actually felt her consciousness detach from her body, and imagined herself looking down at both of them from somewhere far above the ceiling, the boat, even the sea. Briana had no idea how much blood he drew, or how much time had passed. Had he drained her to the point of no return, as he had feared? Had a few seconds of nourishment stretched into an eternity? Then again, what did it matter? They were together—complete.

The most pleasant darkness she had even known followed, along with a silky, peaceful silence, the kind that might accompany a deep, perfect sleep.

Like every deep sleep, though, this one had an end.

Sebastian kept massaging her cheeks, tapping them lightly. "Briana. Come back to me."

It took more effort than she'd expected to open her eyes. When she finally did, she found herself propped up against his chest. One of his arms encircled her waist, pinning her against him so close that she could feel the front button of his jeans—or Graham's jeans, more accurately—pressed against her hip. His other arm looped under hers, his hand supporting the back of her head. His lips were wet, and redder than she had ever seen them. Color bloomed in his cheeks and warmth radiated from his skin.

"It's over," he said. "You did fine."

"And you?" she asked.

This time, his smile showed no trace of sarcasm, bitterness, or anger. "I did fine, too. I took only what I needed and stopped right on cue. Your neck is already healing."

She touched the bite and felt no discomfort. The skin seemed a little puckered, but her fingers came away clean. Gently he released her, and she quickly found her balance again.

Her eyes moved from his face to the gaudy decal on his sweatshirt. His instincts proved correct. Modern pop-culture attire didn't suit him well. He should always wear the finest tailored silks, perhaps with vests or old-fashioned cravats. When he had to wear anything at all, of course.

She touched the site of his wound, sensing no indentation through the cloth. His smile widening, he raised the hem enough for her to see him fully healed, the flesh there as pink and glowing as the rest of him.

"I think we're ready for the Coast Guard now," he said. "Let's go and get those flares."

Chapter 20

Before the last of Graham's flares burst and fizzled against the night sky, the boat came alive with uniformed visitors. Briana felt a bit dismayed to see the female deputy still tagging along with Will, assuming her presence would facilitate her own re-arrest. Fortunately, Joel had remained coherent enough to explain that she was the victim, rather than the perpetrator, of the strong-armed jailbreak. Skeptical, Will spent the short voyage back to Darkisle peppering them with questions. Only Graham refused to cooperate. Exercising his right to remain silent, he lay on the deck of his own boat in handcuffs, smug and defiant. The sight of her former lover, now her kidnapper, made Briana shudder. She realized now that she'd never trusted him completely, but never could she have guessed at the depths of his depravity. Worst of all, he'd tricked her into doubting Sebastian—a mistake that had nearly cost her more than she cared to dwell on.

A fresh contingent of Coast Guard and emergency personnel, not to mention a fair number of gawkers, waited for them on the wharf. Ruby stood there, too, cradling an odd bundle that Briana mistook for a baby. Then she realized that she held Sebastian's discarded clothing to her chest.

"I'm taking Briana home. She's been through enough for one night," Sebastian announced as they finally docked. He looked around as if daring one of the rescue workers to contradict him. "I assume no one has any objection."

"All right," Will said in a guarded tone. Briana couldn't tell if he were relieved or annoyed at being forced to accept their innocence. She suspected that his sudden desire to cooperate had something to do with Sebastian's repeated mentions of legal action—something about an incompetent police force that had allowed her to be abducted from its own facility. "I'm sending Todd to the hospital though. His head wound looks pretty nasty—and besides, it's evidence. We'll need photographs, that kind of thing."

"I want to go with him," Briana protested. She felt Sebastian tense up beside her, ready to object, but Will made any further argument unnecessary.

"You can see him tomorrow. I'm dropping the charges against you on the condition that you go home and stay there for the rest of the night. I'll need an official statement from all of you in the morning, and I don't want your testimony cross-pollinated. That goes for you, too, Morgan. No discussing the case for now."

"You have my word," Sebastian said. He looked down at the makeshift outfit he'd thrown on. "For my part, I would just as soon forget this little escapade ever took place."

"That's not an option." Will snorted. "Just so you know, I intend to keep investigating this. I plan to sort out what happened between the last time anyone saw Ami and tonight. The evidence exists somewhere. Now it's a matter of me finding it."

Sebastian nodded. "Briana and I would expect nothing less."

"What do you think he meant?" Briana asked as Sebastian held the Maserati's passenger door open for her. Her own car, parked a few spaces away, was already decorated with bright yellow crime tape. She wondered if she'd ever get it back, and in what condition.

He waved her concern aside with a sweep of his hand. "Don't worry about it. He's fishing."

Briana shivered and turned her head away from the water, the boats, and Will loading Graham into the back of the police car. "Please, Sebastian, don't ever mention fishing to me again."

"Agreed." He reached down to slam the door and then paused. Briana saw that Ruby had appeared beside them, still holding his clothes. Sebastian turned to her with a touch of impatience. "Are you coming with us?"

"No thanks. I'm going to follow Todd to the hospital, but I'm not planning to take this stuff with me." Unceremoniously she dumped the clothes on Briana's lap.

"They won't let you into Todd's room," Briana pointed out, though she felt as relieved as Sebastian seemed to be that Ruby had no plans to intrude.

Ruby gave an unpleasant laugh. "I don't wait for permission to do anything."

"Just be careful," Sebastian warned. "Best not to stir that particular pot for the time being."

"Oh, brother dear, loosen up and live a little. I can handle the likes of Will Garvey and his flunkeys."

Turning, she slid away into the crowd, leaving Sebastian with his hand on the half-closed door. Still grimacing, he slammed it and walked around to take his place in the driver's seat. Briana couldn't help but enjoy the sight of him operating the Maserati barefoot.

As they crested the hill near her house, the acrid smell of stale smoke and charred wood assaulted her nose. The car picked up speed as Sebastian attempted to fly past the entrance to The Dunes, trying to spare her from the sorry remains of her motel. She laid her hand on his arm.

"Take me there, please."

"Are you sure?"

"Yes. I need to see it."

He spun the wheel to the right and rolled into what had once been her motel's parking lot. Two fire trucks remained in the center of the blacktop while a few emergency workers in thick yellow jumpsuits and protective face masks milled around, dragging hoses and chemical tanks.

Where the crisp white façade of the office had once stood, there now lay blackened beams, crumpled sheets of vinyl siding, and shards of broken glass. A few gutted mattresses and heaps of singed bedclothes, dragged from the rooms as the firemen searched for victims, sprawled pitifully in front of the trucks. A single wooden door, torn from its hinges, lay at an angle against an upended bureau. The piece of twisted metal in the exact center of the carnage had perhaps been the ice machine. So little remained that she couldn't be sure.

The rest of her family business, everything, was gone. The big wooden planters that flanked the main entrance, the shutters her father had painstakingly painted every spring, and the cheerful sign with its design of a seabird lifting its beak toward the waves were all destroyed.

"Will was right…it's nearly gone." Her words emerged as little more than a whisper. Her throat burned as she fought back tears and the bitter taste of charcoal. "How could he have done this?"

"Don't dwell on it," Sebastian urged. He stepped on the gas and screeched out of the lot. "We'll deal with this another time."

His use of the word "we" gave her food for thought as they continued up the hill to her driveway. Though the air around—and inside—the house still reeked of smoke, Briana had never felt so happy and relieved at the simple act of walking through own her front door. Without a word, Sebastian followed her up the stairs to her bedroom. He stood by and averted his eyes while Briana stripped off her jeans and sweater and headed into the master bathroom. The whole outfit smelled of jail, Graham's boat, and smoke. No way would she ever wear any of those clothes again.

She emerged from the shower fragrant with strawberry bath oil and the fresh cotton smell of the long white t-shirt she used as a nightgown. Sebastian still hovered in the same spot, though now that she was dressed again, he permitted himself to look up at her. Briana saw his nostrils quiver and knew that he enjoyed the fresh scent of her hair and nightie, too.

"I know you can't stay long," she said, pulling back the sheet and settling against her full stack of pillows.

He shrugged. "We have a little time. The sun won't rise for a few hours yet."

With the bedclothes still pushed to one side, she swept her hand over the empty spot beside her. "I know it's killing you to wear that sweatshirt, even though I think it's kind of sexy on you. I won't be offended if you want to take it off."

His thin lips quirked in a smile as he picked up on her meaning. Discarding the shirt with obvious relief, he climbed onto the bed beside her. Briana settled her head against his bare chest, her hand resting on the cool plane of flesh just below his rib cage. The site of the vicious wound Graham had inflicted shone unmarred and ivory-smooth.

"I see my blood had the desired effect," she said, tracing the spot with her fingertips.

His arm slid around her shoulders and pulled her closer. "Did I hurt you?"

"No. It was incredible. While I fed you, I felt as if we had become one person."

He nodded. "For a moment, we did. I shared your emotions as well as your life force. You are a more passionate woman than I ever suspected, Miss Dempsey."

"That's the only excuse I can offer for the foolish things I do at times—like sending you away when you came to see me in jail. Can we please forget that ever happened?"

"You weren't being foolish, though. On the contrary. Leaving me was the most sensible thing you've done since the evening we met. I admit it isn't what I wanted, or what I want, but your reasoning remains sound. Selfishness led me to ask you to join your fate to mine. I can offer you many things, but safety and stability are not among them."

"Maybe I've played it safe long enough. Where did that get me, really? Graham had a point about one thing—I feel like my old life went up in flames along with the motel tonight. It's almost like a chance to start over, to make better decisions. I can do what I want, not just what's best for Todd, or what my father expected of me." She sighed and rubbed the flat of her hand over his middle. The way his muscles tightened and quivered pleased her. "Maybe I'll rebuild The Dunes as a gift shop, or an art gallery. The tourists will come if I give them something worth buying. I can build up trade over time."

"You could also take the insurance money and leave Darkisle," he said.

"I could…but somehow it just seems like this is where I belong." She pushed herself up on her elbow and faced him. "You can take me into your world, Sebastian. I'm not afraid. And you can take my blood anytime you need to."

His expression darkened. "I had no intention of using you as a donor. Tonight was an aberration—an emergency. I plan to resume my usual course of treatments as soon as possible. I would never use you so callously."

"But I don't see it that way, Sebastian. You see, when you bit me tonight, I tasted your emotions too. I could tell how much you needed me. You could never have put that into words. I don't think I can either. But I can tell you that it turned me on more than I ever thought possible."

Leaning forward, she rested herself against his body. Her breasts molded to the harder sinew of his chest, the peaks of her nipples stretching the fabric of the t-shirt taut. When he didn't resist, she let her right hand drift lower, settling over the swelling front of his jeans. When she toyed with the zipper, she heard the metal groan against the surging force of his desire.

"Maybe you could think of me as a sort of dietary supplement," she whispered. "Take your injections—live as normally as you want.

But when you feel weak, or the need becomes too much to bear, turn to me. I'll always be there. I promise."

Sebastian groaned, too. When he spoke, his voice sounded thin with tension. "The arrangement you suggest requires a level of trust most humans are not capable of."

She placed a finger across his lips. Her other hand finished wrenching open his jeans. "Don't be afraid. You need to feed. I'm here. And I long for your kiss, Sebastian. Your deepest kiss."

He was ravenous now. She could feel the need pulsing in him, concentrated in the part of his body that strained against her palm. Pushing the t-shirt up over her hips, Sebastian pulled her on top of him and nudged her thighs apart. Briana gasped as he thrust into her with such force that she rocked backward. His hands curled around her wrists, dragging her back toward him. Impatiently he peeled her nightgown over her head and tossed it on the floor. Then he lifted his head and fastened his mouth to hers.

Sharp teeth dragged across her lower lip, splitting it with razor-like precision. A warm, liquid sensation took the place of the pain she expected, followed by the metallic taste of her own blood. When she opened her mouth, Sebastian's tongue swept inside to cleanse her wound.

As he drank, his body grew warm against hers. Soon his nipples burned like twin coals pressed into her skin. She could feel him swelling still larger inside her as his mouth pulled away from hers and slid down into the hollow of her neck.

The sharp, sweet pain between her thighs erupted at the precise moment his teeth broke through the tender flesh at her throat. Another flood of warmth, thicker and heavier this time, pooled around his pursed lips. Briana moaned, siphoning pleasure from his body as needily as he savored her blood. Her lust burned as raw and as feral as his appetite.

The harder she twisted and bucked against him, the more securely his teeth and his cock held her in place. A single chord seemed to stretch from his ravenous lips to her most feminine center. Sebastian strummed it, and her, with his whole body until he brought her to a perfect crescendo of pleasure.

When it ended, he extracted his teeth from her flesh and lifted her off his still-rigid erection. A thread of warm blood still trickled from the mark his kiss had made. Tilting her head with both hands, he applied his tongue to the gash and massaged it shut with a series of slow, tender strokes. The gentle laving swept away not only the last flecks of moisture, but any trace of pain. The quick pulsations of her flesh as it healed merged with the lingering throb of her orgasm. Briana felt herself dissolve into a puddle of pure bliss as stretched out beside him.

They'd kicked away the sheet and blankets, and Sebastian's jeans had been cast aside, too. Nothing remained to hide them from one another. Briana let her eyes rake his body while he did the same. She loved looking at him, especially now, when his skin glowed hot and flushed with her own life-warmth coursing inside him.

His lips swelled ruddy and hot, too, moist with her blood and slick with his own healing saliva. She brushed her fingers over his mouth and delighted in the tiny kisses he bestowed on her fingertips. Then she curled up against him and rested her head in the crook of his shoulder.

Briana wasn't sure how long they lay together in the moonlight, her mind drifting on a wave of physical satisfaction and fatigue. Her insides still pulsed with the aftershocks of their joining, but the loss of blood had left her sleepy and weak. That boneless feeling would be temporary, she knew. For the moment, it felt oddly pleasurable. She closed her eyes in perfect contentment.

Eventually she opened them and noticed that Sebastian had covered her with the quilt. He lay on his side next to her, his head propped up on his left arm. His soft gaze seemed to warm her bare skin as his eyes trailed over her.

"I don't know where this will lead, but I'm willing to try," he said.

"You're sure you won't leave me and run off to Paris? That's where all the wild women are, I've heard."

He shook his head. "You must never compare yourself to Amelia. The man who wed her is long dead. Morgan House is my home now, in a way I don't think it ever was before."

"I'm glad." Briana fell silent for a while. "There is something else," she said at last. "What about Ruby? Will she accept me? I doubt she's in the market for a step-grandmother."

His jaw hardened. "Forget Ruby. She is a bit lacking in self-control, admittedly, but she would do nothing to hurt me. Especially where you are concerned. I will see to that. Always."

"All right. I believe you." The last word he had spoken lingered in her mind. So many couples spoke of being together forever. If things worked out with Sebastian, she realized they really could share an eternity.

But they could sort all that out later. Right now, she needed to sleep. Though she knew he would have left by the time she woke up, he'd be back soon enough. That was what real trust meant.

She closed her eyes again and drifted off.

* * * *

Standing in the center of the same jail cell he'd taken Briana from only hours before, Graham stared at his lone visitor with undisguised contempt.

"What the hell do you want?" he growled. "Who let you in here in the middle of the night?"

"Let's just say the cops owed me a favor." Ruby shrugged and threaded her fingers through the bars. The front panel slid open with a screech of metal. Graham's eyes widened as she stepped inside and closed it again.

"How'd you do that?"

"I dated a burglar many years ago. He taught me a few tricks. Maybe I'll show you later. Right now I want to talk about what happened on the boat."

"Don't start on me. I know what you want. You want to make sure I confess, so Briana and your brother can sail off into the sunset. Well, forget it. I'm pleading not guilty to everything. Let them prove it if they can."

Ruby laughed. "You have no idea what you're talking about. Somehow, you've failed to notice that I can't stand Briana. I'd be happy to keep her away from my brother. And Ami? You did me a favor. Now at least Todd and I can get it on in peace—once they stitch his scalp back together, that is."

"Yeah, I'd been waiting to deck him for a long time. I don't know what you see in that wimp anyway."

"I admit that you have a point there." She crossed the cell, sat down on the bed, and patted the spot beside her. Cautiously he moved closer. "When it comes to testosterone, there's no doubt that you're gallons ahead of Todd. Sensitive guys are fine for a while, but it's nice to have one who can win a good old-fashioned fistfight too. I always liked you, Graham, though you got too worked up over Briana to notice."

Brightening, he moved closer. "Yeah?"

She looked around the cell. "It must be pretty lonely here."

"It's all right. I'll get out. They don't have any real evidence against me."

"Sorry to burst your bubble, but that's not what I heard. Briana, Todd, and my brother are all eyewitnesses to kidnapping, assault with a deadly weapon, and an admission of murder. I'm not saying I believe them, of course."

He sat down. The side of his hand rested against her thigh. "That's just it. They're all liars. A good lawyer will get all that thrown out before my trial even begins. Anyway it was all self-defense." He paused, scowling. "What is it with your brother, by the way? I jabbed him with that stick and nothing happened. He just…pulled it out."

Her smile turned to one of pity. Why did these humans take such pride in their powers of observation? So little good ever came from their nosiness. "My brother practices martial arts," she explained. "He has some pretty impressive moves."

Graham considered this, chewing his stubbly upper lip. His weather-beaten face split in a grin. "I'll bet some of your moves aren't bad either."

"So I've heard." She smiled as his hand moved onto the flat of her thigh. Half-turning, she cupped his face in her palms and stroked his earlobes with her thumbs.

"You know, I had you all wrong. You're not so bad after all. Nothing like your brother," Graham murmured.

He shuddered as her long, exquisitely manicured fingernails traced twin lines from his ears to his jawbone.

"Now that we can both agree on."

He leaned in to enjoy her kiss.

Her nails flashed against his throat, as quick and decisive as the striking of a match. Before his moan of anticipation could turn to an airless gasp, she bent and feasted on the crimson flood that erupted. Soon his limp body, wet and red, slumped to the mattress.

Ruby stood, straightened her clothes, and licked her fingers clean. It took only an extra moment or two to tear a strip of metal from the bottom of the bed frame and place it in his unmoving hand. Tomorrow, the whole town would be abuzz with the bizarre tale of Graham's attempt to escape criminal charges. What a shame, the humans would say, that Graham had become desperate enough to cut his own throat. Something simply had to be done to prevent these dreadful—and appallingly messy—jailhouse suicides.

Too bad they would never know that he had actually died in a spasm of idiotic bliss, the kind many of his fellow mortals would envy. Among her many other talents, Ruby prided herself on her efficiency. Sebastian might, erroneously, —have called it mercy.

Of course, not all her victims surrendered as willingly as Graham Smith. Some of them put up quite a struggle. The woman in Amsterdam, for example. So relentless. It was just a matter of time before Sebastian gave in to her demands for immortality, or she betrayed him out of spite. He'd probably never realize how much heartache his devoted granddaughter had saved him. Hopefully Briana would never figure it out either.

Because she wanted to give Briana, and her inexplicable ability to make Sebastian happy, a chance. For a few centuries, anyway.

THE END

ABOUT THE AUTHOR

Cassandra Pierce has been a fan of Gothic literature for most of her life, even studying the origins of the genre in college and graduate school. Before long, she got the urge to create paranormal romances of her own and is now hard at work on the second Darkisle novel (among other projects). When she is not writing, she teaches English at a small New England college and is active in a charity that rescues and rehomes abandoned pets.

Siren Publishing, Inc.
www.SirenPublishing.com

LaVergne, TN USA
10 April 2011
223644LV00006B/70/P